Doin' It

Doin' It

JO-ANNE SOUTHERN

PRIMIX
PUBLISHING
THE WRITE CHOICE

Primix Publishing
11620 Wilshire Blvd
Suite 900, West Wilshire Center, Los Angeles, CA, 90025
www.primixpublishing.com
Phone: 1 (888) 585-7476

Published by Primix Publishing   03/20/2021

ISBN: 978-1-953397-95-9(sc)
ISBN: 978-1-953397-96-6(e)

Library of Congress Control Number: 2021902068

Children begin by loving their parents; after a time they
judge them; rarely, if ever, do they forgive them.

Oscar Wilde: 1854-1900

CHAPTER ONE

"Hand it over."

She felt a thrill of terror as Ed stood over her like an avenging angel, his black leather jacket glistening in the harsh overhead light Her hand came out of the pocket holding the compressed bills, damp from the rain, scared to hand him the paltry amount.

"It's been a bad night," she gabbled, "everybody says so, Linda and Sheila and the others. We were dragging in old men and they don't like to pay so much." As she saw his expression of displeasure, she backed away, her stomach clenched with nerves. "I know you told me not to bother with oldies, but nobody else was about. It rained all evening and I'm soaked."

"I said hand it over." He put out his left hand, his right clenched into a fist. When she saw that, she felt afraid but offered the damp notes, put them on his outstretched hand and smiled. Hoping.

His fist hit her even as she tried to dodge it. "Stupid whore," he spat as she fell backwards onto the one chair. Her leg touched the small electric fire and it seared.

"Ouch, that burned." Tears of pain filled her eyes as she lowered her head to look at the burn.

He glared down at her, the bare bulb looking like a halo behind his head. "All right, don't start with the water works. Grow up!"

He doesn't care about me, Christine thought, nursing the hurt, he could care less. She glanced up at him as he continued to rant, his fists clenched, wondering if he would hit her again. She resented it when he hit her for almost no reason, because no one else had ever lifted a hand to her, not even her parents. Yet she lingered under his control, detesting his chauvinistic attitude even as she appreciated his protection.

When he turned as if to leave, her heart began to slow and her stomach muscles relaxed.

"I don't know why I bother with you," he snarled. "You're useless. Why am I paying for this place, if you can't earn the blasted rent? Now get out there and hustle your buns, and don't come back until you've made your quota. I want at least four hundred from you before morning."

Silently she began to cry, averting her face so he would not see her silent tears. She was so tired, so very tired and wet, too. When the night turned cold and rainy, all the tourists returned to their warm hotel rooms, and even the older hookers called it a night. It wasn't fair that he forced her to work in the cold rain.

Ed turned to face her as he opened the door. "Don't start with the waterworks. Fix your face. You look horrible. Then get going."

She wiped her sleeve across her cheek. "Okay," she whined, "but it's cold and nobody is walking around. How am I going to find anyone?"

"That's your job, not mine. Other girls seem to make out all right. Try the bus depot and the station. Why don't you try fixing yourself up? Wear something tighter, show more of the goods."

"You'll have to give me some money to do that, and I know you won't."

"Damned right! You'll only fritter it away, you stupid kid." He slammed out and she was alone.

Moving to the chipped metal sink on the back wall of the small room, she examined her reflection in the cheap cracked mirror. Her cheek looked swollen where he hit her, but it was not too bad.

This is a dump, she thought, as she caught the long view of the room as she held a cold washcloth to her face. The narrow bed, a too low second-hand table, the single upright chair, an ancient rug with half its nap missing, so that long threads caught at your feet, dirty walls, and a window covered with aluminum foil so she never got any daylight. What a life and somehow she dared not break free of him. Yet could she? It had taken her a long time to realize he was taking advantage of her.

Towards morning she got lucky at the bus station and spent ten minutes in the back seat of a rental car. The john gave her a brand new hundred-dollar note. Then, hoping to find more game, she hung around the depot lobby where a fat old banker type asked if she were free for some fun. That was better because they went to his motel room and, as was usual with most fat men, he came when she put her lips on him. That earned her another hundred. When he asked for more, she raised the price and walked out with nearly two hundred and fifty bucks. That, plus the other hundred was only fifty short: she decided Ed would accept it, and forgive her for the earlier slip.

Then it occurred to her that she could buy herself a bus ticket and get away from Ed. Simply vanish. He would never think of looking for her, probably not even miss her.

A pimp, they called him, and he had other young women in his stable, all young street walkers like her, all hating every minute, yet reluctant to forgo the tenuous stability of his protection. He professed to love her and even as he said the words, lately she began to wonder if he said the same to the others. Ed had spent many hours in her small bed teaching her new ways of making the johns climax quicker, explaining that the more men she serviced, the more money she would make. She, the world's stupidest idiot, tried her best to please him, tried to prove what a great hooker she was. Stupid, stupid, stupid! Anyway, how could a man love a female that slept with anyone who asked? A woman who did it with winos, druggies, old men and married men? Why had it taken her so long to realize it? She grimaced at the thoughts that raced through her mind, wondering how she could be so dense when she knew she was not.

"When am I going to get some of my money?" She recalled once asking him as he lay smoking.

He blew out a long plume of smoke. "It's safe, sweetheart, safe in the bank, earning interest. Don't you worry. Another year and you'll be rolling in it."

"Can I see the bank book?"

He laughed and coughed. "I don't carry things like that around with me, you know. It's in my safety deposit box. I'll fetch it next time I visit."

"Promise?"

"'Course, chicky," he had said. However, he never did fetch it, so she became convinced he hadn't banked her earnings, but spent the money on himself.

Her doubts were proven when one day last week, when walking aimlessly around downtown, lonely and penniless, she saw him driving a new grey Jaguar, a beautiful woman by his side. They were both well dressed and laughing at a shared joke. Dodging behind a street vendor's stall, she stared as they got out and walked up the steps of the Dorchester Hotel. He was so attentive, holding her elbow and leaning forward so as not to miss a word of her reply. His suit was well tailored, better than the suits her father wore, and his shoes shone brilliantly. It was the only time she had seen him wearing anything other than his motor cycle leathers and those huge heavy boots.

Once, desperate to use the bathroom, she had sneaked into that prestigious hotel. Its marble and glass lobby awed her, as did the brass and crystal fittings where obsequious well-dressed staff stared at her as if she were a monster in their midst. No, that was no place for a common tart.

So, she thought, Ed has a gorgeous companion and is accustomed to dining in style. With narrowed eyes she watched the doorkeeper greet them and hold open the huge brass door. This discovery of Ed's other life had opened her eyes.

Now as she huddled in the doorway out of the rain, rage surged through her and she knew she must leave him and his stable to their own devices. He wasn't going to push her around any longer. Time to leave, time to grow up, time to become part of the real world.

Quickly deciding, she snapped out of her revery and went to the wicket where she bought a one-way ticket to Toronto, her hometown. Surely her parents would be pleased to see her.

♥

Christine dozed as she sat on the bus, warm and dry for a change. Past glimpses of her life flashed into her mind: tiny glimpses of her luxurious home, glimpses of the parents who cared nothing for her. At one time she had secretly harboured the hope that they would look for her, have her picture on milk cartons and on TV, but nobody had rescued her.

In her years at home, she would sit beyond the curve of the circular stairs every night and listened to them talk. It was her way of finding out things, had been since she was small and able to get out of her bed. Neither of them talked to her, never had a conversation. They ordered her around, assigned chores, and nagged about her bad grades. Christine felt sure they did not love her, that she was an imposition that interfered with their social life. Neither showed her any form of affection, both constantly told her of her bad habits, bad behaviour, bad school results.

So why should she try? To please them? Her father was not so bad, but he was too demanding of her.

"She's uncontrollable these days, Jeff." She had heard her mother say once.

"I don't think you're talking to her properly, Milly. She's almost fourteen now. Try talking to her woman to woman, not as mother to a daughter. Those old-fashioned methods are long gone."

"Too right, Dad," Christine whispered, straining to hear the answer. She sat huddled into a ball, arms wrapped around her knees. Her mother was at the sink, clattering dishes, rinsing them before putting them in the machine, and talking toward the window.

"I'm not talking about anything she shouldn't already know. She's old enough now to pick up after herself, to help with the chores, to run a few errands." That whining tone her mother affected grated on the ear.

"Now, Milly, we both know she's not easy to deal with, but she's a reflection of you and, as such, you should make allowances."

Christine heard the sound of pottery breaking. "Exactly what is that supposed to mean?"

She heard the scrape of her father's chair as he rose and smiled. Good old dad.

"Come on now, Milly. Most teenagers go through this stage and all I want is for you two to stop scrapping. You're too much alike, both headstrong and stubborn."

"Oh, get away from me. I am *not* stubborn. I don't know where you get that idea."

She could hear the desperation in her father's voice, thinking 'he'll do anything for a quiet life, will Dad.' His tone was patient and smooth, trying to stop the argument from escalating. "Look, all I meant is that you stick with things, that you're not a quitter, but then neither is Christine. She's just as stubborn, but right now her ideas don't gel with yours. Let's face it. This isn't the age we grew up in, Milly, things have changed, and she has the same outlook on life as her peers. Girls are no longer servants to their mothers, they don't jump to attention because you give an order. Leave the girl alone for a while, let her stew on things. She'll get the idea on her own if you don't do everything for her. Let her dirty clothes lie on the bedroom floor."

A pan clattered. "Honestly! I don't know why I bother talking to you. She'll wear them creased and filthy and bring shame on us."

"I doubt that. Once she realizes you won't wash and iron, she'll start to get the message."

'Yeah, sure, Mom,' she thought grinning, 'and when did you ever wash or iron? You've got Mrs. White to do all the hard work while you sit around giving orders.'

Jeff's voice of reason was calm, no hysterics for Dad. "She's always had the nicest clothes we can afford, hasn't she? She won't want to let her image start slipping. Christine isn't as stupid as you seem to think."

She leaned forward to hear every word. 'Right on, Dad.'

The dishwasher door slammed, ready for Mrs. White to start in the morning. Her mother was now facing the hall door. "Stupid? I never thought for one second that she was stupid. Stubborn and intractable, uninterested in the things that matter most, yes, but not stupid. If anyone is stupid around here, it's you."

After sitting through an interminable argument about her father's faults, she got bored and returned to her room with its white furniture and flounced curtains. Petal pink and cool white, the colours she had chosen herself last year when they started on the annual 'beautification' as Mom called it. She jumped into bed and pulled the down comforter around her as she switched on her new white TV with the earphones. Soon she forgot the argument raging downstairs and fell asleep almost as soon as the television movie started.

Christine came back to the present as the bus brakes squealed. How long ago that seemed now, and she strained her eyes to see out the dusty window. Nothing out there but dreary streets, run down tenements and boarded up stores. Sitting slumped with her shoulder against the window for so long made her feel stiff and she winced as she sat up straight.

♥

The bus lurched around corners as it bumped and rolled through the centre of the city. Too bad this was not one of the newer buses that had movie screens and reclining seats. The stench of diesel fuel made her nauseous as she stared out the window and took in the sights. Old houses leaning against each other, boarded up windows, faded paint peeling off 'For Sale' signs, winos standing in doorways, smoking or drinking out of paper bags. What a dump it seemed, then again outbound buses always used the back streets, not the smart roads the tourists usually saw.

After an hour, she started to doze and, since the seat beside her was empty, let down the arm rest and lay with her head on her coat.

As she dozed, her mind returned to her childhood home where she had been safe and well fed. She pictured her father, a tall man, good looking, who dressed well, shined his shoes and always wore a hat. Her mind flipped back to when she was six or so and her excitement when her father bought a new car, his second new car in two years.

"You're a superlative salesman, Jeff," her mother said and Christine wondered what superlative meant. She asked her mother later.

"It means your father is very clever. Complete strangers trust him, and he can converse intelligently with many people from many professions. That, together with his after sales follow-up calls bring him repeat business."

"Daddy is clever?"

"I just told you that, Christine. Pay attention. The company will soon promote him to Floor Manager and he'll earn a bonus for every car sold through the dealership. Yes, your father is an ambitious man."

She recalled thinking that selling cars did not seem like much of a job, not for a father.

She sighed and changed position as she thought about her mother. Millicent, tall and slim, with dark-brown eyes that glared like gimlets when she was angry, did not work outside the house, but played at housekeeping. She belonged to all the best local clubs, volunteered at the library and the resource centre, played bridge with the ladies, and took tea with the Wednesday afternoon Fine Arts league. What a laugh! What her mother knew about art she could inscribe on an eyelash.

Of them both she had inherited her mother's dark eyes, her slim frame and energy. From her father came her looks, the straight teeth, and his confidence. Neither of her parents was worthy of a second glance, but their combined genes had given her the best of their good points, and she knew she was sometimes beautiful. Ed had told her that countless times, but then again that was probably part of his pep talk. Yet she knew she was attractive, even when she was dirty.

Come to think about it, life before she left home had been good, and only now did she appreciate it. Maybe if she had stayed, she would have come to accept the scolding, the constant subjection to what she had interpreted as misery. They knew nothing, her parents, didn't see that things had changed in the world, that their rules were idiotic, that other girls in her class had more freedom, had large allowances, could stay out late.

She sighed fitfully. Too bad she had run away because that had not turned out anything like she expected. She thought back to all the nights when she slept in shop doorways and winos accosted her, or slept in garages or sheds. The nights when she almost passed out with hunger, when her stomach was aching for sustenance, so much that she ate left overs from fast food garbage cans. She slept on room floors when other runaways took a shine to her and lost her virginity to a youth who promised her a home. Somehow she had survived, and, as the weather warmed, had found a life on the streets, stealing clothing from markets and food from market stalls. The only thing she shied away from was drugs.

Christine had used her savings, money saved from birthday and Christmas gifts, to travel as far as she could. Her money took her to Edmonton. Then Ed took her in, gave her a home. When he found her, she wore stinky old clothes and her pasty face was a mass of pimples. He took her with him to a small apartment, had given her new clothes, let her bathe and rest.

Too bad she had ended up paying for his largesse. Come to think of it, she had not had a good bath since she had left his home, a nice long bath that made her fingers and toes wrinkly, a soothing bath where she could doze and dream. In the past three years, all she had was a washbasin and a small ragged towel. Ed did not care.

Yet why had she stayed so long? What had Ed offered that she could not do without? His presence was reassuring, his maleness and comfort always available when she felt like ending it all. He seemed caring enough then, those times when she said she wanted to quit. Always he had talked her around, had made love to her as if he cared.

She changed position and tried to fall asleep again.

CHAPTER TWO

"Look, mother, you simply can't live here alone." Milly's anger rose as she contemplated her mother. "Talk about stubborn. Why don't you sell this place and come to live with us? I could look after you."

"I'm *not* alone because Mrs. Grant comes in every day. You want my money, that's what you want." Her daughter's Good Samaritan act did not fool Evelyn, who knew Milly thought only of herself. They had driven away the child, the girl that Evelyn loved, because she and Jeff thought only of themselves and had no patience with Christine. Evelyn had searched for her, had paid for advertisements, contacted Child Find, placed ads in local newspapers, whereas Milly simply washed her hands of the truant.

"I do not! We have more than enough money of our own. You surely realize you shouldn't be alone in this huge old place. Anything could happen."

"You listen to me, Millicent, *this* is my home. I've lived here for almost fifty years. Your grandfather bought this house for us before we were married. I'm at home here."

"Oh, Mother," Milly raised her hands and eyes to heaven. "You're not getting any younger, and you know how we worry about you."

Evelyn laughed bitterly. "Oh yes, you worry all right. If I didn't call you occasionally, you'd forget I was alive. I can't recall one instance where you called me. Too busy with your committees and clubs, too busy wining and dining with customers that Jeffrey hopes to impress. You don't fool me for an instant."

Milly tossed her head and started to examine the Chinese antiques in the china cabinet. "You're becoming impossible, but then all old people get crotchety. My friend Jane found a lovely retirement home for her mother. You'd like it there."

"What's the matter with you? Can't you hear straight? I am *not* moving to any home, or to your house. This is my home and here I'll stay." She glared at Milly and put up her hands as Milly opened her mouth to speak. "Why don't you try to find Christine? That's a better use of your valuable time. Maybe she's sick or in prison, or . . . I don't know what. Just go away, go home, go and bother somebody else."

"Oh, mother, what are we going to do about you?" Milly picked up her purse and smoothed on her fine kid gloves. "I'll be over occasionally to make sure everything is all right, but don't think for one moment that we're going to accept this ultimatum of yours." She looked over her shoulder at her uplifted leg, making sure she had no runs and that her shoe heels were clean. "Jeff knows, as you do yourself, that you shouldn't be on your own."

Evelyn watched her and sighed, knowing Millicent was vanity personified; all that constant checking that nothing was out of place. "Do leave off, Millicent. Jeffrey doesn't like me, any more than I like him. Go home. I've managed without you both for years now, and I'll continue to do so."

Milly slammed out of the house and stood for a moment on the wraparound verandah. It was a beautiful house. Victorian and well maintained, it stood proudly among the great old beeches. The carefully groomed acres set it apart from its neighbours.

Jeff, she knew, would not be pleased because he promised the bank manager, who coveted the house, that her mother would sell when asked. After all, he said, an eighty-seven-year-old could not possibly manage the upkeep for much longer. Mind you: her mother had money, lots of mutual funds and investments about which Milly could only guess.

Her father, a good businessman who died when she was twenty, had amassed millions. He had willed two million to her as his only child, set up trust funds for his favourite charities and left her mother with more money than she could ever spend. It was Milly's money that had bought their social clout, her money that had built their house and afforded them a life of luxury. Jeff played at being a businessman, but he had no real feel for work. If her mother would move in with them, they could sell the old house, free up funds for Jeff. No way would she deign to use her own money for his foolish schemes.

Now she gazed at the garden with its massed perennial beds and sighed. She had always loved this place. Admiring the garden, she headed down the crazy paved front walk to her car, and as she turned the key in the ignition, she looked up at the three storey house, thinking how majestic it looked. A 'painted lady' as Americans called Victorian houses, ginger breaded and shuttered, gabled and stained glassed. Her mother always ensured the paint was kept fresh, the windows cleaned once a month, the gardens tended weekly. Oh, she could not fault her in that regard, and had always thought of it as her mother's wish to leave the house in tip top shape for her, her daughter. Now things had changed. Jeff needed the money more than she needed the real estate.

"She's put her foot down, Jeff," she said later when they sat drinking their pre-dinner martinis. "She won't budge from that house until she's in a coffin."

Jeff snorted with annoyance. "Damn and blast the old fool. Mr. Jennings is willing to pay market value and that's somewhere around four hundred thousand plus. With that amount of money I could buy the dealership."

She put down her glass and glared. "Still, it is not *our* money. It's *hers*."

Jeff looked at her, disappointment evident in his stare. "She's not long for the top now, and you'll get the lot when she goes."

"Don't talk that way. She's my mother."

"Too bad you've ignored her for so long, then. If you were closer, you could have moved her out, no trouble."

"I suppose you've been the perfect son-in-law?"

He shook his head. "No. I haven't, but she's never liked me and lets me know it."

"That's true. Well, you'd better think up another plan to get the money since she's not moving. Even if she did, she'd bank or invest the proceeds."

He filled a tumbler with Scotch and ice and glared at her. Milly had more than enough money and yet she staunchly refused to offer him any help.

♥

Christine woke with a start when the air brakes screeched. An accident? No, only another scheduled stop. Her empty stomach rumbled, but she knew she must conserve her cash. Maybe a doughnut and a Coke would suffice to ease her hunger.

What would she find when she reached Toronto? Would her mother welcome her home? Somehow she doubted it. Better that she invent a good story before she arrived. She could say a cult had brainwashed her, spirited her away to Edmonton and held her with many others. They had made them sell flowers on the streets and the airport, made them beg on street corners. That happened all the time and her parents would surely accept her explanation. She would say they had starved her until she did their bidding, and that always two of them worked together so neither could steal the money.

Yet how then did she get the money for the bus trip? She could say she found a wallet that had no identification. Did that sound logical?

Sighing, she stared at a wino begging outside the terminal, wondering why the police did not move him on. They had moved her on enough times, and that's when she was cold, sober and a juvenile to boot.

A man boarded the bus and sat next to her. He kept trying to talk to her, but she was having none of that.

"You going far?" he asked.

"Nope."

"Going to school?"

She glared at him, knowing she looked untidy and dirty, knowing the makeup alone set her apart. He was persistent, but she ignored him. Eventually he gave up and she put back her head and dozed.

Again Christine thought back to her days at home and the reasons she had run away. Her mother was the worst, always nagging. Her father was always at work, or attending meetings of the Chamber of Commerce and other organizations that could further his career. Why were her parents not like those of the others in her class? Parents who said they loved you, took you to concerts and shows, attended school plays, let you take tennis lessons, ballet and tap? All they wanted was for her to study, to stay home and do chores. Her mother had driven her out with the constant harping on the same old subjects, and her attempt to turn Christine, who she took to calling Tina, into a model child. No, she had done the right thing, although it had not turned out the way she had visualized it back then.

All through her young years she had longed for a good friend, a real pal. Someone to talk with about her problems: the problems that had seemed so enormous to her juvenile mind. Every time she got close to a girl in her class and invited her back to her home, her mother went out of her way to be rude and monosyllabic, making it clear that the girl was not welcome. She had forced her to give up any hope of a long lasting friendship with her own peers. Now she wondered if her mother had changed.

Did her mother still dress to the nines? Did her father still wear a well-tailored three-piece suit? Was the house still the same, expensively expansive? She did not miss them though, not at all, but they were her parents and surely should take her back.

The one person she did miss was her grandmother. Her Gram was a sprightly old thing, always well dressed, her hair always neat, her manner one of confidence. Yes, she would be glad to see Gram.

♥

It was eleven fifty at night when they arrived in Winnipeg and she saw the man leave the depot with an obese wife and two teenagers. At ten minutes to one, the next bus would leave for Thunder Bay. To kill time, she sat at the lunch counter and bought another doughnut and Coke. Soon she would need to eat properly because already she could feel the lightness in her head, feel the strange sensation in her legs, as if they could not hold her weight. She spent the remaining time walking around the terminal, trying to get the cramps out of her legs, getting some air into her lungs.

At twelve fifty-five the bus door closed and the driver pulled out onto the street. Thunder Bay was the last change, so when they stopped again, she would be close to home. Strange how it took so long to cross the country by bus when buses always took the shortest route. Maybe she should have taken the train, but too late now.

The vehicle was packed and a woman sat next to her. Not that she was talkative, but Christine noticed how she held herself away from contact as if Christine might have a disease. She smiled into the window, and looked at the passing downtown stores.

CHAPTER THREE

Evelyn smiled as the lady from Meals on Demand set the neat tray in front of her.

"I do appreciate this kindness," she said. "I could make my own meals, of course, but the lady from the social agency told me I would have a better diet this way. She came when someone sent her to find out if I needed Meals on Wheels."

Evelyn peeled back the foil. Today it was roast beef and roast potatoes with peas, gravy and a whole wheat roll. At one side stood a small green salad and she smiled at the container of Jell-O and whipped cream. "This is very nice."

The woman picked up the insulated container and smiled down at her. "Eat it up now, like a good girl. Oops, that sounds silly that, doesn't it, Mrs. Wallace? Never mind, I know you'll enjoy it and I'll see you tomorrow. Leave the tray on the counter and I'll take it back with me tomorrow. Don't bother washing anything. We have a sterilizing washer for that. Have a good afternoon, now. Bye, dear, I'll let myself out."

Evelyn ate her meal and decided it was very tasty. This all started when a lady from social services and Meals On Wheels had come to see her. The official asked questions about her likes and dislikes, if she had any allergies, what medication she took. They were nice people, though she could not fathom how they had come knocking at her door. Then the woman asked questions about her income and lifestyle.

Unfortunately, the lady explained, that since she was not penniless, and had a woman coming in every day, she did not qualify for Meals on Wheels. That was all right with Evelyn since she had not known of their existence. However, the woman gave her the name of Meals on Demand and Evelyn called them. The very next day they brought her a meal, saying she would get one every day from now on, except Sunday.

Whoever had sent the woman had done her a favour, though. The meal meant she did not have to make a big production out of supper. The woman from the agency had told her eating a large meal at noon, was better than eating a lot in the evening. She did not say "at your age," though Evelyn knew that's what she meant. Mrs. Grant, her daily woman, was a passable cook but her meals were heavy on starch and fat, something Evelyn found nauseating these days.

When Mrs. Grant arrived late because of a dental appointment, she saw the tray and pulled a face.

"You getting Meals on Wheels now?"

Evelyn shook her head. "No. Meals on Demand. A kind lady told me about them. It's nice of them to look after me like this."

Mrs. Grant grunted. "You have to pay, you know. Not that paying will bother you, I dare say. You enjoy and don't worry about a thing."

"I'm not worried, why should I be? Don't wash the tray, the lady said not to."

"Sure!"

"What's the matter?"

"Oh, nothing." Mrs. Grant pushed the tray to one side and started on the kitchen counter.

"Is something wrong?" Evelyn asked, wondering why her daily looked decidedly cross.

"It's simply that once you get on the list of shut-ins and elderly, the people at City Hall begin to take an interest."

"And?" Evelyn looked puzzled.

"There's a housing shortage, you know. This place could house about sixteen or eighteen, if not more if they come from a third world country. They'd want you to sell up and move out, put the place on the market. They're converting old houses like this into apartments."

Evelyn sat, stunned. "They could force me out?"

"Sure enough, Mrs. Wallace. You're too old to be living alone."

"I'm not alone. You come every day, the gardener comes about twice a week in summer and every day in winter to shovel the snow. The man comes to clean the windows, the cleaner comes to pick up and deliver, the grocery store brings my order, the paper boy comes every morning. I see enough people on a daily basis who know that I'm self-sufficient."

"I know you are, but that's as maybe, Mrs. Wallace. Them people down at social services are a law to themselves. If they think you should live in a home, they'll do it, with or without your consent."

Evelyn thought about that later as she sipped the tea Mrs. Grant brought her. Thinking that anyone could remove her from her home was ludicrous.

Then it dawned on her. Millicent, Millicent had done this! This was what devious Millicent had intended: she had sent those people from Meals on Wheels to get Evelyn's name on the rolls of elderly. Well, darned if she would let them push her around. The doctor had told her she was in exceptionally fine health for her age and she did not even need glasses. No, she would stay here in her home until it was time to meet her maker.

♥

Milly, well aware that social services and Meals on Wheels would alert the authorities, all of whom knew that allowing an aged woman to live alone was precarious, had made the anonymous phone call.

"So she accepted. At least I know they called on her," she said triumphantly to Jeff who nodded and grunted. "Well?" He sat impassive, expressionless. "Don't get too excited, will you? Don't you realize what this means?"

"It means your mother might get a return on some of the millions she has spent in taxes over the years and good luck to her."

"Oh, don't be so pedantic. It means the authorities have her on their files. It means that sooner or later they'll force her to move into a retirement residence where they have nursing staff, it means . . .,"

Jeff glared at her. "No, it does not. It means you're determined to move your mother from her home to get your hands on her money before you're entitled to it. Anyway, she doesn't qualify for social services. She's living in a mansion with servants."

"I notice you were the one who suggested she sell the house, so *you* could get your hands on her money. Why now am I the heavy?"

Jeff picked up his crystal tumbler and headed for the tantalus. "I managed, as you very well know, to get a bridging loan and a line of credit from the bank." He splashed scotch into his glass. "I own the dealership now and we're doing very well. I don't need her money and neither do you."

She eyed the crystal glass that held far too much single malt. "Oh honestly, you'd think I was the wicked witch of the west the way you talk. It's not right that she lives alone like that. Anything could happen. She could fall down the stairs or something and lie there for days. Then nobody will know and she'll finish up in a home anyway."

He set down the drink on the obligatory coaster and lit a cigarette. "You know, Milly, you sometimes astonish me. You don't give a fig about her welfare. You haven't done so since you left home to marry me and now here you are, all gracious sympathy, worrying about your poor old mother. Anyway, she's got enough people at her beck and call. She can well afford them." He rose and left the room. She heard him rummaging in the refrigerator and the snap of the ice tray. Cubes tumbled into the ice bucket.

She sighed, another evening of listening to his rambling as he slowly got drunk.

♥

Christine sat on the edge of her seat as they sped along the highway. It was nearly five o'clock and the sky had lightened considerably. How large the outskirts of the city seemed and it was only four years since she left. Huge malls stood among acres of parking areas, houses had sprouted like weeds, the highway had gone from four lanes to twelve, and cars streamed past endlessly. Where were they going so early in the morning? To work?

The downtown terminal looked depressing and unclean, as did most bus stations. Even the pigeons that pecked at invisible specks seemed grimy as they wandered around, unafraid of human feet. People struggled with unwieldy packages and enormous suitcases tied with leather straps, vagrants mooched around looking for handouts or a handy piece of luggage to steal. The air was thick with diesel fumes and she coughed as she waited for the driver to remove cases from the luggage compartment, and a crowd of passengers blocked the walkway.

Home, this was home. Christine wandered around the corner onto the main street. A busy thoroughfare clogged with cars, trucks, buses and a few people. Strange, she mused, how white faces were the minority so early in the day. A horde of people emerged from the subway and rushed along the street, all in a hurry to get to work. They almost knocked her over. She browsed along the store windows, admiring the latest styles of shoes and cast an anxious glance at her own ancient running shoes, a cheap copy of Adidas that had not worn well. Once she had worn real leather shoes, shoes with labels, shoes that cost nearly a sixty dollars and her only a child. Now look at her.

She stopped in front of an arcade and eyed herself in the large mirror. Although partially obscured by the neon lettering: "Exotic Dancers! Peep Shows! Lap Dancing!" she saw enough of herself to know she looked like a tart. Cheap clothes, too tight, too short, too everything, shoes run down, too much makeup, too many split ends in the unwashed hair that hung lank against her blue jean bomber jacket.

How could she go home looking like this? How could she expect them to welcome her if she looked like a hooker? And she was a hooker: she had no doubt about that. Her mind skipped back to all those hours of the talking, about how they wanted her to attend college, wanted her to become something, wanted . . . . . yeah, well, that's why she had run away, because it was all about what they wanted, never what she would like. Maybe, though, they had changed, would accept her as she was now, might like having her back.

With her mind in turmoil, she slouched along, brushing past those men and youths that tried to speak with her. To her men were all the same now, wanting only one thing. Too bad she was a walking advertisement for her profession. When she saw a cop watching her, she flipped him the finger. He frowned, but did not move as she turned toward the bus stop and waited in line.

As she sat, watching other business bound passengers steer clear of her seat, she felt her heart sink. She must look horrible if no one wanted to sit near her. Maybe she smelled, probably did. Hunching her shoulders, she sat looking from under her brows. A load of old farts, was all, a bunch of sanctimonious do-gooders who were afraid she might give them a disease. She had no venereal disease and had always attended the free clinic for a weekly checkup. No fear, she wasn't going to get aids or herpes or VD or any of the other horrible things.

How to smarten herself up, that was the question? Then she thought of the gas station on the corner of the street one road over from where she lived. They had a washroom and she could get the key from the office. Too bad she'd forgotten that if she had gone to the train station, they had cubicles for that purpose.

Walking boldly into the gas station office, she took the key off the wall and nobody even noticed. She opened the toilet door and locked it behind herself. Ugh! The washroom was putrid. Why didn't gas jockeys bother about hygiene, she wondered as she stood to pee? Oily fingerprints covered the toilet seat and the toilet bowl looked like it had never been cleaned. Above the foul sink hung a small mirror and she looked at herself, knowing she must do something about her hair. Her only choice was to tie it back with the old scarf she had in her pocket. Then she washed her face, without soap because the dispenser was empty, and dried herself with rough paper towels. It took ages to get the mascara from around her eyes but when she had done all she could, she thought she looked better. Not clean, but better.

CHAPTER FOUR

Milly glowered at the chairlady on the podium and leaned close to the woman sitting next to her. "How dare she hand the plum assignment to Mary after I did all the spade work?" she whispered.

All those weeks of carefully cultivating Mrs. Beresford had been for naught because now Mary Greenberg was chosen to entertain Forest Hills queen bee at a social tea. While Mary's house was much smaller than hers and lacked many modern conveniences, Mary wore the best furs, the most expensive jewellery, custom made high heel shoes and let everyone know it. She had no class, Milly thought, but then Mary's parents were *nouveau riche,* having made their money through a chain of pawn shops. True, they had achieved the pinnacle among the higher echelons of the financial world and their home was in Forest Hills, enclave of the rich and famous, but that was not the point. She, Milly Armstrong, a seventh generation Lancastrian, had proven her worth to the club, had worked endlessly to promote the club's objectives. If it were not for her efforts, they wouldn't be sitting here in a private room at the prestigious Granite Club.

"It isn't fair. I find it disturbing and a public slap in the face."

The woman patted Milly's Versace clad arm in sympathy but did not agree.

Milly rationalized that they were all jealous of her, jealous of her looks, jealous of her fine home, jealous of the new Mercedes she drove. Time and again she had run for office, urgently seeking the nomination for president knowing that is where she would shine, but this group of menopausal old tabbies refused to acknowledge her existence.

"I should quit this club, that's what I should do. Then they'll sorely miss my hard work."

"Don't take it so seriously, dear," the woman said softly and turned away.

She sighed as a show of hands seconded the motion to have Mary hostess the tea and reluctantly raised her own hand. No, no way would she quit. Whether they realized it or not, she was the glue that held this group together.

♥

Jeff's stomach plummeted as he read the latest Profit and Loss statement.

Harry watched his expression and said, "I think you're over extending yourself, Jeff. Do you need four hundred cars on show? More to the point, can you sell them without cutting prices?"

Jeff glared at him over the papers. "Leave that to those who know, Harry. I know what we can and cannot sell. We'll show a decent profit this year, all things being equal."

"Jeff, Jeff," he said quietly. "Did you read the Financial Times? Things are not equal this year and won't be for a long time. We're heading into a recession and the first thing people will do without is a new car. They'll hang onto what they've got."

"Bullshit! I know we'll clear the lot this summer. People love the new models. Look out there," He gestured out the office window at the show room where people were admiring cars and talking to salesmen. "Does that look like we'll have unwanted stock? It's been like that since the new season designs arrived."

Harry shook his head. Jeff only saw what he wanted to see. "It's always like that when the new cars arrive, but that doesn't mean they'll buy."

Jeff's eyebrows rose. "What a negative attitude! Leave it to me, Harry. You concentrate on making a few adjustments to last quarter's figures to keep the tax people off my back."

"I can't keep doing that, Jeff. Sooner or later they'll come after you and then where will you be? I've already altered sales figures three times, but before our year end, you'll have to pay the whole whack. So far you owe the government about £56,000.00 in back taxes, about a hundred thousand with your arrears. Where will you find that amount?"

The amount struck a chill into his bones. "Do leave off, Harry. The bank will refinance my loan again. We've done it before. No problem."

Harry stood and went to the door, pausing with his hand on the knob, "I don't like this one bit. I want to get it straightened out now and put us in the clear. I'd lose my licence if anyone found out what I've been doing for you."

"Worrywart." Jeff laughed and shoved the papers in his top drawer. "Get back to the books and make us look rich."

Harry slouched across the show room floor. He glowered at the salesmen, all wearing confident smiles, dodged sticky fingered children, then smiled at a junior salesman who waited, duster in hand to remove hand marks.

With narrowed eyes Jeff watched his progress and lit a cigar. Harry was a pessimist who let his conscience bother him too much and that would not do. He must do something to get Harry back into the proper mood, a mood that allowed him to cheat the authorities with no qualms.

Still, that was not his only problem with Harry. Inevitably Harry would catch him out in his fiddling. So far he had covered his embezzlement by the late posting of invoices, but Harry would realize it the minute he saw the still hidden paperwork. Darn Milly and her search for social standing. What she spent on clothes would keep the average family for a year in luxury, and him, he was a fool to allow it.

He lit another cigar and put his feet up on the desk. As he blew out a satisfactory cloud of aromatic blue smoke, he considered his wife of twenty years. Her beauty had drawn him into her trap years ago and, weak willed and easily led, he had allowed her to cuckold him. What a strange word to pop into his head, *cuckold*. However, that was exactly what she had done, fooled him, and him with his eyes wide open. Sure he had gained stature in the community, wore the finest suits and shoes, drove the best car, but what had he accomplished? A runaway daughter, a few thousand in the bank, plus pile of debt that would suffocate a lesser man, and all because of his wife.

How had he let himself take all those orders, knuckle under to her demands? It was her looks and ancestry, of course, of the way people thought of him with her as his wife. His wife's family, once the corner stone of city society, had employed about half the local population in the cotton mills and foundries they owned. The last mill now stood shuttered and decaying because a multinational, who thought nothing of mass layoffs, bought it out when the economy was bad. Evelyn was worth millions, as was Milly, because both were astute with their investments. A rich wife was usually an asset, but Milly was not the ordinary run of the mill wife, she was too independent for his liking. No matter what her worth, she considered every penny *he* earned as her own.

Putting down his feet, he dug into the bottom drawer and pulled out a large ledger. Here he recorded his deals, the secret deals made with both customers and suppliers that comprised his getaway money. In another town under another name he had a large bank account about which nobody knew. When the axe fell, and unquestionably it would, he would simply drive away from the city with Jennifer. To hell with Millicent.

CHAPTER FIVE

At ten o'clock, Christine arrived at 27 Grosvenor Court, her Forest Hill home. The cul-de-sac looked quiet with no neighbours around to gawp. Around the centre hammerhead, with its lavish circular flower bed tended by the tenants' gardeners, stood the largest houses. Their house was the biggest, with strong lines and deep bay windows. The shiny black front door stood at the top of six wide deep granite steps, guarded by two Chinese dragons.

How pretentious it is, she thought as she gazed at it through new eyes. The gardener's truck stood curbside and she spotted him industriously weeding the flower beds in the middle of their lawn. A recent addition was a small fountain and a large bronze statue of a heron, waiting for fish that would never appear.

All three garage doors were closed so maybe her mother was out at one of her interminable meetings. She ran up the steps, the house key in her hand. How glad she was to have kept it, although often she felt tempted to toss it away.

Mother had redecorated the hall, but that was her standard practice. She grinned. How awful if anyone saw the same furniture for more than a year. Now a long mahogany table stood along one wall with two mirrors at right angles, reflecting the circular staircase and the leaded cut-glass French doors to the living room. Putting back her head, she looked up the staircase, now wearing claret red carpeting and carpet rods that shone like gold. Large oil paintings, her mother liked to say were ancestors, still lined the walls, glaring or smiling down on those lucky enough to gain entrance. Christine grinned, knowing her mother had purchased them at a classy antique dealer and chose them for some small resemblance to herself or Jeffrey.

Pausing before the hall table, she considered her reflection. Not bad, but not good. Still, if her mother were out, she could go upstairs and have a bath and wash her hair. Tenderly she touched the large floral display and inhaled the sweet scent of stargazer lilies - the aroma of money. Her mother had fresh flowers delivered twice weekly and the house usually had a splendid arrangement in every public room.

Going into the living room, she paused: not a thing out of place. It could be a museum or show room. The thick carpet muffled her steps as she walked through to the other door, the one leading to the breakfast room, which in turn led to the kitchen.

"Good grief!" Her mother stood and almost toppled the chair. She had been writing at her desk.

"Hello, Mum." Christine tried to sound sincere but it did not come out that way.

"Christine?" Milly stared at her, her mouth agape, as if she could not believe this was her daughter.

"Of course. How many other girls have keys to this house?" Milly swallowed as Christine watched and said scathingly, "No 'welcome home?' No, 'we've missed you?'"

"Of course, dear." Milly put a hand to her face as if in dismay. "Why don't you go up stairs and take a bath? I can smell you from here."

"Sorreeee!" Her tone was insolent. "Boy, some homecoming! You don't even want to know how I am or where I've been. Go and have a bath, is all you can say. Use disinfectant too, I suppose." She turned on her heel, peeved and irate, but knew being angry with her mother achieved nothing. "I'll talk to you later."

"I have a meeting this morning." Milly said, handkerchief to her nose, following her through the living room, as if her long lost daughter had not suddenly appeared. "I was getting my notes together."

"Still trying to climb the social ladder? Nothing changes, does it?" She walked to the stairs.

In her room she looked in the closet where her clothes still hung on the rails, neatly lined up in plastic dust bags with lavender pomanders. She wondered if they would still fit. At least she could get herself clean and look half decent before her father arrived home. Dad was easier to deal with, and sometimes he listened to what she had to say.

It was heaven to lie in her bath, to which she added half a bottle of fragrant bath oil. She had washed her hair first and now it was under a towel turban. Good old Mom, she thought grimly, she makes everything so easy. Her mother still kept the cabinet stocked with deodorant, shampoo and other necessities. In case anyone popped in here when they visited the house, she supposed.

After a complete make over, she eyed herself in her dressing table mirror. She looked good now. The pale blue blouse, the only one that still fit, matched her eyes and her skin looked fresh and young under the slight touch of foundation. Whatever else had happened in the last four years, she was now a young woman, a lovely young woman. She dug through her old jewellery box, one that Gram had given her years ago, and found a pair of blue earrings. Tossing back her hair, she posed for a moment, a smile on her face. This is how she must look when her father saw her.

♥

"She suddenly appeared while I was writing in the morning room." Milly said into her cell phone as she drove to her meeting.

Jeff smiled. "That *is* good news. How is she and how does she look?"

"Terrible. She looks like a tramp, a no-good street urchin. I could smell her!"

Jeff chuckled, pleased that she was home. "I bet she's been living rough. No wonder, with nobody to support her. Where has she been?"

"I don't know. I had to leave for my meeting. I told her to bathe."

"Some mother you are, Milly. Didn't you show any relief that she was home? Did you welcome her back?"

"No, I did not! She's a dirty little wretch who has a lot to answer for. Why, we gave her everything and how did she repay us? She shouldn't have run away."

"Look, Milly, she ran away from you . . . from us. It's now time to find out *why* she ran away, what we did wrong. These past three years you've tried to pretend that she never existed, but she does and now she's back. I'll be glad to see her. Tell her I'll be home early tonight."

"Well, I suppose I should be glad something gets you away from that company, even if it is only Christine."

"Thanks a lot." Jeff slammed down the phone. Why did he put up with it, with her?

♥

Later that afternoon Milly walked slowly up the front steps wondering what she would find. She mentally shuddered to think the girl had come back to disrupt her life.

The hall was empty, but nothing seemed out of place. Somewhere she could hear loud rock music and figured Christine must be upstairs. On the hall table lay the mail and she picked it up, riffling through the envelopes to check for invitations. Not a one, she tossed them on the table: all bills and Jeff would handle those.

She walked through the living room and stopped to pick up a book placed face down on the chair. "Really!" The girl knew better than to treat a book like that, knew it broke the spine.

The kitchen was aromatic with roasting meat and her daily woman, Mrs. White, smiled as she saw her. "Good meeting, Mrs. Armstrong?"

"Not bad. I still think it's a bad idea to hold yet another bazaar but those women are scared to change a thing. We have so many ways to raise funds these days."

Mrs. White dried her hands on the tea towel. "That's for sure. I spent a hundred dollars on a ticket for the hospital fund raiser. The chances of winning are one in twenty and the prizes are fantastic. I could win a brand new house and a car."

"Hmm." Milly knew the odds were much higher and grew larger as someone won each prize, but advertising was advertising, and who was she to pop Mrs. White's bubble?

As she set out the cups, Mrs. White looked at her mistress. "Nice to see Christine is home, I must say. You must be ever so pleased. She looks lovely too, now all her puppy fat is gone. She's a real credit to you. Breeding always shows."

Milly regarded her with puzzlement. Christine was not exactly a model child, had never displayed any depth of character or shown any breeding. She was a walking complainer, always whining, always . . .

"Oh, so you're home," a voice said from behind her.

Milly turned to see Christine clad in a pale blue blouse and black skirt. Her patent leather shoes were years out of date. Darn it all. She would have to buy a complete new wardrobe for the child.

She nodded, satisfied with what she saw. "You look much better. By the way, how often do I have to tell you not to put an open book face down?"

Her face contorted into a grimace. "Boy, oh, boy. Welcome home, Christine. We all missed you. We're so glad to see you. We can hardly wait to start nagging at you again." She turned on her heel and left.

Mrs. White stood listening and Milly turned to her. "Don't you have any work to do? If you're finished, you may leave."

"I've got the veggies to do, then I'll go. If you ask me. . . .,"

"I did not ask you, Mrs. White. I never ask you. Please get on with your work."

Milly went to look for the girl. She did not find her downstairs, so went up to her room but Christine was not there. Oh my God, Jeff was coming home early and the little fool had run away again.

♥

In a newly opened pizza parlour, Christine sat eating pepperoni pizza. The store manager kept staring at her and made her feel uncomfortable. Strange how that had never bothered her before. She had enjoyed people looking, had flaunted herself. Had he never seen a hungry person? She sipped at her Coke and took another bite as he sauntered over.

"Excuse me, but aren't you Christine Armstrong?" he asked, hands on hips.

"Who wants to know?" she asked, neatly patting her lips on the paper napkin. 'Dab gently, dear, don't make it look like you're drying your face.' The grating voice came back like a burp.

"I'm David Chesterton. I sat next to you in class."

She looked up at him. He was good looking but not very personable, and maybe that's why he worked for Pizza-Pizza. She smiled. "Hi, yes, I'm Christine."

"Heard you left town and saw a notice asking for information about you, that you were on the run. Did they find you and fetch you back?"

She grimaced. "Boy, diplomacy is your middle name, Dave. No, they didn't fetch me back. I wanted to come home for a visit, but I'm not staying long. This place is a dump." She gestured around with the hand that held the pizza. "So I guess you made the big time, eh? Manager of a pizza joint."

"No need to be sarcastic. I don't think you've changed much. You always were sarky."

"Thanks a lot." She turned back to her pizza. Boy, if only he knew what she knew about life. "I'd like this to go, please. I don't much care for the staff in this place."

His lip curled. "Certainly, madam. Please let your friends know about our restaurant."

She laughed in his face. "Boy, they sure have you brainwashed."

As she strolled home with her pizza, she wondered if her mother had yet discovered that she had stolen the money from the earthenware jar where they kept petty cash for household needs. Still, she had not asked for food, had not put them out looking after her, so what the heck?

CHAPTER SIX

Jeff doodled as he thought over his options. Too bad he had borrowed money from Arthur French because without that particular debt he thought he could deal with the others. His mistress, Jennifer, was worth every penny, though: warm and caring, she was the antithesis of Milly. So far he had managed to put aside a tidy amount for their future.

He smiled, then started as a voice said, "Good news, I hope?" Harry stood in front of his desk.

Jeff flushed angrily. "Do you usually walk into an office without knocking?"

"The door was open, and I did tap but you were deep in thought. I saw your smile and thought you might be in a better mood."

"Well, I'm not. Get the hell out, Harry, and fetch the figures for the month." He glared at the accountant, all good humour gone.

"No way. You'll start changing them again and we're getting close to the end of the quarter. We have an accumulation of taxes due this time and I don't want you insisting on more double entries."

Jeff stood. "Am I, or am I not the owner of this company?" he said through clenched teeth.

Harry stood his ground. "If you want the honest truth. No. Your name might be plastered all over the outside walls and the door, but no, you don't own a thing. The bank and people who bankrolled you own seventy-five percent of this place, the government owns the rest in unpaid taxes. I don't know how we've managed to hang on this long, and if it wasn't for some very tricky and illegal book keeping, we would already be in bankruptcy."

Jeff drew himself up and let out a deep snort of disgust. "The trouble with you paper pushers, is that you're short on balls. All companies sail close to the wind and we're no exception."

"Well, I don't like it, and I won't do any more of your so-called paper pushing. I'm out of here and now." He turned to go.

Jeff rushed from behind the desk and grabbed his arm. "Wait a minute. Sit down and let's talk this out. You know how much I rely on you. I can't afford to lose you."

Harry reluctantly allowed Jeff to propel him to a chair, then snorted with derision. "The only thing you want me for is to steal from the government, plus I'm the only one who knows of your true financial status. Don't try to kid me, Jeff." He stood again. "Anyway, I've accepted an offer from another company and start next week."

Jeff flushed deep red, then the blood seemed to drain from his features and left him looking pasty and distinctly unwell. "Please, Harry," he begged, "We've always worked well together, and I know I've asked you to do some things that you don't like, but don't leave me like this. How could I ever replace you?"

Harry stared at his shoes. "I don't know and I don't particularly care. I've got to get out before the tax man comes calling . . . and he will, you know." He raised his head and stared steadily at Jeff, leaving Jeff aware that he could not talk him around this time. "I don't think many top end dealerships have such low sales figures. It looks suspicious."

"I thought we were buddies, Harry, I thought you were a good friend." Jeff turned to stare out at the showroom. What could he do? How could he talk Harry around? "To leave me in the lurch without notice is hardly ethical."

Harry sighed and nodded. "That's very true, but what do *you* know of ethics?" he said and Jeff felt a tingle of hope. He turned to face Harry and smiled, but Harry said, "That doesn't mean I'll go along with any more falsification of your books. What I did was illegal, and I'd like to point out that when they catch up with you, it'll be muggins here, the accountant, they'll come after. I'm licenced and should know better. Too bad I didn't quit two years ago when you first started this juggling. Sorry, Jeff, but I have to leave."

"Look, I'm the owner, I carry the can for everything, not you."

"Sorry, but that's not true. You didn't sign the tax returns. I did."

Jeff slumped into the visitor's chair and sagged, a picture of misery. "Come on, Harry, you have to help me get out of this mess."

Harry stood and walked to the door. "No can do, Jeff. I wish I could say it's been a pleasure, but I can't."

Jeff wanted to accuse him, say that he was a crook, knew it was wrong and yet did it because of the hefty bonuses he paid him, but he did not want to make an enemy of Harry. Not right now.

What could he do? To hell with everything. He took his overcoat and hat from the brass stand and left. Jennifer would change his mood.

He forgot all about his daughter.

♥

In the hushed privacy of the 'originals' area in Creeds, Milly posed in a Ralph Lauren gown that fit her like a second skin. Far too young for her, it revealed too much wrinkled cleavage.

Milly, blind to her own faults, decided that the weekly massage and her sessions with the new personal trainer had paid dividends. "What do you think?" she asked her companion, Joyce Rawlings.

"Nice," Joyce pondered for a moment. "I hope you won't mind me saying so, Milly, but I think it's too young for you."

"What do you mean? The saleslady wouldn't have pointed it out if she had thought so."

Joyce coloured. "Sorry. Do you like it? Well, that's all that's important, isn't it?"

Milly turned around. "Where is that woman? Ah, there you are. Is this dress too young for me?"

She smiled and said softly, "No, madam, only someone with a figure like yours could wear that style."

Joyce pulled a face. These women all worked on commission, so anything, no matter how unsuitable a garment a customer liked, they obsequiously agreed looked wonderful. She could not think why she had agreed to come out with Milly today and already regretted it. Still, Milly was very generous to those she considered friends, and she anticipated a delicious lunch at a top class restaurant.

"I do think it looks good on me." Milly postured in front of the three-way mirror, pleased to notice how the fabric skimmed her form, showed no evidence of fat or lines. "Yes, I'll take it. Charge it to my account." She turned to Joyce. "This will knock their socks off at the art gallery dinner next week. I can hardly wait."

For the next hour they spent time selecting shoes, earrings and a necklace to match the gown. Milly bought perfume, silk stockings, new underwear, made an appointment for a facial, massage and hair styling for the afternoon of the event. Then they had lunch at the best hotel.

"Not a bad morning's work, eh Joyce?" Milly said as she sipped her tonic water. "I can't eat too much." She turned to the waiter. "I'll have sole, broiled or steamed without butter, and a small salad with no dressing." She had not even looked at the menu. "I'd better not gain even one ounce if that dress is to fit properly. Good job I dieted these last two weeks."

Since Milly was paying, Joyce ordered lavishly. "Jumbo shrimp cocktail to start, then prime rib with baked potato and carrots." She handed him the menu. "Oh, and I'll have another martini, please."

Milly regarded her with contempt. "Really, Joyce, how cruel you are. You're going to sit in front of me and eat that much food? I think you should monitor your intake, dear, you're getting chubby."

'Oh no, you don't, lady,' Joyce thought, 'you'll pay for dragging me around the stores today.' She smiled widely as if she had not caught the hint. "My Marty likes me with a few extra pounds. He says I'm voluptuous." She smirked and patted her rounded tummy.

"Then he's not got much taste." Milly sniffed. "You owe it to him to keep yourself trim and fit."

Joyce drained her glass. "When I went to that spa with you and lost nearly twenty pounds, he didn't like it at all. I had to eat like a pig for a week to get back to my usual weight. I don't know about Jeff, but Marty doesn't like thin women. He likes to feel he's holding something other than a bag of bones."

"Well, really!"

Joyce reached across and patted Milly's hand. "Not my words, Milly dear, his."

Milly made desultory conversation as Joyce ate her way through the lunch. She nibbled at her salad, ate one bite of a dry bread stick, picked at the sole and drank four glasses of water. Joyce asked for the dessert menu and ordered Black Forest cake with ice cream.

"This is absolutely the last time I bring you with me when we shop," Milly said, her face contorted with anger. The down turned mouth made her look much older, and the rows of discontent on her forehead ran deep as tram lines.

"That suits me," Joyce said as she forked up the last of the cake. "Are we having coffee, or is that off your list?"

"We're leaving." She looked around and signalled for the check. Joyce sat back and waited, for once silent.

Milly picked up her purse and stood. "Well? Come along, don't dawdle. We have things to do."

Joyce followed in her wake as they stalked from the restaurant, grinning like a fool, knowing she had eaten her way through at least sixty pounds of Milly's money and enjoyed every mouthful.

CHAPTER SEVEN

Christine slept late the next day. Accustomed to being awake all night and sleeping all day meant it would take time for her body to adjust. Last night her father had not come home and her mother's mood was volatile.

She stretched and yawned. Today she would keep a low profile, wait for the storm to pass. Reaching over, she picked up the new novel she had taken from the downstairs library. Her mother purchased every best seller for display on the library shelves of Whites. Not that Milly ever read any of them: she only scanned the reviews and the jacket blurb. Still, she had to give her some credit because Milly could discuss the books at length as if she had read every page. Most of this was information gleaned from other people who had read the novel.

She opened to the first page. 'A Novel by Rosamunde Pilcher.' Of course, she remembered her, she wrote "The Shell Seekers," a book she loved. Snuggling down into her pillows, she began to read.

Hunger forced her out of bed two hours later. As she entered the kitchen, she spotted Mrs. White in the adjoining laundry room taking things out of the dryer. She looked in the refrigerator and took out a plate of sliced roast chicken.

As she looked for the butter and bread, Mrs. White came in. "Oh no you don't, young lady," she said snatching up the Saran wrapped plate and putting it back in the fridge, "This chicken is for the tea sandwiches. Your mother has company coming today."

"I'm hungry. What else do we have that you haven't earmarked for mother?"

"Well, we have cheese and bread of course, not the fancy stuff, but we've got some white bread in the pantry."

"Make me a toasted cheese with tomato," Christine ordered. "I'll be in the office. I need to check on something on the computer."

Mrs. White glared but said nothing. No use causing another upset, what with Mrs. Armstrong in the mood to kill Mr. Armstrong, and a gaggle of posh ladies coming to tea. With bad grace, she got out the cheese slices.

Christine sat in the home office and switched on the computer. People kept all kinds of secrets in computers and she needed to find out exactly how their financial arrangements were holding up. If her mother could buy designer originals, then surely they were rolling in it.

She discovered many of the files were password-protected and whiled away an hour trying to break into them. Using words that would probably mean something to her parents, she finally hit the jackpot when "Millicent" opened a financial file. While she had no knowledge of the particular accounting program 'Quicken' she soon found her way around and sat reading the state of the company finances.

Surely this had to be wrong? Maybe her father didn't know how to use the program. How could they owe so much money to so many people? While she had cut short her education, she was intelligent enough to know that low income and high expenditures made for bankruptcy. Wow! Did her mother know? How did they go through life knowing of this horrendous debt load? Her mother went out shopping almost every day. Nothing was from regular shops and everything wore high class labels. Where on earth did she get the money from if they owed so much? She shrugged, thinking maybe they had Swiss bank accounts and investments.

Christine knew her mother had money of her own but found nothing in the computer that she could access. She sighed, knowing that was par for the course. Her mother was secretive about her personal worth and she'd often heard her telling her father that he must pay for something or other, that she had no funds. Oh well, it was none of her concern, but she felt a twinge of unease about the company affairs. Surely they could not continue to live in this manner? On the other hand, maybe these were old files.

♥

Jeff stared at the balance sheet. God, he owed over £518,000.00 to the bank and various others stupid enough to make him loans, plus the taxes he must submit. Arthur French constantly called to ask for figures, making it obvious he would soon want a proper accounting.

He knew he was in trouble with Arthur, who owned a large manufacturing concern and was intent on gaining entree into supplying auto parts. Jeff, always fond of exaggerating his powers, had given Arthur impression that he was very close to those in power at the Jaguar manufacturing plant, and thus Arthur thought he was doing himself a favour when Jeff went calling to ask for a loan.

Where had the money gone? He knew that his own sizeable salary and Milly's constant demands had taken the largest share. Harry had insisted from day one that they paid the sales associates on time, but the dealership building with its plate glass walls and marble tiled floor required much maintenance. Its eye-catching summer flower beds were imperative to draw attention to the stock and in winter snow removal was essential. To top off this outlay and, to his chagrin, his embezzlement loomed greater than he had imagined. Because he had always procrastinated if anyone important were around, his personal ledger was missing more than a few entries. He down loaded a copy of the accounts onto a diskette to take home. Maybe he could make more sense of them in private.

Darn it all! Other than leaving with Jennifer he saw no way out. At least the half million in his secret account was collecting interest until it was time for them to leave.

He dialled her number.

"Hello?"

Her soft voice, almost a whisper, always made him smile. Jennifer was such a lady in every sense of the word. "Hello, sweetheart, how are you?"

"Oh, Jeffrey, I was thinking about you, and here you are. It must be telepathy. I'm fine and how are you?"

This silly conversation was the norm when he called her, even when they had seen each other the previous day. Yet he did not mind, though it would have made him angry if Milly had ever called with such inanities.

"All the better for hearing your voice, my love. I was thinking about the future. You did think about my suggestion?"

"About moving to the Bahamas? Oh yes, it sounds so lovely and I can hardly wait to go."

"Me too. Well, it might be sooner rather than later, Jenny and I thought I had better let you know so you could make your plans."

"Oh," He heard the sharp intake of breath, then an ominous silence.

"Is there a problem?" His stomach prickled with nerves.

"Oh, no. I don't suppose so, it's just that I must visit my mother and let her know I'm leaving As I told you, she's very sick right now."

Jeff felt a cold chill settle on him. "How ill is she? You never told me anything about it being serious."

"I didn't want to worry you, sweety. After all, you don't even know my mother. She's dying, Jeff, dying of cancer. They say she can't live much longer and I had thought everything would be finished before we moved away."

The tears were flowing, he could hear her stifled sobs and his heart went out to her. Poor little Jenny, so warm and caring, and he was dragging her away when her mother needed her most.

"I don't mean tomorrow or even next week, Jenny, but definitely within the next six months."Could he ask how long the old lady would live? He shook his head. It hardly seemed the Christian thing to ask.

"Thank you for caring, Jeffrey. I think that would be more than enough time and then we would have nothing to worry about."

"I hope they're taking very good care of her." He hoped she croaked and soon.

"Oh yes, they're wonderful with her at the hospice. I'm going to see her today and I'll tell her all about my plans. I won't mention you, though, as that might not be wise. My going there will be something nice for her to hear. She loved the tropics and went to Nassau or Barbados every winter."

They chatted until a sales associate knocked at his door.

After dismissing the man, he thought about Jenny's mother. The old lady, or so Jenny called her, had never entered their conversations until lately . . . around the time when he asked her to go away with him, now it sounded too much like an excuse. Next time they met he would ask what hospital she was in so that he could send flowers. That was one way he could learn the truth.

♥

Two weeks later Christine, wearing a new dress and matching coat, sat on the bus. Today she was visiting her grandmother and wanted to look her best. Milly had taken her measurements and had a fashionable shop send over a selection of appropriate clothing, from underwear to outerwear. Choosing those items that appealed to her, she had told her mother that the others were 'crap and get them out of here.' Milly said nothing: her glare said it all.

Catching her reflection in the window, she smiled. This was not the young teenager who worked the streets of Edmonton. This was a sophisticated young woman with more than her fair share of looks. Patting back her newly styled hair, she admired herself.

Since her arrival home she had seen her father only once as he was going out the door. He nodded and said, "Nice to see you again." Her mother ignored her most of the time, being completely involved with various charity works and social clubs. When they did by chance meet at the table, Milly always found something to criticize, and they fought over trivialities. Strange that her father was never present for any meals.

When she asked Mrs. White, she said, "Your father has odd hours, but that dealership is open all hours. He can't take time away when he's that busy. Anyway, if he can't be here when the meal is ready, he eats out. Your mother doesn't like the routine upset."

"He could eat in the kitchen then, couldn't he?"

"Oh my dear, your mother wouldn't like that. Eating is done in the dining room."

Christine found it incredible that her mother was unwilling to allow any leeway. Surely a working husband should have some license, could come and go as his work demanded?

She sighed, she would never figure out her parents, but then why should she try? They did not seem to care about her. Left to her own devices, she grew bored and started to frequent a coffee shop in a nearby shopping centre, the Cyber Web Cafe, where she surfed the net and talked to others like herself. Getting away from the weekly influx of chattering, wealthy women became essential to her state of mind because when her mother gave a lunch or a social tea, Milly trotted her out, dressed in her best, to announce her return. One afternoon of passing around canapes and cups of tea was enough.

Her grandmother would welcome her back. That was a given.

♥

Evelyn sat in the conservatory reading when a movement caught her eye. A large butterfly had somehow found its way inside and flitted from plant to plant. How refreshing it was to watch nature at work, she thought, wondering simultaneously if the gardener had sprayed anything toxic on the plants.

Mrs. Grant came bumbling into the area where she sat. "You've got a surprise visitor," she announced, her face gleaming from hard work, her hair a mess. "You'll never guess who!"

Evelyn's face lit up in a broad smile. She loved surprises and it did not seem like it could be Milly, or Mrs. Grant's expression would resemble an undertaker with bad news. "Do not start playing games, Mrs. Grant, show them in."

She turned her head and sat upright. Who could it be?

With a gasp, she saw the young women enter and cried out with delight. "Christine, my dear Christine." Standing, she opened her arms, and Christine went into them.

"Hello, Gram."

"Welcome home, my little chicken." She hugged her close ands kissed her cheek. "I've missed you so much. Sit down with me and tell me all about your travels."

The tears misted her eyes as she sat by her grandmother. This was the homecoming she had wanted. For an hour she talked and Gram made no comment, other than 'tutting' or smiling. Christine told her the unvarnished truth, knowing Gram would not castigate her.

"So there it is, Gram. I've been so stupid. I know it now and thank heaven I didn't catch some horrible disease. I had another checkup last week. Everything is okay and I can put the past behind me."

Smiling widely, Evelyn patted her hand. "And that's where it belongs, darling. Now, we must have tea and scones." She picked up a small crystal bell and rang for Mrs. Grant.

"She's getting Meals on Wheels now, your Grandmother, or should I say Meals on Demand," Mrs. Grant announced after taking Evelyn's order, her face a mask of distaste, as she came into the conservatory. "I told her, yes I did, the authorities will be putting her out of this house soon. You mark my words . . .,"

Evelyn put up her hands. "Thank you very much, Mrs. Grant, but I've heard it all before. Please serve us, then leave us to talk privately." Evelyn grumpily waved her away.

Putting her hand on Christine's, she leaned forward and spoke quietly. "She takes too much on herself, does Mrs. Grant. Her nose is out of joint because I didn't ask her to cook my meals, though she likes the money I pay her. She'd like to live in now she's on her own and to tell you the truth, I'm thinking of inviting her. I need someone here full time at my age. Your mother's actions brought that home to me, as did the woman who brings my meals."

She grinned. "So why don't you ask her? Isn't she a good cook?"

Evelyn pulled a face. "Not really. She specializes in fry ups." She laughed and Christine joined her.

"How are the meals they fetch you? Good?"

"Oh yes, dear. Only the best ingredients, I'm sure, and a certified dietician makes up the menus. I'm sure they're well balanced."

Christine wondered why she would bother with an outside service. "Oh Gram, you're such a good cook yourself that it must be awful not being able to cater for yourself."

"It is, child, it is. I do sometimes manage to make a grilled cheese sandwich, but my arthritis is so very bad some days that I can't peel potatoes or lift anything heavy." She paused and smiled, "But I shouldn't call you a child anymore, should I? You're a lovely young woman now and a credit to the family."

Christine frowned and sighed. "My mother doesn't talk to me and I never see Dad. Neither asked me where I'd been so they obviously don't care and they didn't even welcome me home." The ever present tears misted her eyes. She felt more alone and abandoned that she ever did when living on the streets.

Evelyn put her arms around her granddaughter and comforted her. "Would you like to come and live here?"

She drew back, eyes wide, as tears trickled down her cheeks. "Could I?"

"Of course." It did Evelyn's heart good to see the radiant smile. "I'd love to have you here. I could teach you how to cook and we'd could tell Meals on Demand not to bother."

She hugged her grandmother. "Hurray! I can live here in this lovely house and look after you, Gram. I don't mind paying penance by learning how to cook."

"Now, now, don't start with your back talk, missy, or you'll be out of here."

They laughed and Mrs. Grant came to see what was so funny.

It made them laugh harder when Evelyn whispered, "Here she comes, the nose of Toronto."

CHAPTER EIGHT

"How's Miss Christine doing?" Mrs. White asked Milly when she served her tea in the breakfast room one morning.

"I have no idea. I must say she manages to keep out of sight very nicely.

"I mean, since she left." Mrs. White eyed her mistress with some alarm. How could any mother not notice that her child had gone?

"She left?" she shrilled. Milly's eyebrows rose to her hair line.

"The beginning of last month. 0I asked her where she was going with the suitcase and bags and she said 'somewhere else.'"

Milly's face shut down and her lips compressed into a straight line. "That will be all, Mrs. White. Do not disturb me again this morning."

She glared after the woman as she left. So the little fool had run away again, had she? This was all Jeff's fault. He had never as much as attempted to speak to the girl since her arrival. He also had a lot to answer for because he had cancelled Milly's credit cards, an embarrassment of the highest order. Things were not right in her world and she wondered what else he was hiding from her.

Picking up the phone, she called him.

"Jeff, she's run away again."

He did not ask who was calling. Who could mistake that shrill, whining tone?

"So, let her run. She's not a baby and you're not exactly a good mother."

"I beg your pardon? When was the last time you spoke to her? She's been back about three weeks, yet you never even came home early to see her. Don't blame me, because you're as much at fault."

"Come on now, Milly, she's old enough to look after herself. You said so yourself." He eyed the portly man who was haggling over the sticker price on a top of the line car and watched his sales rep.

"I thought you should know that she's gone. Anyway, that's not why I called. I've had my credit card seized and that's your fault. Didn't you pay the bills this month?"

At last, she had come to the reason for her call. "Yes, I did. However, if you're talking about that card you wangled for yourself from American Express, I didn't and won't pay that. I don't mind paying legitimate bills, but you spend like money is no object and I can't afford it."

"How dare you not honour that bill? My debts are your debts. You've *got* to pay it."

"No, I don't." His voice was smooth, knowing an attempt at sarcasm or vituperation would rile her even more. "I wouldn't try to use the other cards either, because I've had your name taken off as signatory."

He smiled malevolently, holding the phone away from his ear, as she shrieked, "What? You can't do this to me, damn you. You can't!"

He kept his voice low. "I can, and I did. We're having some financial problems. You wouldn't understand, so I won't bore you with the details. Suffice it to say, we have to cut back on expenses, and I do mean drastically. The government wants our taxes paid up to date. We can't afford not to pay, or they'll seize our assets."

Milly felt a cold chill. What else had he not told her? "Good grief! Don't you have an accountant to look after such things?"

"Not any more. He quit."

"Oh my God, what are we going to do? I can't survive without my cards."

He chuckled, picturing the look on her face. "Of course you can, Milly, don't be stupid. What's so hard about not shopping for a month or two? It's not as if you need anything."

"They can't see me in the same old clothes, Jeffrey. You know that. The ladies would be sniggering behind my back."

"Even more reason why you should stop your eternal quest for equality with the upper class and try being yourself for a change. These are not the days when your family ruled the neighbourhood."

"Don't I know it! I never thought you could be so heartless, but it just goes to show how wrong I could be. I'll expect you home at seven. We need to talk."

"Sure." He put down the phone and grinned. She'd have a long wait because tonight he and Jennifer were dining at the Empire Club.

♥

After two months Christine was so at home with her grandmother that she felt she had always lived with her. Every day she would learn a new dish and was now a capable cook.

"I suppose you'll be messing up the kitchen again today, eh?" Mrs. Grant did not like coming in to face a messy kitchen. Christine never bothered cleaning up, because, as Gram said, she paid Mrs. Grant to clean.

"Yes, and why not? Gram is teaching me how to cook and that means I have to use pots and pans."

"Too bad she didn't teach you about cleaning up after yourself. How hard can it be to rinse pots out and put them in the dishwasher?"

"I sometimes put things in there, but you always take them out and wash them in the sink." She shrugged. "I don't know why you bother. The machine does a good job."

Mrs. Grant, one of the old school, did not trust the dishwasher and liked to know things were spotless.

Christine smiled. "I bet you even do your washing by hand, don't you?"

"No, I do not. I have a washing machine. I do like to pre-soak things, though, with some soda or borax."

"You're so old fashioned, Mrs. Grant," she said as she laughed, "You could have been the cleaner on the ark. Why don't you take it easy and let the machines do the work. I do."

Her face reddened. "Yes, and I get to clean up after you. I'm not here to look after you, you know. Mrs. Wallace is my only concern. She pays me."

"She is my grandmother, and she wants me here. I don't think you have any say in that."

"You've got a big mouth on you, that I will say. There's nothing wrong in speaking your mind, but don't be so hurtful."

"I didn't mean to hurt anyone. All I did was state a fact."

Mrs. Grant slammed down the tea pot and faced her. "Well, I . . .,"

"What's going on in here?" Evelyn stood at the door.

"Mrs. Wallace, I will not have this, this, this . . .," She flung her hands around searching for a word, "*girl,* telling me what to do. I was working for a living before she was born. Telling me that I'm old-fashioned. What's so bad with that?"

"Nothing at all, Mrs. Grant," Christine said, before her grandmother could answer. "All I did was point out that half the things you do are unnecessary. Pots rinsed out and put in the dishwasher will be spotless without your scouring them *before* putting them in the machine."

Evelyn nodded. "I must agree with Christine this time. That dishwasher is the top of the line and used in many restaurants. Spare yourself, Mrs. Grant. Take it easy."

Mrs. Grant huffed and puffed as she pulled out the vacuum. "I like things clean, Mrs. Wallace, you know that."

"Yes, I do. Do try to get along, you two. I don't like bickering."

"Yes, Gram." Christine looked suitably chastened, and Mrs. Grant scurried away to vacuum the living room.

"You were right, Gram. She's jealous because I'm doing the cooking now."

"That's as maybe. Well, she'd better get over it or I won't ask her to live here. Now come along, I want to show you something."

♥

Milly decided to bring things to a head and went down to see Jeff. Things looked quiet enough, she thought as she drove up to the dealership, so he could not make the excuse of being busy. The new models glistened in the morning sun, reflecting glaring light from their sharply sloping front windows and she had to look away, dazzled.

She blinked rapidly, hoping to remove the dots imprinted on her retina as she turned into the lot. In front of the plate-glassed marble-floored showroom stood one of the salesmen who immediately came to the door. She smiled. They knew she was somebody, unless, of course, he had recognized her. He had.

"Good morning, Mrs. Armstrong," he said as he opened her door.

"Good morning. Leave the car here. I won't be long." She wiggled her fingers at him as she entered the glass door.

"Would you like the car washed?" he asked, squinting at her through the glare.

"Not today. I won't be here long enough."

One of the staff was polishing finger marks off the cars as she walked through the showroom to Jeff's office. She caught a glimpse of him as he talked on the phone, his face wearing a broad smile. It irked her when she saw his expression change as he caught sight of her. It was almost one of hate.

"Well?" she said, as she entered his office. "What's the matter? You look as if you've seen a ghost."

"Oh, I was thinking about you and there you were." He laughed not very sincerely, and added, ". . . like I had conjured you up out of thin air."

"Hmh!" She stood looking at him and decided she didn't like what she saw either. He looked washed out, tired, almost exhausted with bags under his eyes and a badly creased jacket. Surely he had not worn the same suit two days in a row? "I'd say something was wrong, and you've not yet told me about it."

She lowered herself into the visitor chair, showing the right amount of silk clad leg, her hands neatly placed in her lap. Putting back her shoulders, she stared at him. No way was she going to start this confrontation. He had to go first.

Jeff slumped in his chair, looking defeated. He put out his hands as in supplication and cleared his throat. "Er, Milly . . ."

"Yes, Jeff? What is the problem? Obviously one exists since you stayed out all night."

She knew about his mistress, everyone did. They all laughed at him behind his back because Mistress Jennifer belonged to anyone with the right amount of money in his pocket. Relaxed, she waited, watching his throat contracting as he swallowed, could almost see his mental gyrations as he sought the right words.

Someone tapped at the door but she did not turn around.

"What is it, Tyrone?" Jeff asked sharply.

"I wanted to talk over a deal for Mr. Waterton, boss. He's almost ready to sign."

"Not now. Can't you see I have someone in my office? Come back later and take Mr. Waterton to lunch. Charge it to the company. Keep him sweet until I can get back to you."

Tyrone shut the door and Milly again glared at Jeff who was still debating with himself. Eventually, she stood and put on her gloves. "I can't see any point in sitting here while you ignore me. What on earth is the matter? Has that little tramp dumped you? Is that what this is about?"

He looked up at her, startled. "What do you mean?"

"Jennifer.Has she dumped you for someone with more money?"

His face was a picture, she thought, as she put back her head and laughed. "Come on now, did you think I was stupid and didn't know about your affair? Everyone knows about it, including our friends. The wives keep me up to date on things, like when you bought her that ranch mink and the Mustang. Oh yes, you treat her very well, Jeffrey, much better than you treat me."

Staring open-mouthed, he swallowed again and stood. "Looks like you know everything then. I was trying to find the words so it wouldn't be so painful for you. From the minute you got pregnant, we were finished, and you know it. If it wasn't for your looks and background, you'd be another housewife with nothing to offer."

Mentally she controlled her temper and spoke in a soft voice. "Really? I notice you like people to see us together. It does your image good, doesn't it? I like people to see us together too, but for other reasons entirely. I think a tame husband on one's arm sends the right message to those of our set who thinks faithfulness is a virtue. They all know about Jennifer and regard me as a saint for putting up with your adultery."

"How very noble of you, my dear, considering you've not got an ounce of sentimentality in you. You let our daughter run away, made no effort to find her, and when she did come home, ignored her. Now she's gone again. Have you tried at all to trace her?"

She flapped a languid hand. "That's not necessary. I cannot believe that you don't appreciate what I have done for you all these years. I exercise, diet and groom myself properly and you don't even notice. I've put years into becoming the type of wife any man would love to have. Yet you, you've let yourself go, haven't you? Put on weight, never exercise unless it's to play golf with someone who could help you in your search for financial gain. Oh no, Jeffrey, do not confuse me with someone who cares about your present problems. As for Christine, we are probably better off without her in the house God only knows what sort of life she had been leading and what horrible germs came with her. Anyway, that is irrelevant. We must discuss this trollop, Jennifer, who, I might add, has been to bed with almost everyone we know."

"Milly, I will not have you talking that way about a woman who offered me comfort when you did not A warm and caring woman."

Her face contorted. "You make me sick. You know that? She's a prostitute of the highest order yet I bet you've spent more on her than you've ever spent on me!"

"That is likely, but then she's worth every penny. As I said, you're not exactly the most caring woman I've ever met. Then again, your . . .,"

Milly, anger surging, jumped to defend herself. "This is not why I came today. I came to discover why you didn't pay the bills again this month. The bank called about the mortgage because you've missed two payments." She almost smiled as she noticed the blood drain from his face. "The store seized and cut up my credit card and I don't see any transfer into my cash account this month. Now, what is going on?"

He seemed to crumple in on himself and slumped in his seat, his face strained. "Look, I didn't pay the bills because I didn't have the money. Before I can pay myself, I must pay the taxes and the staff. We can't operate without clearing our taxes."

She heaved a martyred sigh and regarded him with incredulity. "Why weren't the taxes paid? What did that fool Harry say about this? And why did he leave?"

He blew out a breath, a deep trembling breath that came from his soul and she felt a frisson of alarm. Had Harry been embezzling?

"Harry left because we owed so much in back taxes. I got him to do some creative bookkeeping, but we had to clear everything this quarter." He waved his hands around helplessly. "You know how it is."

"No, I don't know how it is." She squared her shoulders and raised her chin. "This company has always made a decent profit. Through the hard work of the previous owner, everyone knows it as a square dealer, and I had thought you cherished that image. You're stupid, Jeff, plain stupid. How did you ever think you could fool the government?"

"I had no intention of fooling anyone. Think back, Milly, think back to January when you called in that idiotic interior designer to make over the house. Where did you think we got the money for that little venture, all two-hundred and ninety thousand pounds? Then you had to have a new car because the old one was last year's model." He clapped his hands to each side of his face. "Oh my God! What would your posh pals say if they saw you driving a car more than one year old?" He pointed at her, leaning over the desk. "You could have had a company car but, oh no, you had to have a Mercedes. You make me sick. You know that?"

She stood tall and held her ground. "I don't care what you say, Jeff, one cannot cheat the government. They always catch the criminals."

"Oh, la-di-da! Listen to her, would you?" He appealed to the invisible beings that hovered overhead. "She's a walking library of government rules now." Leaning across his desk, he shook his fist at her. "If it wasn't for you, madam, and your penchant for being better than anybody, we might have managed to keep our taxes up to date. I can't understand why you can't comprehend that we can't keep spending above our means. Nothing you see is ever off limits, is it? No matter what the cost, you must have it, and you must have it *now*."

She smiled smugly. "It is your role as man of the house to provide for me. Surely that isn't asking too much?"

"I can't afford you, Milly, not anymore. Get yourself a job, make your own money. I know you've got stock certificates and other goodies stashed in a safety deposit box at the bank. I know your maternal grandparents left you a tidy sum, as did your father, and yet not once have you offered to help me with the business."

She sat up straighter and stared at him. "As I have said repeatedly, why should I? My money is only on paper."

"What are you saving it for, Milly? A rainy day? To my mind you'll never have a rainy day if I keep working the hours I do. You've never lacked for anything, nor would you now if I could afford to keep tipping my hard earned money into your bank account. Face it, those days are over."

Milly sat through his monologue thinking Jeff only thought of himself. "That's why I came here. To find out why you have not paid the bills, and why you have not transferred my allowance to the bank."

"The money is gone, all gone." He waved around his arms, willy-nilly and smiled at her. Not a real smile, more of a grimace.

"What on earth do you mean? Where has it gone, and why haven't you told me about this earlier? The company is still functioning, I can see customers out there, Look there," she pointed through the vertical blinds, ". . . salesmen writing contracts."

He sighed. "Oh yes, they are writing contracts, and we are making sales. However, those sales are not enough to get us out of the hole. I think we must declare bankruptcy. Then we will divorce."

She stood and stared down at him, breathing hard. "Over my dead body will you declare bankruptcy! Neither will we divorce. We'd be the laughing stock of the county." Then she sat down again, trying to think.

"We have no other option unless you are willing to open your coffers to bail us out."

For a moment she considered that option but shook her head. "No, I will not bail you out. You got yourself into this mess."

He crossed his arms over his chest. "Then I call in the bankruptcy trustees."

She stood again, her face expressionless. No way could she let him see the fear she felt. "I don't think so, Jeff. I'll call the bank manager and request a loan. My collateral will more than cover that."

As he frowned, Milly knew she was again controlling his future. How he must hate that. Jeff looked befuddled, as so he should, and beads of perspiration dotted his forehead. He must want to talk to his paramour Jennifer right now, she thought, smiling grimly.

"What will it cost me, this largesse? I know there has to be a catch. I'd sooner declare bankruptcy and get it over with."

Her lip curled. "You turn my stomach. I will not have our name connected with anything as abhorrent as bankruptcy. My family has never. . . ."

"Your family, my dear, never had to live in the real world. They had money enough to cover their every debt. This company would be in the black if it were not for your inbred arrogance and utter disregard for our financial situation. Never would you talk about our finances, not even when I told you we couldn't afford to keep spending money."

"Of course not. Why should I? I expected to lead a life much as mine had been before I married. My mother is a prime example of how one should handle money. She's loaded, even now, even after all these years of living alone."

"Goddamn you, Milly. I don't give a hoot about your mother's financial perspicacity. We're in big trouble and taking out another loan is not going to solve the problem."

She regarded him with pity. "I don't understand why you have such a hard time understanding why bankruptcy is the last resort. You must apply yourself, start cost cutting, cancel all those full page ads in the paper, cut staff if you must, but you must start economizing." With complete aplomb, she smiled as if offering him the answer to his every question.

"What about you?" His face was crimson with rage and he took a deep breath in an attempt to calm himself. "Does this edict apply to you? I don't want to receive any more bills for designer gowns or interior decorators, because I can't, and won't, pay them."

She smirked. "I shall manage. As you so rightly pointed out, I *do* have money of my own." She smoothed her skirt, picked up her purse and smiled evilly. "I will go to the bank now. I think you can expect a call from the manager some time this afternoon."

With an airy wave of a kid gloved hand, she swanned out of his office and left him gasping with anger.

Jeff sat down heavily and pounded the desk with his fists, angry as he had ever been. Another loan would only add to the debt load that was crippling them. No, bankruptcy it would be, whether she liked it or not, but only after he had arranged for a tropical home for himself and Jennifer.

To think she had known all the time about his affair, yet had said nothing. Maybe Milly also had a lover, he thought, maybe she was also having an affair. Yet in his heart he knew Milly would never stoop to an affair, would never want another man to hold any power over her. One whiff of scandal attached to her name might send her mad.

Nevertheless, if she knew about Jenny, why had she let it continue for so long? If, as she said, everyone knew, why had no one mentioned it, even in a joke? Men talked among themselves, everyone knew that, and risque material was the norm. They looked upon a man with a mistress as an idol, someone with the guts to do what they would dearly love to do. Not one word, nothing said at Chamber of Commerce dinners, at the golf club, at the country club, not a word.

Then it struck him, maybe Milly had warned them off and he grinned. He would not put anything past her.

CHAPTER NINE

"**I** think you should think about continuing your education, dear," Evelyn said as she read the badly written recipe Christine had pasted into the ledger. "I find your spelling deplorable."

Christine looked up from the table where she was icing a cake. "Who cares, Gram? When I send things by e-mail, the spell checker does all that for me. I don't need to know how to spell."

Evelyn sighed. To get the girl to do anything she had to resort to trickery and flattery. "Unless you know the word and can spell it, a spell checker can't make sure you have the right one. Some words have many variations, all with different meanings. I think you should attend a good school in the city so you can come home at night. I think I could get you in . .,"

She slapped down the spatula. "No! No, no, no, and no. I won't go back to school and you can't make me."

"But, dear . .,"

"No!"

"I still think . .,"

Christine picked up the icing tube. "Who will look after you? Who'll cook your lunch and supper? Do you want Mrs. Grant's fry ups or Meals on Demand again?"

Evelyn shook her head as she watched her fashion butter icing roses, thinking Christine had talent. Her decorated cakes looked sensational, so attractive that it was a shame to cut into them.

She changed the subject. "That's extremely good and so pretty, darling. I think we'll enjoy our tea time today."

"Yes." She brushed back her hair with her arm. "I like decorating cakes. I got a book from the library last week and I thought I'd try with a basket of flowers for Easter. What do you think?"

"That would be lovely."

"Uh-oh, she's ba-ack," Christine looked over her shoulder as she heard the back door slam. "Here comes another lecture."

"I got everything we needed, Mrs. Wallace," Mrs. Grant announced, looking pleased with herself. "The store is delivering the heavy things tomorrow at nine." She looked at Christine. "I hope you'll be out of bed by that time and can sign for them."

Christine grinned. "All right, Mrs. Grant, I always get up at seven and you know it. I suppose you'll want your kitchen back now."

Mrs. Grant looked at the dirty table, the used pots and bowls, the scattered flour. She sighed. "I don't suppose you'll be clearing up after yourself?"

"That's your job, Mrs. Grant," Evelyn said with a touch of asperity.

"I know, but it's not my job to run downtown to place an order, is it? This young lady could take the bus too, you know."

Christine grinned. "But *I* wouldn't have gone downtown. *I* would have picked up the phone and called in the order Honestly, some people!"

As she started to clear the table, Mrs. Grant eyed the cake. "You expecting company, Mrs. Wallace?"

"No, not today." She looked up at Christine, "I think I'd like to take a walk now, dear."

She rose and waited for Christine to take her arm. These days she could not trust her legs. Twice she had collapsed as all feeling went from one leg.

"Where shall we go today, Gram? The park?"

"I don't think so." She glanced around but Mrs. Grant was in the pantry and lowered her voice. "I wanted to get away from Mrs. Grant for a while. Her face would sour milk."

She laughed and hugged her grandmother's arm to her side. "Come on, we'll have a few turns around the garden and see what that man has been doing."

'That man' was the gardener. He had his own agenda and planted only those flowers and shrubs he considered appropriate for his design. No matter how much Evelyn pleaded for Black Eyed Susans, he would not plant them, saying they were weeds. When she purchased a container from a local nursery and planted them among the massed perennials, he had spotted them the next day and removed them. Now she watched and said nothing, knowing his work was excellent and it was more his garden than hers.

♥

Evelyn wondered if Christine had called her parents and one evening when they were sitting in the living room watching a TV biography, she asked.

"Christine, dear, you know I told you I would never interfere with your life, that it was your own life to do with as you wish . . . ." Christine nodded and smiled. ". . . but I am now about to break that promise."

"What do you mean, Gram?"

"I am going to ask you a question and I want you to answer it truthfully."

"Okay." She wondered what it could be. Maybe about her past life on the streets? She hoped not.

"Have you called your mother to tell where you are?"

Her face grew stony. "No, I have not, and I'm not going to, either, Gram. She'll be over here interfering and I couldn't stand it."

"That's enough of that. This is my house and what I say goes."

"Oh, Gram, ask yourself why she has never come to see you in the last months. Why she ignores you."

"I've asked myself that many times, dear, but that is not what I asked you. Surely you should let them know where you are."

"No. I won't," she wagged a warning finger at Evelyn, ". . . and don't you dare call them. They don't care about me, only themselves. Mom is so busy with her charities that she can't appreciate how she treated me like a pest that had insinuated itself into her well-organized life. Oh, she bought me things, like clothes and stuff. If I asked for something I usually got it, but that's not loving someone, is it? Just because she's got lots of money is no reason to ignore me. She never put her arm around me or hugged or kissed me. She always talked to me as if I were an adult and should know the way to behave. Then when I made a booboo, she acted as if I were a mad thing that required punishment."

Evelyn listened and knew much this rhetoric was hot air, exaggeration for effect. Yet Millicent had an arrogant manner about her that did not lend itself to demonstrations of affection, so the girl was right about that much. On one hand she wanted to agree with the child, but on the other knew that Christine needed a firm hand if she were to become a well-adjusted woman.

"I think you should think about this, darling. Call them, leave a message on the machine, but at least put their minds at rest. Your mother can do nothing about your living here with me. If you like, I'll call my solicitor and discuss a guardianship."

Christine's face lit with hope. "Would you, Gram? I like it here with you. We have a great time and I'm learning such a lot from you."

Evelyn sighed. "Darling, you should go back to school and I think you know that yourself. Why not think about what career you would like? I'll pay for your tuition and you won't have to leave home."

"All right, I'll think about it. Hush now, the second part is starting."

Christine, Evelyn knew, had no intentions of ever setting one foot inside a school and as for her calling her mother, she decided Christine would conveniently forget all about it.

♥

Jeff sat in the darkened bar in their usual booth. Jennifer was late but, that was usual. He ordered another scotch and water.

It was almost an hour later when she arrived. As she sauntered through the tables, he smiled, all thoughts of argument dissipating. Dressed in a pale pink slubbed silk suit with a frothy lace blouse, startlingly beautiful, every eye followed her.

She air kissed him when she reached the table. "Sorry I'm late, Jeff. My mother kept me so long and was so upset that I could hardly bare to leave her."

"How is she?" he asked.

"Not good." He thought she had tears in her eyes and reached for her hand. "She's very low right now. The matron told me they don't expect her to live for much longer."

Jeff's heart soared. Soon the old lady would be gone, and so would they. Already he had rented a villa in Nassau via the Internet and hired a couple to look after things.

"That's so awful for you, sweetheart," he murmured, caressing her hand. "She'll have a far better life on the other side, though. She'll be happy and will watch over you from heaven." Jeepers, from where did he dig these inanities? It turned his stomach to talk in such a manner, but Jenny always seemed so grateful.

"I know, Jeffy, and I'm sorry to see her go, but it's the best thing since she caught this horrible thing. I wish they could put her to sleep, like they do with cats or dogs, then she wouldn't have to suffer so much."

"I'm sure the doctors are doing everything possible. She'll have drugs to stop the pain. In which hospital is she?"

Three times he had asked, and each time she had managed to change the subject. Now she smiled widely and flickered her eyelashes in a way that had once driven him mad with lust.

"I'd love a nice dry martini right now, Jeff. Call the waitress."

He smiled grimly. She had done it again, but this time she was not going to fob him off. When the drink arrived and she sipped, he asked said, "I'd like to send your mother a floral arrangement. I'm sure it would cheer her day."

Jennifer smiled and he waited for an answer. She smiled and patted his arm. "Give me the money and I'll get her something. I know she'd like to see me fetching it."

Damn it all. The old saying popped into his mind, 'foiled again!' He took her hand and squeezed it firmly as if that would make her understand. "I'd like to send it from both of us, dearest. Now which hospital and what room?"

"Oh Jeffy, I don't want to hurt your feelings, but she doesn't know about you and I don't want to upset her. She thinks I'm uninvolved with men and that's the way she wants me to be. I don't know if I ever told you about my father. . ."

Jeff sighed, knowing she was lying again. The number of times she had told him about her dead father, usually when he wanted to talk about their planned visit to Nassau. Was she that stupid? Did she think *he* was stupid? He knew she was about to launch into another saga about a cruel father who beat her and her mother, who abandoned them and turned the mother off men for life. "No, I don't think you ever did."

He listened to her tall tale, knowing she invented every word even as it came out of her mouth, continually contradicting herself. Jenny lied badly, and while he should dump her and get on with his life, he didn't want to lose her. She was the only person who made him feel like a real man, who admired him for his business acumen and position in society. He would be lost without her, but part of his mind knew she was only out for what she could get from him. That was all right, though, because he was using *her* for his own selfish motives.

♥

Her granddaughter had taken to going out after tea and staying out until late. Evelyn didn't bother waiting up for her, knowing the girl was trustworthy enough to lock the doors on her return.

"What time does she get home, I'd like to know," Mrs. Grant said, her face grim. "She's always going out. Are you alone all evening? 'Cos if you are,that's not good enough. A woman of your age shouldn't be . . .,"

Evelyn checked a sigh. "That will be enough, Mrs. Grant. She comes home at a reasonable time for a person of her young age. I think you've forgotten what it's like to be eighteen."

"Hmph! No, I have not. Young people these days get far too much freedom. God only knows what she gets up to, I mean, with all the drugs and stuff."

"She does not indulge in drugs or alcohol. Tina is a good girl and we'll have no more of this. Please sit. I want to talk to you."

Mrs. Grant sat gingerly on a small side chair. Unused to being treated other than staff, she felt uncomfortable.

Evelyn smiled. "Mrs. Grant, you have worked for me now for more than twenty years."

Her face fell. 'Oh my god, she's going to fire me,' flashed through her mind and she felt the tears spring to her eyes.

"We have always muddled along together," Evelyn continued, "I am used to you and you are used to me. I know it has been hard for you since your husband died and yet you have not said a word about your loss. I admire that."

Mrs. Grant nodded, her eyes fixed on the carpet. The carpet she had cleaned on her hands and knees only yesterday.

"I would like you to come and live here, Mrs. Grant. We have more than enough room and it will be more convenient for you in the winter. I would like someone else in the house when Tina is out." Mrs. Grant's head shot up and she stared at her employer. "I will understand if you refuse. Selling your home won't be easy. The home where you and your husband lived for so many years."

She stood, her legs shaking. "Oh Mrs. Wallace, it's so good of you. I would love to move in and look after you and Miss Christine."

Evelyn smiled widely, realizing Mrs. Grant accepted that Christine would stay and she liked her all the better for that. "Move in when you like. Take the back double bedroom. It's large enough for a sitting area, and you can fetch your treasures."

"Oh, thank you, thank you. I'll move in this weekend. The realtor can sell the house without me in residence. I'll be so glad to get away from that place. It has too many memories."

Evelyn nodded and glanced around her spacious living room. This too had many memories: of her and her new husband exploring the many rooms, of when Milly was a toddler and had learned to navigate the hazards of stairs, slippery floors and family cats. No, this was a house of happy memories.

". . . and the drafts in winter are something else." Mrs. Grant chattered on, excited at the thought of moving.

Mrs. Grant stopped talking eventually and Evelyn smiled and ordered her tea and toast. Mrs. Grant sang as she made her way to the kitchen and Evelyn chuckled. At long last something had brought a smile and a song to her daily cleaner, though now she would call her a 'companion.' That sounded much nicer and would please Beth Grant. In her heart she knew she should not be left alone in the evening so often.

She should ask Christine where she was spending her time, she supposed, but that would be prying and surely the girl had enough of that when she was at home. That was another thing, Christine really should call her mother.

At one point she had picked up the telephone to call Millicent, but then changed her mind. What good would her calling achieve? Millicent would storm over to the house and start ordering everyone around and cause hurt feelings. No, better she did not interfere because she knew Millicent would arrive one day, if only to be nosy. Not that Millicent, Evelyn knew, cared much about her, but felt sure her daughter had expectations from her mother's will.

Yes, her will, she must take care of that, must contact her solicitor to have it changed.

"Mrs. Grant will you get Arthur Appleton on the phone for me?" she asked as she accepted her tea.

"So where's her ladyship right now, or should I not ask?"

"She's gone to the library to change my books. I would like you to stop complaining about the child."

"Here's Mr. Appleton." Mrs. Grant handed her the phone and stood hovering.

"That will be all, Mrs. Grant." Evelyn said firmly.

♥

In the mall coffee shop, Christine sat at a computer chatting to a pen pal in Australia. She had found the place by chance one day while window shopping. The Cyber Web Café was a no-frills restaurant that had cosy places to sit and read, computers for access to the Internet, and tables for card games and dining. The clientele was of her own age and she had made many friends.

"Hi, Tina."

Looking up she saw Harvey Wright, his latest hair style a Mohawk of brilliant day-glo orange. She smiled, eyes wide with shock. "Hello, Harvey. Got a new hair style, I see."

"Yeah. Real with it, eh?"

"I thought Mohawks went out years ago, but it suits you."

Harvey pulled a face. "Come on now, Tina. It's bloody awful. I only did it to make my mother angry. She kept telling me to get it cut, so I did."

She laughed. "Wow. That takes some nerve. What did your father say?"

"He laughed and said it would soon grow out. If it wasn't for Dad, I'd leave home, but he's a good sort and sometimes we get along. Not often, though."

They stood chatting, then moved to a long table when the rest of their clique arrived. For the rest of the evening they ate and drank, talked and laughed. At ten thirty, the group rose as one and left.

As Christine rode the bus home, she thought about her friends, Harvey in particular. She grinned as she visualized his haircut. Horrible and a particularly gruesome shade of orange. Good for him, though. He had stood up to his mother and had won the battle. Too bad that she couldn't get the better of her own mother.

Harvey's father was a bigwig with the Regal Bank and dressed in the corporate uniform of navy blue pin stripe suit with a white shirt and understated tie. How he must hate to see his only son dressed like a hobo, too long baggy pants, tattered tee shirt proclaiming 'life sucks!' The hair cut and dye job must surely have brought on his corporate dyspepsia. They were all the same, these parents with money, she thought then, all wrapped up in themselves, all actively dedicated to acquiring more money and possessions.

Gram was still muttering about her going back to school. She had toyed with taking a course in computer programming and then dropped the idea as it seemed such a boring occupation. Cooking she also dismissed as a possibility, because while she liked trying new recipes and eating the results, she didn't want to make it a career. So what should she do with herself? Up to now, she had always had it in the back of her mind that her parents would support her until their deaths, when she would inherit everything.

Harvey laughed hysterically when she told him that.

"You're priceless, you know that?" he spluttered as he wiped his eyes. "You need a job, something to keep your mind occupied. Nobody sits around waiting for their parents to drop dead. Boy, and I thought you were intelligent!"

"I am! And what about you? You're not working."

"No, but I *am* looking, which is more than you are. Boy, waiting for them to die!" He laughed until he saw her looking hurt.

She felt deeply embarrassed because he was right. She was a moron of the first order. Sighing, she considered her options. Tomorrow, she decided, she would read the want ads, see what was available for someone with her abilities.

CHAPTER TEN

Milly sat in her car, watching the dealership. Jeff had arrived at work at the usual time and it appeared business was normal. Last night she had found a travel agency wallet in his dresser drawer holding two tickets to Nassau. The man was about to skip out on her, unless, of course, by some wild stretch of her imagination, he was planning to take her on vacation.

At twelve he left, hopped into his car and drove down the road. She followed a few seconds later, thinking herself very foolish. Why had she not hired a private detective to do this? She banged the wheel with the flat of her hand as the answer came to her: because she had no money in her checking account and she was not going to touch any of her own money.

He stopped at a small mall and went into a florist. Buying his mistress flowers and yet he had told her he was broke? She smiled grimly. Soon Mr. Jeffrey Armstrong, you're going to get yours, and I will be delighted to pull the trigger

♥

Jennifer admired herself in the new faceted brass and crystal mirror. She had ordered it from a television shopping network and thought it lovely.

The door bell chimed but she did not move. That pain in the butt, Jeffrey Armstrong, she guessed.

Jeffrey stood with his finger on the bell, waiting for her to answer. He looked across to the parking slots and noticed the Mustang stood in its usual place.

Eventually Jennifer could stand the noise no longer and opened the door. She put on her sweetest smile and stood braced for his firm grasp on her body. He never kissed her in greeting, just grabbed.

"Why, Jeffrey, you caught me in the bath," she exclaimed, sharply stepping out of range. "I was talking to the nursing home about mother and they said that . . .,"

"Come here, sweetheart, give me a hug." He advanced into the room as she stepped into the bathroom and shut the door. The click of the lock sounded loud.

"Jenny?" he said into the silence, listening for her. "Is your mother dying? What is it?"

Jenny sat on the toilet seat and dialled a number on her cell phone. Let old Jeffy wait, make him pay for his supper, so to speak.

Jeff paced the living room, glaring at the closed door from time to time. Then he heard her laugh and moved closer to the door. Cupping his hands around his ear, he attempted to hear what she was talking about. That didn't work so he jammed his head against the panel and heard her say: "I'm going to tell him today. I've had enough of him and his clutching hands. I can do much better for myself than a car salesman." She paused, "Who? Oh him. He's useless in the sack and no fun at all. No, thank you very much. The tall dark man that was with Linda at the theatre. Who's he?" Really? Do you know him and can you introduce us?"

Sickened, Jeff slumped onto the couch. To think he had set his hopes on her, had planned to take her away, to live with her. The story about her mother was false and those other far-fetched sagas were probably more of the same. No, she was as bad as Milly, out for what she could get. Milly, at least, stood by him, always appeared as the caring wife when they were out in public. Jennifer was not exactly top drawer material when he thought about it and he was probably better off without her. Taking his floral offering into the kitchen, he tossed it into the garbage can. Then he slammed out of the place.

He stormed over to his car and got in, not even seeing his wife's Mercedes in the lot. When Jeff drove past, staring straight ahead, jaw set, his expression thunderous, Milly knew Jenny had dumped him and laughed with delight.

♥

Mrs. Grant muttered as she pushed the mop over the kitchen floor. That young woman was a blasted nuisance, all this mess and trouble. Mrs. Wallace did not make things any easier either, always taking the girl's side. Trouble was that Mrs. Wallace was too soft hearted by far.

Today Christine had taken her to the doctor for her annual checkup and the house was, for once, silent. "Not that I object to music," she muttered, "but you can't call what she plays music. All that jangling and drums pound right through to my spine. What a din!"

The front door bell chimed and she went to answer.

"Why, Mrs. Armstrong. We haven't seen you for ages." Mrs. Grant stood aside as Millicent Armstrong pushed past her. From the expensive fur coat to the alligator shoes, she shouted class.

"Where is my mother?" she asked, peering into the parlour.

"Gone to the doctor for her checkup," Mrs. Grant said, delighted that Mrs. Armstrong had wasted her time. A horrible woman, Mrs.

Armstrong, only out for herself and bugger everyone else. She smiled as Milly glared.

"Did she take a taxi?" she asked, patting at her hair as she admired herself in the mirror.

"No, not today. Went on the bus."

"What?" Milly's face expressed her shock. "How could mother travel on a bus? She knows nothing about public transportation."

Mrs. Grant knew Christine had not told her mother of her whereabouts as she had listened to many conversations. "Oh, she's not alone. Oh no, they often travel on the bus these days."

Milly's face lost all expression. "Who are they? Who is this person who is taking my mother out?"

Bet's she's thinking it's a man, a man who might marry her mother and get her inheritance. Mrs. Grant thought this a wonderful situation and played it cagey. For once she held the upper hand with Mrs. 'Bossy Boots' Armstrong.

"They sometimes go to the theatre and out for supper," she said. "They went to an art gallery last week." Milly started pacing as Mrs. Grant mentally laughed. "Oh yes, Mrs. Wallace is so much better now. She's got a new lease on life, as they say."

Milly stopped and almost stamped her foot with anger. "Who is this person and why are they treating my mother in such a cavalier fashion? She's almost ninety now and should not be tramping the city streets."

"Oh, I don't think she does much tramping, Mrs. Armstrong, but she's got a whole lot more energy now she's getting so much exercise."

"What time will she return?"

"Who knows? You know how doctors are. We all sit waiting and waiting for hours when our appointment has already passed. I don't know how long they'll be. They might go shopping afterwards or have tea at a hotel."

Milly faced the mirror and surveyed her appearance. "I have an important meeting to attend. Inform my mother of my visit and tell her I expect her to be home tomorrow. No, not tomorrow. Tell her I will call again later in the week and expect to see her."

"I think you should telephone before you come. She often has appointments these days, like you do. I'll tell her you were here, and that you'll telephone her." Damn the woman, always giving orders. I'm not her blasted servant and I won't kowtow to her.

As she put her hand on the door handle, Milly turned. "I do not like your attitude. When I see my mother, I will inform her of your rudeness."

Mrs. Grant smiled and turned on her heel. "Please yourself and don't slam the door."

Sniggering, she held her stomach as Milly said, "I *never* slam doors. That is the prerogative of the lower classes."

As the door clicked quietly shut, she laughed aloud. "Stupid stuck up bitch. Wait 'til I tell Mrs. Wallace and Miss Christine."

♥

For a couple of hours Jeffrey Armstrong contemplated suicide but did not have the guts to carry it through. No, he would have to make the best of it, go to jail if necessary.

Arthur French had consulted a solicitor who was now sending legal letters demanding an audit. Jeff had used every delaying tactic possible, and all in vain because French's solicitor was sending in his own accountant to check the books.

What could he do? Leave town, of course: go to Nassau and live in the rented house, live on his embezzled funds, find himself another mistress. To hell with Milly and her demands. Even the huge loan she had wangled for him had not covered much other than the outstanding taxes. No, he had no other option than to leave.

♥

Harvey glanced at his mother, the old trout as he privately called her. She sat erect, back straight as a ramrod, knees together, hands lying loosely crossed in her lap, every inch the reigning monarch.

"I would like an answer, Harvey," Grace said, "Your father is very concerned, as am I."

God, she is a bloody idiot, all airs and graces that went out of fashion with Queen Victoria. So what if he had quit his job? He had done it before and his father always managed to find him something. Not that he had stuck any of the jobs for longer than a month: all too boring, too confining, too everything.

"I don't know, mother. Something will come up, and I'll soon be back at work. I'd like to get into computers, you know that, but Dad hasn't got any contacts."

"I fail to see that your penchant for playing games on that stupid machine qualifies you for anything. Why don't you go back to school and learn something useful?"

He groaned. "Don't you understand that computers are the future? Computers will soon run the world and all its offices. Can't you see that?"

She waved aside his statements. "Honestly, Harvey, sometimes you talk like a five-year-old.Your father knows the value of computers to the financial world, and the bank has many dedicated floors of such machines, but I honestly can't see you fitting in anywhere."

"Mother, I know a lot about computers, about programming and stuff like that."

She sniffed. "Games, that's all you know. Games."

Harvey sighed and huddled down in the chair. His mother knew nothing. His father knew a little, but was not a hands-on type of guy because his lackeys did the work under his direction.

"Do sit up properly, Harvey. You'll develop round shoulders."

"Yes, mother."

♥

Christine listened to his tale of woe and had to smile. She was sure his mother was not the gorgon he made her out to be and must have some redeeming qualities. On the other hand, her own mother sounded like his mother's sister.

She said, "My mother is as bad, you know. That's why I won't ever talk to her again. She doesn't care about me, and I don't think she cares about my father, either. Finally she got around to calling on Gram and said she's coming back to see her. I wish I knew when, because I don't want to be around."

Harvey nodded. "Yeah, she'll start bossing you around again. Mothers are like that. I hope you miss her visit."

"My father ignores her. He once told me that he only married her for her money, and that once she'd had me, he never slept with her again."

"Oh, how gross." Harvey rubbed a hand over the bristles sprouting where they had shaved his head. It felt like sand paper. It soothed him to rub at it and he figured he should quit before it became a habit. He had seen a documentary on mental cases where patients sat around rubbing at their heads and had worn all their hair away. He stopped rubbing and rested his elbows on the table. "I don't know about my parents. I once heard mother saying something about Dad's philandering so maybe they're the same."

"Yeah, I guess we're two of a kind."

He nodded. "Two of a kind, yes. I like talking to you, Tina, you always understand."

Strange how Harvey's abbreviation of her name never bothered her, he was the only person other than Gram that she let call her Tina. "Yes, I do. Strange how our parents are so much alike. Mom has piles of money that she inherited from my granddad, but she won't let Dad have any of it. I heard him begging her once and she laughed at him. Poor old Dad, he doesn't have much of a life."

"My father is always at work. He's real 'establishment,' know what I mean? I guess being the head honcho takes a lot of time, and he's responsible for everything that happens at the bank. I don't think I'd like that."

She felt puzzled at the way Harvey shrugged off his father's achievements and yet she could care less about anything her own father had accomplished, since he had done nothing noteworthy.

"He's famous," she said, looking at him under her brows. "I see his photo in the paper a lot and he's been on television."

Harvey sighed. Girls liked famous men. He had seen the envy on their faces often enough. "Yeah, Mom thinks that kind of publicity is super. She loves it when he's quoted and tells all her friends to watch the news or read the paper. She's got a whole scrap book filled with his triumphs."

Christine pulled a face. "My Dad never does anything anyone cares about. He's always at work, selling cars."

"Well, both of us are poor little rich kids, eh?" He pushed at her, laughing now. "We've got prospects, but nothing else. I'd like to have had a brother or sister, wouldn't you?"

She nodded. "Yeah, someone to share the strain. An only child gets all the blame and, in our instance, not much of the praise."

♥

Jeffrey Armstrong made his way home, praying Milly was attending one of her eternal fund raisers.

Her car was not in the garage and he smiled as he let himself in through the mud room and into the kitchen. "Hello? Anyone home?" he called into the echoing space. Not a sound. Good.

Chuckling, he went through to the front hall and ran up the curving staircase. Where did she store suitcases, he wondered? In his room he tossed the suits onto the king size bed and emptied drawers of underwear and socks. The suitcases . . . were they in the attic?

Going up the short flight of stairs to the attic, he paused. Was that a sound in the kitchen? Had that blasted housekeeper returned? He realized he had been holding his breath, and relaxed his stomach muscles. How silly to be afraid of the staff, how silly to think even Milly would suspect the reason he was packing. He often went to conventions and symposiums. She had always fetched him the cases, though. Not the Gucci cases, those were hers, but 'no name' cases, cases that were disposable. In the attic, he found the built-in shelves that held a variety of cases, trunks and travelling bags. Taking the two largest Louis Vuiton cases and two smaller soft sided Gucci bags, he returned to his room.

In fifteen minutes he had packed everything: everything he thought he might need. Clothes still half filled the closet and the drawers. Even if Milly came in to check his room, she would hardly notice what was missing.

Should he leave a note? He paused. Surely that was the more polite way of saying he had left her. Milly was always aware of the correct way of doing things. No! To hell with her and her snobbish manners.

As he carried the two large cases through the kitchen and out to the car, he saw her car rounding the corner to the hammerhead. Quickly he stuffed them into the trunk and went back inside. If she saw him carrying anything, it would be the two small bags and that was no cause for alarm.

"So, Jeffrey? You're not usually home at this time of day," she said acerbically as she met him in the front hall.

"I could ask you the same thing. Is your meeting here today?"

He surveyed her as she posed, one hand on hip, the other adjusting her fine pearl necklace. That hat must have cost him hundreds, her accessories the same. Still and all, she was a beautiful woman and the doctors' bills proved to what lengths she went to preserve herself.

"No, I have a free afternoon for a change. My manicurist has come down with some horrible sickness and I wouldn't dare show my hands in public without gloves." She waved a perfectly manicured hand in front of his face. "What do you think?"

He grinned. "Looks like you just got them done."

She pulled a face of disgust. "Oh you! You never do see anything obvious. Shall we have some tea? I don't think Mrs. White is in this afternoon, but I can make tea."

He put down the small bags. She had not even mentioned them. Grinning, he turned on his heel. "Come along then, let me see you working in the kitchen for a change."

She took off her coat, hung it on a hanger for Mrs. White to remove to her room, placed her purse and gloves neatly on the hall stand and followed him.

Jeff thought it amusing that she wanted to play housewife. He would have preferred a strong drink, but dared not since he was to drive to the airport.

She opened cupboard doors, took down china cups and saucers. Found the sugar bowl, the milk jug and placed them on the table. He grinned. "All you need now is the teapot, some boiling water and the tea."

Milly glared at him and went back to searching the cupboards. "I do know how to make tea. Mrs. White has her own little places to hide things. I prefer a nice tidy kitchen, so I can't fault her."

Jeff looked around. "It looks like it's a display in an interior designer's showroom. Not very homey, is it? I like a bit of clutter myself."

"I know. Your room could do with a good turn out. It's a horrible mess, all those bits and pieces lying around on everything."

"Oh? So you do visit my room, do you? I thought that part of our marriage was finished since we don't cohabit. I suppose you prefer that to me saying we don't have sex?"

She flushed angrily. "I don't want this afternoon to deteriorate into a long drawn out battle. We've discussed the bedroom situation too may times to start again."

Putting back his head, he laughed. "You can't even say the word, can you? Sex, sex, sex."

"That is enough. Please stop it, Jeffrey. Now how does one switch on this range?" She busied herself with the stove top and finally managed to turn on the burner. As the kettle warmed, she went into the pantry and came out with the ornate tin of imported Swiss biscuits, the finest the food court at Harrods of London could offer. She hunted around and found doilies and placed one on the china plate before she set out a few cookies. Her affectations made Jeff smile.

"Black or white?" she asked, as she sat with the filled teapot.

"What?" Didn't the woman even remember how he took his tea?

She glared at him. "Your tea. Do you want milk or lemon?"

"You madden me, you know that?" he said heatedly. "We've been married for over twenty years and you don't know how I drink my tea? I bet if I were one of your cronies, you'd know all right. You wouldn't need to ask 'black or white,' then."

Milly put down the teapot and stared at him. "I don't recall that we ever drank tea. You prefer coffee."

"Too true . . . but do I drink it 'black or white'?" He smiled grimly.

"Black . . . no, white. Oh, what difference does it make?" She poured her own tea and pushed the pot toward him.

"I'll tell you what difference it makes, shall I? You don't know me very well after all these years, but I know you. Oh God, do I know you! You're so self-centred that you hardly see me. If I bring home money for you to spend, you could care less. I won't be doing it for much longer, though."

Should he tell her? No, let her wonder when she suddenly missed him. In his reckoning that would probably be in about three weeks, the time he usually transferred the housekeeping money into her account. She sat gazing into space, not even listening to him.

"Come now, Jeffrey. Why this sudden urge to pick on me? I don't think you realize how hard I work to keep our name viable in the community, or how much good I do your business."

He snorted. "My business? Don't you mean *your* business? You've made sure I'm forever in your debt. Now the government has their tax money and I paid most of overdue bills, we are again on the brink of bankruptcy."

She blanched and drew in a sharp breath. "What do you mean? What have you done with the huge loan I got you?"

"I told you." He watched her face as he listed things, seeing her become red with anger. "I paid the back taxes, paid the outstanding invoices, paid the salesmen, paid you your housekeeping money, paid the mortgages on the house and the showrooms, paid your outstanding credit card bills."

"So what now?" He could see she was trying to control herself, would not allow herself to raise her voice. 'Only those who are uncouth and uneducated raise their voices' she had once told him.

His fingers bet a tattoo on the table. He knew it annoyed her but did not care. "If you wish to avoid bankruptcy, you have no choice but to put in some of your own money. I told you it was our only recourse, but you insisted on borrowing more money."

"I will *never* declare bankruptcy! I will hire an accountant to go over the books and we will sort this out. Before I would entertain using any of my capital, I must know where we stand."

Jeff stood. "You do that, sweetheart. Well, I've got to be going." She did not ask where and in fact had not even mentioned his packed bags. "Toodle-oo," he said as he walked out.

He laughed aloud as he drove to the airport. Wait until her tame accountant got a look at the books, and wondered if Arthur French's man would get there beforehand. She would be more than angry, and he would bet she would scream instead of shout.

CHAPTER ELEVEN

Milly phoned her closest friend of the moment, Monica Sterling. Monica's husband worked for the largest accountancy firm in England Soon she had arranged for a complete audit and hung up, pleased at her own competence.

Mrs. White arrived the next morning and started work. Milly went to the kitchen to give her orders. She ordered supper for six. Tonight she would entertain the Sterlings, the Goldbergs and another couple for bridge. Jeffrey would have to come home early for once and act the part of the loving husband, she thought grimly. He had mortified her yesterday at tea time, but she was above holding a grudge.

The chatty female who answered the dealership phones said Jeff was absent. Then Milly's mind flashed back to yesterday. He was packed to go somewhere when she arrived home. Oh, why had she not asked him where he was going? Unless she invited another man, his absence would ruin her table arrangement. Her solicitor, a divorced man, often stepped into the breach on short notice. She called him.

♥

"Gram?"

"Yes, love." Evelyn looked up from her library book to see Christine standing in the doorway wearing her winter coat.

"Do you think I should wear this to the theatre tonight?"

"I think you might find it a trifle warm for the time of year. Look, upstairs in the storage room I have a lovely evening coat. I'm sure it will fit you. It's royal blue velvet with a satin lining and I think you'll like it."

"Oh, how lovely. Come on, let's fetch it now."

As they made their way into the hall, Evelyn leaned heavily on Christine's arm. Her legs were rapidly failing, though she exercised on the stationary bike every morning and evening. Now they had a seat lift installed along the bannister rail and she sat to ride upstairs.

The storage room was a large bedroom that now held racks and shelves. A large double closet held clothing in protective covers and it was to this she went. Many coats and gowns hung from a high rail and she soon found the evening coats.

Christine got it down and eyed it with delight. "It's fantastic, Gram. I love it."

She tried it on and it fit perfectly.

"I wore that coat to a performance of La Boheme sung by Lois Marshall, the opera star from Toronto, Canada. She was in a wheel chair, you know, but she could sing like an angel. She travelled the world and sang at most of the major opera houses."

"Is she still alive? I've never heard of her."

"No, she died in 1997. So how do you like the coat? Your grandfather bought it for my birthday. I think it suits you admirably. Yes, you take it, love, and wear it in good health."

"Thanks, Gram. Harvey won't recognize me in this. My plain old gown will laugh at it, though. Oh no," she put up her hands, "don't start offering me a gown. I'll bet they are outdated and this coat is so fine that nobody will notice anything else. Thank you."

Evelyn smiled. Tina was right. The gowns in their covers were old-fashioned by today's standards. She must have Mrs. Wallace go through things with her. Time to divest herself of anything she no longer needed.

"What are you seeing tonight?" she asked as she rode down the stairs.

"Phantom of the Opera. I hear it's super."

"I wish I could come with you, but it's impossible. I expect you to tell me all about it tomorrow."

"Oh, I will. I'll even buy the record of the show so we can listen to the music as I tell the story. How about that?"

"Lovely."

"Shall I fetch tea?" They were now sitting in the conservatory where the upper windows had been opened and the fans switched on low.

"That would be nice. Let's have iced tea today."

As they sipped from the silver encased glasses, Evelyn listened as Christine talked about her young man. She never called him that, of course, only 'my friend Harvey', but her face revealed she thought more of him than a friend.

"He's so well mannered, Gram. I suppose it's because his family is of old stock. His father is George Wright, CEO of the Regal Bank, you know."

"Oh, my, I *am* impressed. That gentleman is famous around town. He's very influential in banking circles."

"Yes, he is, but somehow Harvey doesn't much like him because of that. Harvey is like me, really. Both of us have parents that don't much worry about them. You know what he did to his hair?" She laughed as she described it and gestured an imaginary Mohawk over her head.

Evelyn smiled. It was humorous when Tina told the story. "Has it all grown back now?" she asked.

"Not all of it. He's still got stubble with orange tips on top but it looks cool."

"What does his mother say to that?"

"She won't talk to him at all these days. Says he defamed the family by being seen in public looking like a clown. His father didn't care, though. He was right when he said it would soon grow back. Not that he pays much attention to Harvey."

"My, oh, my. Young people today live a different life than when I was your age. We were to be seen and not heard, and our parents left us to the attention of the servants."

"What a horrible way to live, Gram," she said, and then thought her own life was much the same. When she was younger, she had a nanny and then the cleaning lady when she arrived home from school. In a way, they had both lived the same type of life, disregarded and unloved. "I suppose they used to trot you out dressed in your best when they had company?"

Evelyn nodded, her mind back in her formative years. "Yes, they did."

"Honestly, Gram, parents are awful. Mine did the same to me, like I was a trophy to be admired in my patent leather shoes and lace trimmed dress, and when I had said hello and drunk a small glass of juice, they expected me to leave, go upstairs to my room and stay there until everyone left." She went to her grandmother, sat on the chair arm and rested her head on the grey hair, holding her close. "Do you see, we both had to suffer in silence."

"Dear me, what a terrible thing to say. I don't think your life can compare to mine one iota. Things are different now. You have television and radio, videos, CD players and the like. I had embroidery and reading, water colouring, piano and dance lessons, classes in deportment and etiquette. No darling, things are totally different today."

"Go on, Gram, tell me all about your life back then."

They sat side by side as Evelyn talked about her life. How strange that the child wanted to listen, nobody else ever did, not even her dear deceased husband. "Life is today, not back then, Evvie," he would bark. "You must learn to forget the past." Yet surely the past made you what you were today, had formed your personality? She liked talking about the past and recalling her love of life.

♥

Milly gazed blankly at the TV screen. She had switched it on simply to hear the sound of a human voice. Mrs. White had telephoned to say she had the flu and would not be in until she was less contagious.

"Of course, Mrs. White, take as long as you need," Milly had said, mentally cursing.

She would have to eat out. Not that she found that too disagreeable because she could spend more time with her friends, visit the newly opened art gallery, or even take a short trip.

Somehow it palled. Why now, she asked herself, why at this point in her life did she feel lost and alone? Surely she had lived life alone since her marriage, having discovered Jeff useless in more ways than one. He was out of town now, and Mrs. White was taking a break from work, so why should she not make the most of this spare time?

Milly went upstairs and changed into her new Versace suit. As she posed in front of her triple mirror, she saw a trim, beautiful woman and smiled a perfect smile. Yes, she would visit Monica and lord it over her. Poor Monica never wore designer labels, but purchased her clothing at C & A's or other department stores. She laughed then, glad she was better off than most.

Monica was not home. "She's gone to a meeting, Mrs. Armstrong," said the woman who answered the door. Meeting? What meeting? When she sat in the car, she checked her date book to see if she had forgotten something. Surely Monica would not belong to an organization that Milly didn't know anything about?

She sulked as she drove away. 'How could Monica go somewhere and not tell me?' she muttered. 'What kind of friend is she?' Now she was at a loose end, it occurred to her to call on her mother. She had not seen the old lady for at least six months, and often forgot all about her. Yes, mother would be delighted to see her.

CHAPTER TWELVE

Harvey gnawed on a lump of bakers' chocolate.

Tina eyed him with incredulity. "I don't know how you can stand that stuff. It's so bitter."

"I like it bitter." Harvey turned to look around the Cyber Web Café. "Not too many here tonight. How about a game of dungeons and dragons with our pal Langley?" Langley was a cyber pal they talked to from time to time, who was deep into computer games.

"Nah, he takes so long to answer. I don't like playing that way. We could talk to my pal Enid in Australia."

"I don't want to talk to that loony tune. She's got a head full of mist."

"So what shall we do?" She looked around and saw nobody she knew. "How about we go for a walk. Say to the mall?"

"All right, but I'm broke so don't start wanting things," he warned.

"Gram gave me a twenty so we're all right. Come on."

♥

Nassau was wonderful. The small rented house stood on a point of land overlooking the ocean and very well equipped.

Jeff, sitting on a verandah thatched with palm fronds, watched the fish jumping as the housekeeper's husband tossed scraps of food out to sea. A breeze cooled him as the sun shone blindingly, making the sea and surf sparkle. He relaxed completely, almost dozing after the meal Anthilla had served. A meal long on fish and vegetables, with fresh fruit for dessert. A glorious meal, made with local produce and newly caught fish. He sighed. This was the way to live. How irritating it was to be here alone, though, with no one with whom to share. Still, that was Jennifer's loss.

"You go to town, boss?" Anthilla asked as she topped up his coffee.

"Yes. I want to walk around the stores." He did not add, 'and check the local talent.'

"Lotsa nice shops, nice peoples on vacation, too."

"How many hotels are there?"

"Lots, boss. You go to Paradise Island. Look around. They got casino and lots of nice places."

"Sounds good."

He lay back on the chaise and thought about a trip to the island. Surely if he patrolled the casino, he would soon find a compatible companion to share his house.

♥

Harvey's parents were on his case. Day after day they made their point.

"Get a job," his mother said.

"Go back to school," his father said

"Sharpen yourself up, find work" she said.

"Try to make something of your life," he said.

"Don't expect us to support you for the rest of your life." Both had said.

They muttered about him to their friends who looked at him like he was a nut case and made remarks about how well their Jimmy or Johnny was doing at his new job.

It was not in his nature to apply himself to some dead end boring job, he knew that from his failed efforts at the new McDonald's and various other fast food places. He'd even worked at Zellers in their pet department: a job that consisted of stacking shelves and fishing out gold fish for little kids. They fired him when he forgot to feed the fish and most of them died. He told his father that he got laid off because they were hiring pensioners. Boy, his dad was pleased with that, him being a staunch supporter of old men who worked. Harvey knew his dad planned to work until he dropped. He loved work, loved being stressed out, loved deadlines, meetings, overtime, pressure. Boredomville!

Sure they lived in high style in a ritzy neighbourhood, so ritzy that the nearest neighbour had their own twenty acres, twenty acres away. The mansion (it was far too grand to be a house) had eight bedrooms. The only people who ever slept in the other rooms were his father's guests, people he wanted to impress.

His own room was huge, large enough for a pool table if he had wanted one. It was too cold and impersonal for his taste, what with the housekeeper forever tidying up and putting away. He had a large screen television, a CD player and a video recorder. His latest game had pride of place on his bedside table, still new enough to keep his attention. He only had to ask and his Dad bought him the latest computer programs and a state of the art colour printer. One thing about his dad, he welcomed the computer age with open arms, and yet did not even know how to switch one on.

Yes, he lived well, but it was all so boring: nothing to do right now and all day to do it. While he wished he could get excited about work, something in him refused to attend boring interviews. When his dad offered him another entry level job, he thought about running away from home, and when his mother presented him with a new suit and leather shoes, then he was afraid.

"Who wants to work with their own father?" he asked Christine when they met at the Cyber Web Cafe.

"Not me for one. What do I know about selling cars?" she said and laughed. "What did he offer you?"

"Offer me? That's a joke. An 'entry level position' which probably means mail sorter or floor washer."

"Money counter maybe?" She laughed. "Boy, I wouldn't mind a job like that."

Harvey pulled a face. "They've got machines that do that now, silly. Dad says that soon the business world will mechanize and computerize everything. That's when I pointed out that people would also be redundant, and why would he want me to work at something so temporary."

"Good for you. What did he say to that?"

"That I had to start somewhere, display my capabilities. You know, his old tirade about proving myself. Mom sat there nodding and smiling at him, casting the odd evil eye on me. I couldn't wait to get out of there."

"They're right, you know. Now don't get mad at me, Harvey, but I listened to what Gram had to say and she's right too. We both need something to work at, to sharpen our minds. I mean we can't drift through life aimlessly."

"Joining the club, are you, Tina? Jeez, talk about brainwashing. We already had this conversation, didn't we?"

"It isn't like that, Harvey." She gazed into the distances, her eyes glowing. "I want to do something, I want to be someone, I want to show the world that I'm a winner. Don't you?"

"I suppose, but we don't know anything or anybody that can help us make a living and I object to working in a low paying job to keep the old parents happy."

"At least you see your parents. Mine don't even miss me."

Harvey put his arm around her thin shoulders and gave her a hug. "Come on, let's go to the mall and have a walk around."

They walked arm in arm to the mall and stared into shop windows. She pretended they were married and pointed out all the things she would like in their new house. Harvey got caught up in the pretense, and they laughed away almost three hours.

♥

Mrs. White looked at Mrs. Armstrong, who looked mad about something.

"Everything all right, Mrs. A?" she asked.

"My name is Mrs. Armstrong, not Mrs. A!" Milly snapped, turning on the woman and eying her with distaste. Cleaning ladies, or housekeepers as they now liked to call themselves, were a scurrilous lot. Hers was no better than the rest of her ilk.

She looked the woman up and down, at the stained knee length jacket. "Isn't it time you purchased a new coverall, or whatever you call those things? I pay you more than enough for you to look respectable. It is little enough to ask that you look clean."

Mrs. White drew herself up. "Now just a minute. Today is my day for cleaning the oven and doing the floors. I always wear this old thing for that. About time you tried to do something in one of your designer dresses, then you'd know what . . ."

"Please! I do not wish to hear about the rigours of your work. I pay you to do it, so get on with it."

She stalked regally from the kitchen as Mrs. White glared at her ramrod straight back. "Right, lady, today things get a lick and a promise," she muttered.

Milly wandered into the lounge. She picked up the latest copy of Vogue and started to leaf through it. About time she updated her wardrobe. After an hour, she rang the bell and Mrs. White arrived.

"Yes?"

"Tea, Mrs. White." Milly didn't look up from her labours over the vagaries of fashion.

Mrs. White stomped off, muttering.

Milly picked up the phone on the third ring.

"Oh hello, Sarah. I was going to call you later. Have you seen the latest Vogue? Some of the Ralph Lauren gowns are gorgeous."

She rose and walked over to the mantel and admired her reflection, patting at her hair and smiling at herself.

"You are? That *is* good news. Your Brian is such a good businessman and Paris is lovely at this time of year." She listened and then shrugged. "Jeff? I think he's on one of his business trips. Probably seeing next season's models. Poor dear, he works so hard."

She froze as Sarah said something and her face paled. With a hand to her forehead, she sat with a plop on the nearest chair as Mrs. White arrived with the tea tray.

"Who told you this?" she asked, her voice shaky.

Mrs. White set down the tray and stood looking at her mistress, noticing her pallor and shaking hand as she patted at her forehead.

"Are you all right?" Mrs. White asked.

"I'm on the telephone, you stupid woman." Milly snapped again and gestured for her to leave.

She left, shaking her head. Something was terribly wrong. She wondered if it had anything to do with Miss Christine.

As Sarah hung up, Milly put her head in her hands and groaned. Now she would be the laughing stock of her clubs. Jeff had left her and was living in Nassau with another woman. Trust him to show up at the Paradise Island Casino while Sarah's best friend Anne was there on vacation. And him! He had made no pretense but said hello and introduced the tramp as his live in companion Brandi, "That's Brandi with a small i," Sarah reported. Her mind reeled with unanswerable questions: God, what could she do now? Who was running the dealership? What about the mortgage? How could she manage with no income? What had she done to deserve this? The stupid man must have lost his mind to be living openly with a prostitute.

As she drank her tea, she considered her options. First she must continue her daily routine, tell everyone she had thrown him out because of his adultery. She must visit her financial advisor and maybe liquidate some of her assets. Things could be worse and she might weather this without too much strain. At least she was well rid of Jeff.

♥

Christine read some of her grandmother's magazines and became interested in an article on self-made women. All had started with problems, worked their way through them and then gone on to make a success of their lives. From baking cookies in a tiny apartment kitchen to becoming a huge conglomerate that sold ten million cookies a day, to mixing up creams and lotions discovered in an ancestor's diary to becoming a multinational cosmetic company that employed thousands. All it took was determination.

"I could do something like this, Gram," she said as she passed her grandmother the article.

"I'm sure you could, love. You've got the same determination and stick-with-it-ness that these women have. Now you think of a service or product and we'll take it from there." Christine's eyes opened wide and Evelyn then said, "Oh, I intend to help you, Tina. Starting a company at my age will be lovely, but I'll only be a silent partner. The glory goes to the one who does all the work and that's you."

"Oh, Gram, you're so good to me. Well, let's have a meeting of the Evelyn and Christine Corporation. First we must get a good name for it."

For some hours they sat in the living room, talking and looking though magazines and books.

♥

Harvey slouched through the mall, hands in pockets, scuffing his old Reboks along the floor as if it were too much trouble to lift his feet. What was he going to do? His life was a mess.

He mooched dejectedly around the British Home Store, disinterestedly looking at things. Nothing much doing in the computer section, he noticed, but then they were not in that business. Moving into the home appliance area, he studied the various CD players.

"Anything I can help you with?" a salesman asked brightly.

"No thanks, just looking," he said, taking in the neat navy blue suit, the polished leather shoes. A wimp, a real wimp, he thought, his lip curling.

"This is the latest Sony model . . . " the salesman said, gesturing to a large black and chrome affair.

"Not interested."

Harvey moved to another department. The sales clerks got on his nerves, all smarm and charm, dressed like they should be in a tailor shop window. He snorted, bitterly realizing that men like those had cushy jobs, they worked in pleasant surroundings, got decent pay cheques.

He blew out a sigh of aggravation. With his basic education, Harvey knew he would never land a steady job. Working at McDonald's was all right, but the pay was rotten and the hours were terrible. No, he needed a job that he could sink his teeth into, a job that challenged and excited him.

Slumping disconsolately, feet scuffling, he wandered into the mall and flopped down on a bench next to a pensioner who watched him approach and noticed his glum expression.

"Had bad news, son?" he asked, friendly.

"Nope," he snapped, shoving his hands into his pockets and extending his jean-clad legs into the aisle. A woman pushing a stroller ran into his feet, the stroller wobbled and she gave a small shriek of annoyance, bending to check the baby.

"Sorry," Harvey mumbled, pulling back his feet. The small child ceased his screeching and started to chew on a bald teddy bear.

"So you should be," the woman snapped. "I don't know what the matter is with the younger generation. No ambition, no courtesy, no enthusiasm. Mind where you put your feet. People walk along here, you know."

"Sure," Harvey said with a peevish expression. Whom did she think she was, his mother?

The pensioner looked at him. "Sit up straight, son, don't slouch like that or you'll finish up with back trouble in the future."

"Get lost, granddad!" he snapped. "Who rattled your cage?"

George Black looked at the youngster thinking him like his son Ian at that age, all mouth and few brains. Nevertheless, Ian had straightened out and was now the vice-president of a high tech firm.

"Now, now, calm down," George said, not at all offended. "Want to tell me about it?"

"About what?" Harvey looked in the opposite direction. These old fogies got on his nerves.

"About what's bothering you. You can tell a stranger easier than people close to you, you know. I bet you can't tell your family, eh?"

Harvey looked at him sharply. Why would he want to tell anyone other than Tina how he felt? Who would care anyway? He was one of the lost generation. No lifetime jobs with pensions for his age group, no solid salaries and bonuses.

"Come on, we'll have a coffee and you can tell me. I'm a good listener," George said, standing and looking down at the young man.

He stood. Oh well, what was a coffee? If the old man was inviting him, it meant that he was paying.

They sat in a booth at the back of the restaurant where George ordered caffeine free coffee and Harvey opted for cream soda as he hid a smile, thinking a decent drop of caffeine might perk the old man up no end.

Harvey told his sad story. " . . . and it's no good applying for half the things they advertise. They want people with certificates, university degrees, and lots of experience."

George shrugged. "So? What does your resume say? What have you got to offer the world?"

He shrugged. The old man was bonkers. He had nothing to offer, nothing but youth.

"I'm young," he said.

"And I'm old," George chuckled, "so I think that gives me some little more smarts than you, Harvey, my boy. Here's a pen. Write on your place mat everything you can do . . . apart from being young, that is."

Harvey shook his head thinking the old man puddled.

"Go on . .," George urged, " . . . write it all down. It might surprise you to see how much you know."

He wrote a list. First he put 'computers': he knew all about them, although he had no degree or certificate. He had even written a couple of game programs for his own use, so he also wrote that down. Then he wrote 'research' He liked doing research. It was fascinating how you could find out about anything and the library was a wonderful place. At school he loved researching odd facts for his essays and now the Internet was a fantastic resource.

Dancing. He knew now to dance. Mind you, not that old fashioned touchy stuff, but he was expert in the modern 'do your own thing' dancing.

He chewed on the pen thinking. He could write. His teachers always gave him good marks for composition, saying he had a good imagination. Imagination, he had that too. Also, he could use a cash register and could deal with the public when the mood took him, so he wrote down 'customer relations' because that sounded better than cashier. Once he worked in an office as mail boy and once he drove a golf cart around the golf course picking up garbage. He added them to the list and recalled he had also worked as a caddy and a delivery boy.

Now that he looked at the list, it was lengthy. Little things kept popping into his mind and he added them.

"Let's see what you've got," George said, putting out his hand for the paper place mat. "I should add something here," he picked up the pen and added an item. "Penmanship. You write a very fine hand, young man."

George sat looking at the list for the longest time. Harvey bought him another coffee and got himself a Coke. Why was he bothering to hang around the old man? He knew why. It was something to do.

George smiled as he looked up. "You've got a lot going for you. I think you've been setting your sights far too low. People are crying out for computer operators and I see that you've even written a couple of programs. You could be an asset to a company, knowing what you know."

"Sure," Eric said wryly, "And when they see I quit school, it's game over. They don't want people like me, hardly educated."

"Why didn't you finish your education? Why didn't you go on to college?"

Eric slumped in the seat. He hated talking about things at home. "Dad was all set to drag me into banking with him and I didn't want that. My mother was always going on about me attending university and becoming a doctor and that wasn't on my list." His face darkened. "I decided to stop them both making plans for me and quit school when I could." He grinned. "They were furious."

"That made you feel better, did it?"

"Sure did . . . for a while, but now I often wished I'd stayed on at school."

Before he knew it, it was all spewing out, things he did not mean to tell anyone. ". . . but they don't care about me anymore. They ignore me or tell me to shape up, get another job. I think they're going to throw me out of the house. Mom once told me to get lost."

George saw the distress in the boy's eyes, knew how hard he was taking it. "I'm sure that's not how she put it, that's the way you're interpreting it. She's only talking, Harvey, she doesn't mean it literally."

"Yes, she does. Last night she threatened to put my things into garbage bags and said I'd better find somewhere else to live. Says I don't pull my weight, that I eat too much, that they can't afford to keep supporting me. Yet they've got all sorts of money, that's what's so rotten."

George shook his head sadly, what a rotten thing to do to a young fellow. On the other hand it could be the making of him, after all, no use being too reliant on a parent.

"When you were working? How was it then?"

His tone was blistering. "Oh, everything was fine, then. When I was fetching money home everything was great. They let me keep it all too, never made me pay board. It didn't matter that I hated it and had to do the rotten things others didn't want to do."

George chuckled. "It sounds as if you're growing up fast, lad. Finally it got through that thick head of yours that people need something more than an existence. They need a challenge."

Harvey pushed himself up in the seat. Sitting back, he rested his head against the wall. Somehow he felt much better for saying things aloud. So maybe the old man *did* know what he was talking about. Not that he had come up with any solution to his problems.

"Anyway, why I am telling *you* all this? It's not going to change anything. I'm still out of work and I'll still have to find some place to live."

"From this list I see you're capable of far more than people give you credit." George tapped the list with a horny fingernail. "Your many attributes show an ability to apply yourself. You speak well and have an air of confidence, when you're not slouching. You're computer literate and that's very useful. So how would you like to work for me?"

Harvey stared at him. What on earth business could this old man possibly have? George sat smiling inscrutably.

"I enjoyed talking with you, son. Talking to a stranger about things that bother you isn't easy, although it does help a lot. Now, how about coming to work for me?"

Harvey nodded. What had he to lose?

Then a harried young woman came hurrying into the restaurant and headed toward them.

"Uncle George, there you are. I've been looking all over the mall for you. Sorry I'm late, the car wouldn't start and I had to get a boost."

She stood at the table as she said this and then turned to Harvey. "Who is this young man?"

"Harvey, this is my niece Emily, Emily, this is Harvey. Your late arrival allowed me to interview this young man. He's going to join us next week."

Harvey gaped at the pair of them. Work at what?

Emily put out her hand. "Pleased to meet you. We need some young blood, particularly enthusiastic young men. I do hope you're enthusiastic."

He nodded, smiling widely now. It was not a con, the old man had a business and he had a job! She sat and talked and he discovered that he would start work for Symelinx Corporation, a company offering Internet and custom programs for business and industry. It also had a branch that specialized in games. The old man, George Stevens, was CEO and Chairman of the Board. Who would have thought it?

CHAPTER THIRTEEN

H arvey felt a shock when he saw George in his elegant tenth floor office clad in a business suit.

George smiled as Harvey stood in front of his desk, stunned. "Welcome to the company, Harvey. It looks like I took the wind out of your sails, eh? Well now, I'm sure you've heard the expression 'never judge a book by its cover?' I'd taken the day off when we met at the mall and decided to wander around the stores after I'd been to the barber. So you see that while you might have thought I was an old codger who had nothing to do with myself but sit around waiting for the grim reaper, you were wrong."

"I sure was, Mr. Stevens, I sure was."

"Glad to see you've got a suit and proper shoes."

Harvey laughed. "Did you think I'd arrive in blue jeans and a T-shirt?"

George laughed too. "Yes, I did. Now, let me get Arnie in here and you can get started on your first day."

Arnie, a young black man from Antigua, ran the data department. He and Harvey hit it off right away and soon were chatting like old friends. Already Harvey felt better, already the tangle of nerves that had beset his stomach were a memory.

♥

Jeff lay on the beach eyeing Brandi in her tiny bikini. Right now he considered himself the luckiest man in the world.

"We're going to the Casino *again*?" she said sulkily. "Can't we eat in Nassau for a change?"

"I like the restaurants at the hotel. At least the food doesn't make you sick. I looked inside some of the kitchens in Nassau when I was on holiday here once and the roaches are huge. They even wander into the dining room while you're eating. Not very hygienic to my mind. . . and we won't talk about the rats!"

Brandi laughed. "You all the same, you whities. Such weak stomachs."

"I know we all eat lots of things that we shouldn't, but roaches that size are not conducive to any appetite. I'll stick with the island hotel. At least it doesn't have rats and mice."

"I don't want to go there. You go eat there, and I'll eat in Nassau."

"No way. I want you with me." He wondered where she went when she said she was going to her apartment or to the bank.

At first she had seemed exciting, but now, three weeks later, the thrill was wearing off for him. Although she looked like a Caucasian with a tan, he now knew she was black. That, too, had given him a thrill but now he saw the specks in the whites of her eyes, the white palms, heard it in her voice. Maybe she had outlived her usefulness, so if she didn't want his company, then he didn't want hers.

Brandi stared out to sea. She sat upright and rested on her back splayed arms so that her breasts jutted sharply and sucked in her stomach. This, she knew, was one way to make a man desire her, make him see things her way.

Jeff studied her. Now he saw the Negroid features that had once seemed so oriental and captivating. He noticed her heels: the toes obviously Negroid and splayed. She would either come with him tonight or they were finished.

"So what's it to be, Brandi? You coming with me?"

She glanced over her shoulder at him. "No, I go into Nassau."

"Fine. Don't come back here again. I call the shots and I want you out of my life."

She stood and glared down at him. "You poor excuse for a man, you little white boy, sulky and petulant. Can't have things your own way, so you lash out. Well, don't you worry about me, whitey. I've got friends all over the island and I won't be alone for long. Didn't you wonder where I got to when I was away for a day or so? It wasn't to visit my parents, it was to see my lover."

Jeff stood also. "I should slap your silly face, you little whore. Get out of here and don't come back, and don't take anything that doesn't belong to you.

"You haven't got anything I want, whitey. Not that paste jewelry you gave me, not the negligees, not that little pee pee of yours, nothing." She stalked off, head held high and he felt a pang of melancholy. What the heck, tonight he would do some trawling.

♥

Harvey and Christine sat in the mall talking about his new job.

"It's marvellous, Tina. I get to write programs and test new ones that other people have written. We have meetings and seminars given by experts. Boy, am I lucky!"

Christine hugged his arm. "What do your parents think?"

He shrugged. "I didn't tell them yet. Mom never asks where I spend my days, but then she never did. I guess she's glad to get me out of the house. Dad is looking stressed out with the year end coming up and I don't want to tell him yet. Not until my three month probationary period is over."

"I wish I had something. Gram and I are still looking for something."

"Look for something that everyone needs or wants and research that."

"Yeah, I'm doing that. We have a list of stuff but I don't think any of them would make me rich or famous."

"It's hard work to start a company, you know. Anyway, it takes years to become rich and famous."

"I know, I know. You can help me with things when you've got time. I know very little about computers and I'd need to learn more."

"Sure." He hugged her. "So get on with it and tell me what you're going to do to become the next dot-com millionaire."

"Silly. I might not have anything to do with the Internet. I might start a hands-on business. Oh well, Gram and I are having another meeting tomorrow. We will call our corporation ET Enterprises. Catchy, eh? For Evelyn and Tina."

"You'd better come up with something for the corporation to do When you decide, you might give it another name, one that reflects the business. Say, I could get Arnie to design a logo for you. He's a real whiz!"

♥

Milly growled when she felt like screaming. "I don't know why you charge so much for one little task. No wonder solicitors have a bad reputation."

She looked at the short letter she held. Took his secretary about two minutes to add the name, address and salutation to a form letter and he charged her twenty pounds.

"Now, Millicent, don't get agitated. I didn't charge you for my time in negotiating your new mortgage, and that has proved a substantial saving."

She nodded ungraciously. "Thank you for that. No matter which way I look at things, I could cheerfully shoot Jeff to collect his insurance. What that man did to me . . .,"

George Fielding cleared his throat. "Er, I was going to tell you about that. Much against my wishes, Jeffrey changed his will in favour of your daughter, Christine. He left you the jewellery he inherited from his mother, and that which his father left him."

Milly stood. "He what? And you let him? This is outrageous. I want that will rescinded and the original left in place."

"Too late for that now. Anyway, a codicil also changed the original to the effect that if the marriage failed, then you were to receive nothing. And the marriage did fail, did it not?"

"Damn it! I will not have this idiot ruining my life in this manner. What can I do to get support from him?"

"Nothing at all. You're a wealthy woman in your own right and no court would grant you a cent."

"He still has to support our daughter."

"No. She is legally an adult now and doesn't live with you."

"I can fetch her back if that will help."

He sighed. "Don't bother. It won't make any difference. Do you know where she is?"

"Not a clue, but I can find her quickly enough if I need to."

"Look, Millicent, this firm has supplied legal management for your family for more than sixty years and I don't like to see the current events any more than you do. The fact remains that you are still a wealthy woman and your investments increase year by year. You have no difficulty in maintaining your lifestyle, so you're wasting your time in pursuing Jeffrey."

She glared at him, but said nothing,

George looked out of the window. "To move onto other things, I would appreciate your attendance here tomorrow morning at ten. I'm meeting with the bank and you should attend. The dealership is bankrupt as it stands. We have to do something about that."

"It's not my fault. Blame that idiot husband of mine. The one who schlepped off to the Bahamas and left me with the mess."

"Millicent," His tone should have warned her. "The dealership is also in your name and, as your partner, the bank. The creditors will sue you."

"Oh my God!" She stood and shook her fist to the heavens. "What else has that bastard done to me?" She pushed back her chair and turned to leave. "I'll be here tomorrow but I won't be very cooperative. You can rely on that." She glanced at her watch. "The time is precisely two-forty-six. Make a note of that. I refuse to pay for any more of your valuable time."

George made a note and shook his head as she clicked shut the door.

♥

At the dealership, the salesmen went on with their work, though most were on short time. The sales manager, Tyrone, who had assumed the position when Jeff went missing and supervisor Brian Beasley left to work for Jaguar, stood around most of the time, wondering if he, too, should call it quits. They had not paid the staff for two weeks now although the bookkeeper would surely sort that out when she got back from her vacation. Right now, since Harry left and Jeff had gone, no one had authority to sign cheques.

Tyrone was talking to his pal on the phone when the bank manager walked into the showroom with another man and he quickly put down the receiver.

"Good afternoon, Mr. Caldwell. In the market for a new car? The new models are in, as you see. We have a . . .,"

Caldwell put up a hand. "Not today. Today we are here to take the books for an audit. I think you should know that we are contemplating placing the company into receivership."

Tyrone rubbed his neck as he felt his felt his hair stand on end. "What?"

"Mr. Armstrong has left the country and cannot be found. The company has not made the loan payments, manufacturers' invoices are outstanding and wages are overdue. In view of this, we will perform an audit and decide what steps to take. Mrs. Armstrong has offered to finance the operation until we ascertain the correct financial situation."

"Bankrupt?" Tyrone could not get his head around it. This place was a gold mine. It made money, it must make money as the turnover of stock was tremendous and the place was always busy at weekends. "How could that possibly be? We've been the best venue in the city for four years in a row. An accounting firm was to come in to do an audit for Mrs. Armstrong but they didn't show yet."

Mr. Caldwell cleared his throat again. "I am not at liberty to discuss such matters with the staff. Carry on with your work." He turned to the other man. "The offices are over here."

Tyrone watched as they entered the offices, but then a customer came in. He hurried to greet him. He saw the two men leave with two large boxes, shrugged and went back to completing the sales form, feeling sure Mrs. Armstrong wouldn't let the place close.

♥

Milly carried on with her life, attended her meetings, did her charity work, even took on the post of chairwoman of the Manchester AIDS chapter. She figured she had weathered the storm and noticed people no longer whispered about her when she walked into a room.

Jeff was a memory and she felt more alive now, more in charge of her own destiny.

A voice cut into her musing. "Excuse me, Milly, but where shall we place the head table today? We can't use the small room because we've invited the press," the speaker was Joyce Rawlings. 'Milly's shadow' people called her, knowing that Milly got Joyce do the work while she took the credit.

"Oh, let's use the meeting hall, it's large but not too large. Too many empty chairs would make us look incompetent and unpopular. We can put the head table across the front of the stage, but not on the stage. This isn't an entertainment."

Joyce nodded and made some notes in her binder. The precious binder was never out of her hands and held notes from hundreds of meetings of several charitable organizations of which she and Milly were members. Not even Milly had seen its contents, though it would have made no sense to her since Joyce used Pitman's shorthand.

Milly tapped the table with her pen. "Refreshment committee? Plans?"

An older obese woman stood and read from a paper. "Finger sandwiches, petit fours, tea and coffee. Served after the meeting, of course."

Milly nodded. "Adequate I think. Decoration committee?"

Another woman stood and announced. "Red, white and blue streamers. Patriotic, looks good. Union Jacks and the new posters."

"Sufficient, but not too much red, white and blue. We don't want to look like a carnival. Understatement is better, don't you think?"

Joyce stuck up her hand. "Madam Chairman, I read that the Doncaster Chapter had the local high school band and choir perform. That sounds like fun. Should I make some calls?"

"No, we don't want this turned into a carnival, as I said before. Let's use some decorum and look professional. I want a decent write up in the press."

Dorothy McCoy, an angry looking woman, slapped the table. "Jeepers. Left to you, Milly, we'd have secret meetings and all wear white gloves and hats with veils. We've got to move with the time. This is no longer the rich bitch club. This is a genuine all-class committee where we should all have a say in things. How you ever managed to wangle enough votes to be elected chairperson, I'll never figure out. We *should* have a band, we *should* have the schools involved, because we'll get more publicity that way."

Milly stood. "Have you quite finished? I think we should comport ourselves with more dignity. If you think having an out-of-tune band of juvenile delinquents play selections from Jesus Christ Superstar will add anything to our meeting, then go ahead and arrange it. Right now I am resigning as chairperson and you can assume the responsibility." She glared at the angry woman, "I know you have many, many years of experience in chairing committees, Dorothy." Swinging her purse over her shoulder, she turned and stalked out. Joyce jumped to her feet, zipped shut her binder and ran after her.

"Milly, Milly, come back, please."

♥

Christine watched a program on seniors with her Gram. "That's what we should do, Gram. Run a senior program for people who can't get out much. You know, those in wheel chairs, or those who have difficulty walking. We can arrange tours to various places, maybe arrange visits to the theatre. We'd need a nurse on hand, of course, and volunteers to help."

Evelyn looked at her shining eyes, the excited expression, her evident enthusiasm as her words tried to keep up with her ideas.

"That sounds lovely, darling. People like me don't get out much other than for doctor and dentist visits. I'd love to go to the theatre.

It would be afternoon matinees, of course, but I'm sure a theatre would welcome guaranteed seats anytime."

They sat in the library and listed things to do.

Christine got the phone book. "First, I'll list all the senior residences within a ten mile radius. We don't want to cover too large an area at first."

"That's good. I'll get the other yellow pages and list the bus companies."

For some time they worked silently and Mrs. Grant popped in with their tea and marvelled at the industry.

"My word, you are working hard. What is it? A school project?"

Christine brushed back her hair and straightened up. "No, you know I don't go to school. Gram and I are going to start a service for seniors. Take them to plays and movies, or to the park, or on day trips."

Mrs. Grant pursed her lips and tutted. "Tt-tt-tt. I don't like the sound of that, Miss Christine. What about the legal implications? Suppose someone dies on one of your trips? Won't the family sue you?"

Christine's face fell.

Evelyn laughed and pushed at Mrs. Grant. "You do tend to see the black side of things, don't you? People will sign a release form when they make a reservation. I don't think we need worry about that, but my solicitor will advise us on any drawbacks. Now, is that the new caraway seed cake Christine made?"

CHAPTER FOURTEEN

Jeff sat at the bar near Bird Cage walk. While the many circular banquettes lining the long corridor held exotic caged birds in their centres, the walk derived its nickname from the many prostitutes who prowled its length. He was watching a young woman in a tight sequined dress flirting with a portly businessman. People eddied around this odd couple as she held out for more money or whatever. The man patted her hand where it sat on his arm and, a deal made, they moved along the walk toward the elevators and his room.

Jeff sighed. The young woman was about the best he had noticed lately. Too many of the available talent wore too much makeup and suggestive clothing. Twice he had picked up pros and twice been disappointed as they wanted it over and done with, no conversation, no companionship, both eager to be back on the scene to grab a likely looking john who had real money.

His life had becoming a bore. The sun always shone, the sea always beckoned, the tourists came and went. Boring. Even the meals became boring and he became tired of fresh fruit. He had nothing to do and all day to do it in and needed someone, someone to share his life. Yet where would he find that someone? Not among the ladies of the evening, not among the tourists who stayed only a week or two, not among the show girls who only came alive on stage and rarely saw the light of day as they avoided tan lines. All the hotel staff was black and he opted against that route after Brandi. No, he must make a diligent search of the hotels and stores in Nassau. Maybe he would find an attractive American female or someone from Europe.

Swallowing the last of his beer, he left.

♥

Millicent, annoyed at the way things were going, took out her spleen on Mrs. White. Mrs. White, accustomed to the way her employer treated her, let it go in one ear and out the other.

"You never listen to a word I say," Milly said in that quiet poisonous tone. "I don't know why I bother."

"That's right, Mrs. Armstrong. Get it out of your system."

Milly turned on her heel and walked out of the kitchen, her back ramrod straight, anger evident in every step.

Mrs. White smiled and did little jig. "Good riddance, you old crone." She chuckled, "Hee-hee. Looks like she's got her broom stick shoved way up her arse today. Talk about sweeping out of a room! Now I can relax."

She set the kettle on to boil and took down her favourite cup and saucer. From the box of imported biscuits, she selected two or three of the delicious chocolate wafers with hazelnut cream filling. When her tea was ready, she switched on the kitchen television and settled in her old armchair to watch the latest offering.

"What's going on here?" Milly's voice cut into her revery as she watched two soap opera stars kiss.

With an aggrieved expression, she stood. "I'm having my break, Mrs. Armstrong. I need a drink and it's not as if I ever sit down when I'm here."

"That is one of my best cups. I did not give you permission to use the good china."

"I see." She scowled, "But you will allow me to wash it, that it?"

"That is your job. I think you are becoming too comfortable here. I want this place cleaned properly today because I am expecting six for dinner. We will have lamb, new potatoes and peas. Something exotic but light for desert."

As she turned away, Mrs. White decided to have her say. "Excuse me, Mrs. Armstrong. To tell me that you are entertaining four hours before a meal is not on. You must have known about this dinner for at least a week. Lamb is out of the question. It's in the deep freeze and I don't have time to defrost it."

Milly raised a plucked eyebrow. "Yet you have time to sit watching television and drink tea?"

"I am entitled to a break. You know that. It's the law. Stop treating me like a skivvy, Mrs. Armstrong. Not many would work for you and you should . .,"

"You're fired as of this instant. Leave immediately. Nobody is indispensable. I can call a service and have someone here within the hour."

"I'll wait for the wages you owe me, if you don't mind. Plus two week's holiday pay."

Mrs. White took her coat from the pantry and stood, purse over her arm, one hand held out for her money.

"I will mail you a cheque." Milly had no cash and she knew she had overdrawn the checking account.

"Now just a minute! You owe me three week's pay and I'm not budging until I get it." She sank onto a chair and stared at Milly.

"I don't have that amount of cash in the house. I don't suppose you want a cheque, either?" She stared at her, daring her to speak. "So stay where you are. I'm sure you'll need to go home sooner or later."

"Huh! Just like you, that is. Talk about a tartar. I want my money, though I think I'll finish up going to the board of labour the way things have gone since Mr. Jeffrey left."

"Get out of my house. I don't want to see your miserable face for another second."

Mrs. White slowly rose from her chair. "Good luck in finding a replacement. I was the only one who could stick you, because, as you so clearly said 'I never listen.'" She walked to the back door and opened it. "I'd call a caterer if I were you, but you'll discover that nobody is going to come on such short notice." Grinning, she left remembering that only last week Mrs. Rawlings had said that if she ever left Mrs. Armstrong, she could have a job with her.

Mrs. Joyce Rawlings was nice, a soft spoken gentle lady. Yes, she would call in to see her on her way home. It would be a right blow for Mrs. A. to see her ensconced with her best friend.

♥

Milly walked around the house muttering. She had done it now: fired the one person who could work for her and could have kicked herself. Such a procession had come and gone when she first looked for a daily helper. Most were sloppy, ill-mannered and lazy, and they always walked out on her if she as much as pointed out dust or finger prints on the silver. Domestics today were not educated in social behaviour, nor were they reliable. Mrs. White was always punctual, always had meals ready on time, did her work quietly and competently, yet, in a fit of pique, she had fired her. For some reason she had thought the woman would stay, but then why should she?

Financially, things were terrible. The bank insisted on repayment of the last loan she had for Jeff which she had co-signed as security, they also sought payment of the outstanding loans Jeff had taken out earlier. Then Arthur French had threatened to sue her for the loss of his investment in the company. What could she do? No way was she going to bankrupt herself because of Jeff's incompetence. Maybe she should leave the country, take a long cruise, then the banks and the creditors would have to wait.

That was running away, she knew, but it would relieve the pressure. In her personal account she had more than enough to pay off everything, including the mortgage, but very few knew of her consolidated wealth. The bank did, of course, and they were very tenacious when it came to collecting debts. Yet running away was not her style, and she was stubborn enough to weather any storm when it came to her own comfort. No, she would stay, continue her work with the charities, wait to see what the bank auditors announced and pray that Jeff returned to accept the consequences of his actions. Maybe she could get him extradited from Nassau. She must check that with her solicitor.

Her mother . . . maybe her mother could help. The old lady was rolling in it, had money she did not even know she had and would not miss. Yes, mother was the answer. What mother would refuse a child anything? Not that she was a child any more, but she was the sole heir and would soon inherit everything.

She hummed as she dressed for her trip. Time to soothe the old lady, time to do some humble begging.

♥

"Tina?" Evelyn called. No answer. She hauled herself out of her chair and reached for her cane. "Tina?" Where had the girl gone? She was usually clicking away at the computer by this time, but the library was empty and the screen black.

Mrs. Grant walked into the hall with a tea tray as she closed the library door.

"Tea up!"

"In the lounge, I think, Mrs. Grant. Have you any idea where Tina is?"

"Gone to the library for something, she said. She won't be long."

Evelyn settled in her chair and took the tea Mrs. Grant handed her. "I'll have a slice of toasted seed cake, I think. I fancy something this morning."

Mrs. Grant smiled. "Having cravings? My word, we should be glad you're past that at your time of life."

Evelyn smiled though she did not find that even vaguely amusing. "Yes," she said, and heard the front door close softly. Her hearing was acute for her age. "Here's Tina now."

As Milly sailed into the room under full sail, her fur trimmed cape billowing around her.

Evelyn grinned. "What are you dressed as, Millicent? Some new comic book hero?"

Mrs. Grant laughed aloud and Milly stopped in her tracks.

"Do you have to make derogatory remarks in front of the staff, mother?"

Evelyn raised her eyebrows. "Staff? This is Mrs. Beth Grant, my live-in companion. I think of her as one of the family."

Mrs. Grant smiled. "I'll fetch you that toasted cake now." She left, glaring at Mrs. Armstrong as she passed her.

"Honestly, mother. Familiarity with the staff is not a good thing. They take advantage."

Evelyn lifted her head and stared at her daughter. "As I said, Beth Grant is my companion. I don't know from where you get these uppity ideas. It's not as if you're a royal."

Milly tossed her cape over a chair and sat facing her mother in front of the marble fireplace. A small coal fire burned.

"No wonder this room is so warm. The central heating is running and yet you insist on a fire."

"A fire makes the room feel homey. When you get to my age, you feel the cold. I like a fire because it makes me dream of the past."

Milly eyed the old lady. She must watch and listen. Maybe her mother was becoming senile.

"How's your new friend?" she asked, recalling the visit she made on the day of her mother's doctor's appointment. "He must be quite the gentleman if you're willing to ride buses with him."

"He?" Evelyn laughed. "I have no 'he' in my life," she could not resist adding, ". . . but then neither do you from what I hear."

"No need to get out the sharp knife, mother. Now, how are you?"

"In the best of health. I get enough exercise and I eat well. I have much to fill my days."

"Hmm. Theatres, art galleries, restaurants and such I expect. Isn't that a little too strenuous for you?"

"Did you come to nag at me? To what do I owe this visit? You don't usually remember I'm alive."

"I wanted to see you, that's all."

Mrs. Grant arrived with the toasted seed cake and handed it to Evelyn. "Anything else?"

"I will have plain cake, no butter," Milly said, looking past Mrs. Grant at a particularly fine painting over the fireplace mantel.

Mrs. Grant drew herself up and pursed her lips. "It is customary to add 'please' where I come from."

Milly looked down her nose. "I wouldn't know. I live uptown, not downtown."

"Honestly, Millicent, you are really too much!" Evelyn said, patting Mrs. Grant's hand. "Take no notice of my rude daughter. If she wants cake, she can fetch it herself."

Milly ignored both of them and poured herself a cup of tea. The cup was for Christine, but she could not know that.

"At least the help won't be sitting in the room drinking tea with you."

The front door slammed and startled Evelyn. Oh no, not Christine. She glanced up as Mrs. Grant almost ran to the door.

Milly did not miss a thing. "What's going on, mother?"

"Nothing." Evelyn drank her tea and poured another cup. Mrs. Grant was talking in the hall and she hoped she had persuaded Christine to go to her room. No such luck.

The door opened and Christine entered She went straight to Evelyn and kissed her. "Morning, Gram. Did you wonder where I was?"

Milly sat straight up and stared at the lovely young woman. "What is this?" she asked, her voice cold.

Christine turned and glared at her mother. "Oh, I didn't see *you*. What's the matter? Come to beg for money, or ask Gram to sell her home?"

Milly coloured. How astute of Christine. "I came to see my mother. What are you doing here? Your place is at home now that your father has left."

"Yes, we heard about that. Left you for good, they say. Good for Dad. He was due for a break and the sound of your vitriolic voice grating on his ears finally got through. I hope he's very happy, wherever he is."

"Young lady, I will not be spoken to in such a manner. I'm your mother."

"Whew! Don't I know it. What do you want?"

"I came to see my mother."

Christine crossed her arms over her chest and tapped one foot. "For what?"

"To see how she is."

"Horse feathers." She snorted, "You're after something. We don't need you here. You've never shown any interest before, other than to try to remove Gram from this house so you could get your hands on your inheritance. What's the real reason for this visit?"

"Any reason I may have is between my mother and me. It is nothing to do with you, you interfering little brat."

Christine laughed and sat on the arm of Gram's chair. She put her arm around her shoulders. "Never mind, Gram, I'll protect you from the big bad witch."

"Really! You are going too far now, Christine. I would like you to leave this room and allow me to talk with my mother."

"No way! You can talk with me here, or maybe I could call Gram's solicitor."

Evelyn patted Christine's leg. "Darling, please leave us alone. I can take care of myself and I have the bell if I need help. Come on now, don't worry and stay out of things that are none of your concern."

"About time too, mother." Milly sat back, relaxing now.

Christine dawdled her way out of the room, picked up the books she had fetched from the hall table, went to the library and switched on the computer.

♥

Jeff Armstrong knew he was in big trouble. Somehow, and it was all so vague; he had lost all his money. He remembered meeting Jose Valaquez, a Brazilian businessman at a bar in Nassau. He recalled the large yacht and the group of men from various places that assembled to play poker. Yet poker was not his game, had never been. For some unearthly reason, maybe it was the drinks, he had felt invincible, known that he could not lose. His mind saw the cards, the stack of chips that he pushed into the pot. He lost everything in his wallet and then some. Now he was destitute.

It was evening and he sat on the verandah drinking coffee and worrying. Jose knew where he lived, having dropped him off here. No money remained in his account, not after Jose had driven him to the bank.

How could he get away? Jose wanted the rest of his money, the other two hundred and twenty-five thousand, and Jeff had not one penny. Lord, was he in deep shit. He sighed. Anthilla and her husband would ask for their wages, which was not much, but more than he had. His wallet held two credit cards and some business cards, but no cash.

With no cash, he must walk to the airport. He would take only the smaller carry-on shoulder bag, leave the rest of his possessions. Mentally he assessed the remaining credit on his cards. If he took the cheapest flight out, to the closest place in the states, maybe he could make a run for it. It was his only option.

CHAPTER FIFTEEN

"Mother, this must stop. Christine must come home."

"She's happy here and you'll ignore her. She will stay with me."

Milly's lips clamped into a thin line, then she said. "I insist she return home."

"So you can either ignore her or nag her out of the house? She ran away once and you're aiming to make that happen again."

"She's my daughter and I need her at home."

"*You* are *my* daughter, but I don't like the person you have become. You're greedy and manipulative. You drove both Christine and your husband out of your house. I don't think you're a very nice person. I wouldn't want to live with you, ever."

She dropped her jaw, unable to believe what her mother had said. "Mother! How could you say such things? Now I'm alone, I need Christine."

"I see. You'd sooner see me, an aged woman live alone, while you take the light out of my life? I won't be around for much longer, Millicent, and the least I expect is to live happily for my last years. Christine stays with me."

"I can fight this, you know, mother."

"Don't be silly, girl. Christine is now an adult according to the law and can live wherever she wishes although I had the solicitor draw up an agreement and she is now my legal ward. I don't suppose you don't count Mrs. White as a real person?"

Milly looked away. "Mrs. White left."

"Ah-ah! So you want Christine to come and be your housekeeper. Too bad she came home when she did, or we wouldn't be having this conversation. Why don't you tell me the real reason for your visit?"

Milly sighed and sat straight up, she looked at the fireplace and did not blink. "Look, mother, I'm short of funds. Jeff left me with a bankrupt business. Now the bank is demanding repayment of his loans and unfortunately I co-signed all of them. One of his silent partners is also threatening to sue for his investment. I don't know what to do. Can you help me?"

Evelyn eyed her with some surprise and started to laugh She laughed so much that she became breathless and started to gasp, put her hands to her chest and collapsed against the chair back.

Milly watched, disapproving of her laughter, sat back and stewed. "I do hope they've got you in Pampers these days, mother."

Evelyn recovered and wiped her eyes. "Honestly, you have a gall, asking me for money. I won't give you anything, Millicent, since I have no cash money. I invested everything, apart from that which I need for everyday living. Please leave and don't come begging again."

"Begging? I was not begging mother, simply asking for help. I intend to repay every penny."

"You won't need to now, will you? I won't give you money."

"Still, everything comes to me when you die, doesn't it? Why can't you give me money now when I need it?"

"How dare you presume that I care about your welfare? An occasional visit in the past twenty years does not make for a close relationship, daughter or no. Go away, Millicent. Leave me alone. Christine will look after me."

"Oh I see, little Miss Perfect is now the heir. Is that it? I will consult my solicitor about this mother. No way is that little brat going to steal what is rightfully mine."

"Nothing was ever rightfully yours, Millicent. If you had been a proper daughter instead of a social butterfly, things might have been different. You never even invited me to Christine's christening, her birthday parties or her various school plays. I knew all about them and used to attend, sit where you couldn't see me. Christine came over every week back then and we were great friends."

Milly gasped and curled her hands into fists.

"I see that surprises you. Neither of us wanted you to know. You would have stopped her coming here. Oh, don't bother denying it. We both know it's true."

"That little. . .,"

"Stop that She is not little, nor is she a brat. It was you that drove her out to live on the streets, you who made her life a misery, you and that stupid husband of yours. I think you deserved each other. He was, and is, a gold digger of the worst kind. You spent your energy seeking the approval of the social set and neither of you had time for the child. I always did and always will. Now please leave." She rang the bell.

Milly enveloped herself in her cape, her expression thunderous. "You have not seen the last of me, mother."

Mrs. Grant entered and stood at the door, waiting to show Milly out.

Evelyn turned to look into the fire.

Milly stormed past Mrs. Grant and opened the front door herself. This time, contrary to her usual practice, she slammed the door.

Mrs. Grant hurried into the lounge. "Are you all right?"

Evelyn turned and smiled. "I feel better than ever. She sure slammed that door, didn't she?"

They laughed together as Christine came into the room. "What's so funny? Did she leave? Did she slam the door, or did you, Mrs. Grant?"

"No, that was her."

She grinned widely. "Wow, you sure must have miffed her. She usually closes a door so softly that you wouldn't know it had been opened."

"I told her a few truths and she was furious," Evelyn said, smiling. "I oughtn't to have done it, but I did."

Christine nodded. "I'd love to tell her some things, but she makes me so nervous and always talks down to me that I get tongue tied."

"What are you working on, Tina?" Evelyn asked, changing the subject.

"Time for more tea and cake?" Mrs. Grant asked as she removed the used cups.

Christine put the milk jug on the tray and said, "Yes, tea and cake, *please*."

"Certainly, madam."

They all laughed.

♥

Harvey loved his job and spent days working on a project, often working at his station for eighteen hours at a stretch. Challenge and excited, he begrudged not a minute of the time.

"I get to do the animation for a principal character in a new game," he said to Christine.

They had made a date for Friday and were sitting in a booth in the Cyber Web Cafe. Across the room their usual chums spent time on line.

"It sounds as if you found your niche," Christine said. "What does your father say about it?"

"I didn't tell him yet. He thinks I'm working for some place where I enter data, nothing else. Boy, he'd faint if he saw my pay cheque. 'Time you found a proper job,' he said last week. 'There's no future in entering data'."

She laughed. "Time to tell him the truth, I think. I'd love to see his face."

"Yeah, so would I. Still, I think I'll keep it to myself for the time being. He's leaving me alone, Mom hardly sees me and I try my best to keep out of her way."

"I told you about my mother coming to Gram's? She sent me a letter, full of insinuation claiming I was trying to steal her inheritance. Honestly, the woman is money mad. I don't want anything from Gram because I love her and she loves me. That's more than I ever got from my mother. Now she wants me to go home, says she needs me. That's a laugh!"

"We sure have some weird parents, you and I." Both nodded. "Ever wonder what their parents were like? Are all parents the same do you think?"

"Not if what they show on TV is any example. Look at some of the soap operas where everyone loves everyone else and they all get along. Parents never tell kids off without making a joke. Parents are always telling them they love them."

"Yeah, guess you're right. We both got dealt a bad hand."

She looked sad. "My dad never writes to me. You'd think he would at least write."

"Still, he would write to your house and you don't live there now."

"True, but my mother is such a stickler for etiquette that she'd make sure I got his letters."

"Maybe she sent them back 'address unknown.' That would be correct to her."

She nodded. "Yes, I think it would. Maybe I should call and ask her."

"Nah. Don't do that. You wouldn't want to know that he didn't write, and maybe he didn't. Maybe he was glad to get away from you, too."

"I guess you're right. He never paid me much attention, so why would I think he missed me?"

"Do you miss him?"

"Maybe. Mainly because he was always on my side. I know that much."

"Never mind. Now tell me about the business. Is it working?"

"Yes, it is. We had four tours last week, and made a profit after we paid the bills. It looks like we might make a success of it. I sent out flyers to all the senior centres in our area and we're getting lots of calls. Gram is in her glory answering the phone. She loves it."

"Good, eh? Let's face it, we've both found our niche. We should celebrate."

"How? Have a nice meal and a bottle of wine?"

"Yeah, good idea. Come on, let's get the phone book and choose somewhere special. I've got money burning a hole in my pocket."

♥

Jeff arrived in Tampa at dusk, relieved to fine the airport packed with tourists. He mingled with the crowds and made his way to the bus station. While in Nassau, he spotted a swarthy looking man eyeing him at the airport and shivered, thinking maybe he was one of Jose's men. Paranoiac, he sensed danger in every glance.

Arriving downtown, he sought an out of the way motel and booked a room. It was small, cramped and not very clean. Tossing his bag on the bed, he washed his face and combed his hair. His hair was long, almost shoulder length. In the months of lazing around, he had not bothered getting it cut, thinking it made him look younger. Now it seemed a dead giveaway. Right, he would get it cut. A brush cut, and he must always wear his reading glasses, maybe grow a mustache. Time to change his appearance.

Two days later with a brush cut and chinos, wearing a baseball cap and second hand shirts, he bore no resemblance to the suave young businessman he had once been, nor the beach bum they sought. He worked his way north, bumming lifts or walking until someone stopped and gave him a ride. Soon he was in Maine.

He found a temporary job as a caddy at a prestigious golf course. As the vacationing business men played, the topics discussed made a lot of sense to him, and he itched to get his hands on some real money. What he could have done with those investments.

"You new around here?" a female voice asked.

Jeff turned and saw an attractive blond. She looked and smelled expensive.

"Yes, I am."

"A tourist?"

"No, a traveller having some exercise and getting paid for it."

"Do you like golf?"

"Sure do. And you? Do you play?"

"I do," she laughed, "Rather badly. Would you like to caddy for me?"

"And your partner?"

"I play alone. I'm not that good yet. Wouldn't want to embarrass myself, you know."

He glanced at his watch. "Okay. I've got two hours before my next foursome."

They headed for the first hole. A foursome had just finished and were plodding away.

"Did you book this time?" he asked.

She smirked. "Of course. I do know the rules."

It was close to noon and no others players were sitting on the bench waiting to tee off. It was hot but a stiff wind blew in off the sea.

She drove off the tee and her ball sliced to the right. "Darn it all. The pro said I had that licked. Oh well, let's hope I'm better on the next hole."

When they reached the ninth hole, she sliced even more and the ball bounced into a stand of trees and bushes.

"Oops, that's going to take some finding," she said, laughing.

"Come on, let's get out of the sun. At least we can cool off for a while."

They did not cool off for long because she almost threw him to the ground as she wrapped herself around him and kissed him. Jeff responded and soon they were having sex in the brush and grass of the clearing. Mosquitos zizzed around but neither heard nor felt them.

"Wow! That was fantastic," she said. "I could do that again, but not here. The darned mosquitos almost ate me alive. Come on, we'll go to my house and you can treat my mozzie bites."

Jeff grinned. Mrs. Janice Merton was a very sexy lady. He already knew she was a widow and lived alone on Jackson's Point. It took no time at all for him to report to the caddy shack that he felt ill and was leaving.

The shack operator watched as Jeff sprinted to the car park and saw him get into the pale blue Rolls Royce. "Guess Janice Merton found another hot one," he muttered.

♥

Milly paced the study. She was managing with a catering service and various women sent by an agency. None of them would live in, and those who would were either Filipino or Jamaican, and Milly did not like black people. She tried a young woman with a baby for a week but the baby annoyed her and she fired her. Now the agency informed her that she must keep the women longer than a week, that they would only send her temporary workers unless she settled on a long term relationship. She put ads in the papers and interviewed some women, but all wanted more than she was willing to pay. Most looked around the huge house and said it was too much for one person to handle. Yet Mrs. White had handled it with ease. Oh lord. She must get Mrs. White back . . . but how?

♥

Christine and her two couriers were meeting in the library. The Eldertrans couriers were homosexuals, both charming and courteous. Because most of their customers were lonely widows aching for attention, the young men were doubly attractive. Some customers came on weekly trips just to speak to Alan or Patrick.

"She was so generous," Alan said of a customer. "She gave me a hundred and told me to spend it all at once, said she would give me another on her next trip. I ask you, all I did was sit with her at lunch. She's got a lovely sense of humour."

"She'd need it, sweety," Patrick sniffed. "All I got from her was a pat on the behind. I mean, she's pushing it."

"Come on, you two. Let's get back to the situation. If they tip you, good, if they don't, don't complain. They're old ladies, for heaven's sake. Anyway, the men that come along are usually grumpy and obnoxious."

"Too true, sweety," Alan grinned. "Know that old fruit cake Mr. Webster? He said he liked me and would I come to his room to play chess. I should cocoa!"

Patrick laughed. "When he was on my bus, he said he wanted me to help him with his memoirs. I've heard it called some things, but that takes the cake."

"Back to business," Christine said firmly. "About the trip to Liverpool for shopping. I've hired three more registered nurses because we have more than enough customers for three buses. Christmas shopping is important to the clients so I'm considering hiring another bus. Some of our regulars are becoming irritated because they missed making their reservation in time, but most have bad memories, and there's nothing we can do about that. Still, I have to soothe ruffled feathers. Anyway, do you know of anyone who could courier?"

"Oh yes," Alan said, "We know all kinds of guys."

"I want someone competent, someone with empathy for the oldsters."

"Someone of our persuasion, were you going to say? No need, sweety, we know the very person."

"Gerry?" Patrick asked.

"Gerry, and maybe Jack."

"All right, now how are we going to handle this? This is a list of four malls. Which one should we patronize, or should we send each bus to a different outlet?"

"Each to a different place," Alan said. "Let's spread out. Some of these places can't handle a crowd, especially since we have so many wheel chairs."

"Right, let's sort that out first."

♥

Mrs. Grant sang as she polished the bannister rail. Christmas approached so she must dig out the decorations and check the lights. As she polished, she mentally organized her Christmas baking. This year Miss Christine would be here and could help her, though that meant twice the cleaning. No matter how she argued or cajoled, the girl would not clean up after she made her messes. Still, it didn't matter because Christine was now a superlative cook and they all ate well.

She smiled. Just look at the young woman now, running a company, while Evelyn, acting as switchboard operator, was in her glory, talking nonstop. Evelyn seemed twice as active as she had been before Christine arrived and it suited her. Not even a cold did she catch this year, yet for the two previous her health deteriorated and she suffered through colds and bronchitis. Yes, Miss Christine had made a big difference to their lives.

"Is it tea time, Mrs. Grant?" Evelyn asked as she left the lounge. "I'm spitting feathers. Such a lot of phone calls today."

"I'll go and make it." She looked at her employer. "Are you sure this isn't all too much for you?"

"No, it isn't. I love it. Oops, there's the phone again."

Mrs. Grant muttered as she went to the kitchen. "Like a telephone exchange, this place is lately."

In the library Christine and the couriers laughed at something one of their customers had said.

". . . and her ninety-two if she's a day," Alan finished.

"I think you both enjoy this work," Christine said as she wiped her eyes.

"I most positively do, " Patrick said. "The old dears are a pleasure to work with, and even the grumpy old men seem to perk up when they get on the bus."

"And if they don't, we perk them up, don't we, Alan?"

"I hope so. I'd hate to be as old as some of them are and without a sense of humour. One old chap wanted me to hold his penis in the stall. Said he couldn't hold it still. I said, I thought it might be better if he did it, because I was unskilled in holding anything still."

Alan laughed. "That's true."

"Anyway, he chuckled, and said I should make sure he pointed it in the right direction. He sprayed the entire cubicle but it was a long slow pee so I managed to stay clear."

"You two are priceless, you know that?" Christine laughed as Mrs. Grant popped her head around the door.

"Tea for three? Cookies?"

"Please, Mrs. Grant. These two must be spitless by now."
"I shouldn't wonder." She closed the door.
"Yum, elevenses. I do feel peckish."
"I know," Patrick said, grinning.

CHAPTER SIXTEEN

Janice's place stood along an inlet off the sound. A large rambling cedar built home with lots of verandahs and decks around a kidney shaped pool, it overlooked the river. Jeff grinned with his first glimpse. In the bright sunshine it looked like something out of a movie as it posed in the perfectly manicured lawns. Bright splashes of annuals stood along the driveway in terra cotta urns.

"Wow!" He couldn't help himself.

"It is something, isn't it? I love this place in summer. Don't stay much after Halloween, though. I go back to Florida or my place in the south of France."

He eyed her with interest. "Jeepers, you must be rolling in it."

She smiled, raising her chin higher. "Not exactly, but I do manage my investments very well. My ex-husband was a rich man."

"And you got the lot?"

She turned to stare at him as she slowly wheeled the car around the circular driveway and stopped below the steps that lead to the porch. "You're beginning to sound a lot like a fortune hunter, deary. Let's drop the subject."

"Sure." He felt suddenly miserable, envying her. Jealous because she had money, homes, a future without worries.

Slamming her door closed, she said, "Come on, let's get inside. I need a shower."

The interior looked very grand. He glanced around the two story entrance hall with its massive chandelier and overhanging second storey. Their feet made little sound on the beige ceramic tiled floors that shone dully in the light from the large windows. A long refectory table stood in the centre of the space on which was a silver dish into which she tossed her keys. He gazed in wonder at the floral arrangement on the table that stood at least four feet high.

She chuckled as she saw him staring open mouthed. "Lovely, isn't it? The local florist used to work for the Vanderbilts. He's a treasure. This way," she said, crooking her index finger.

Janice headed up the stairs and he followed.

Deep wool carpets covered the upper floor and a wide corridor bisected the house front to back. The far walls were floor to ceiling windows and light flooded the corridor from both sides. What a dump, he thought, grinning, thinking the windows alone would pay for a world cruise.

She opened a double door and entered a room, her bedroom: almost a suite with a seating area and a small alcove used as an office. Her computer stood there, its screen saver an underwater scene.

Janice threw open another door. The bathroom.

The bathroom of his dreams, he thought, looking over her shoulder. White marble floors, incandescent with floor to ceiling mirrors, and the sunken tub looked large enough to bathe an elephant. A shower stood to one side with gold embossed glass doors and double shower heads.

She watched his expression in the mirror wall and smiled. "You like?"

"Oh yes, I like very much."

Janice took off her blouse, never taking her eyes off him. "Want a shower, sailor?"

"Sure do."

Jeff fumbled his shirt open and tossed it onto the chaise longue. His pants came off so fast that he wondered at his haste. Naked, she stepped into the shower and turned on the water. By the time he had removed his watch and socks, she was washing her hair.

They each had their own shower head and since they were at opposite ends, he faced the wall. His mind raced. Was this a shower, or did it signify something else? He soon got his answer when her arm circled his waist and she grasped his penis.

♥

Milly thought the young solicitor very attractive.

Seeking further legal advice about her financial affairs and, reluctant to liquidate any more of her stock holdings, she asked her long time solicitor, George Fielding, for his advice. George, not very helpful, told her that she should either find Jeffrey, or ask her mother for an advance on her inheritance. Unwilling to waste money looking for her husband, and now aware her mother would refuse to help, she decided a new solicitor might do the trick.

He essentially told her the same thing, but she felt a physical attraction to him. Not many men appealed to her, but he did as he talked so earnestly and seemed caring. She smiled at him, one of her attractive smiles, almost touched his hand a couple of times, to make sure he knew she was interested.

"Mrs. Armstrong, I can't help you. I think you should take the advice from your bank and clear the outstanding loans. As far as your mortgage, I assume you can pay that."

"Oh yes, I'm solvent, but if that husband of mine shows his face again, I need to know that he will assume his role as breadwinner and pay me back everything I spent to resolve the situation."

"I don't think you could demand that. Not since you solved the problem. He didn't ask you to clear the debts, did he?"

"No, but since I co-signed the bank loans, I am responsible in his absence. This is ridiculous! I shouldn't have to use my money. It's his responsibility."

"Then I suggest you find him."

"Are you busy tonight?"

"Pardon?"

"Are you busy tonight? I would like to invite you to supper."

He looked flustered, and she wondered if she had made a mistake in being so forward.

"No, I'm not busy. I accept your invitation."

She smiled and touched his hand. "I think we can find other topics of much more interest than my finances."

He straightened his tie and smiled.

♥

Christine filled in for Patrick when he came down sick with a cold. She looked forward to her first bus trip.

"Sure you won't come with us, Gram? We've had a cancellation so there's room."

"No, thank you. I'll man the office while you're gone. The phone will keep me busy. I have so many new friends who call to chat."

"Yes, that's true. 'Gram's lonely heart's club' is a good name for it. You've got more friends now than you ever had."

"I owe that to you, darling. I'm so much happier with you here. You've brought such joy into my life, Tina, darling."

Christine blushed with pleasure. "Shucks, t'weren't nothing, ma'am," she said, laughing.

"You could ask Harvey to go with you. It's on a Monday and you told me he sometimes works all weekend, and can take off Monday to recuperate from his efforts. At least you'd have a day out together."

She considered it for a moment, then shook her head. "No, I can't ask him. He wouldn't want to be stuck with a lot of old ladies. You know how they are. I've told you about them and the couriers."

Gram laughed. "Yes, those sweet young men are walking targets. They're so charming and friendly and invite female attention. I've often found that gay men are so lovely and attentive."

Christine looked at her. Gram knew they were gay?

"Oh, don't look so shocked, Tina. I like homosexual men. Some years ago, long before I married, my best friend in the entire world was a homosexual. Not that society accepted them in those days." She shook her head and mentally looked back, her expression sad. "No, as an army officer he hid it very well. So well, in fact, that my parents started to regard him as a future husband for me." She sighed, "Their constant hints and outright suggestions put paid to our relationship. We both knew it couldn't continue, so we parted the best of friends and wrote to each other regularly. Not a soul knew of his torment, apart from me, that is. Not even his parents knew. Hal died during the war when the Germans torpedoed his troop ship in the Battle of the Atlantic. Poor Hal. He was born far too soon, I think."

"Sad story, Gram. I wish you hadn't told me."

"Never mind, your sweet young couriers are blatantly gay and no one shuns them for it. I like them."

"So do I. Too bad Patrick caught a cold, though I'm looking forward to the trip. I can do all my Christmas shopping. Not that I need to get much."

Evelyn regarded her then knowing Christine felt the estrangement from her parents very deeply, although they had never treated her well. Christmas brought many emotions to the surface.

"Never mind. Don't spend much money on me. I don't need a thing. You buy something nice for Harvey and some little things for your staff."

"Jeepers. What on earth can I possibly get for the couriers and the nurses, Gram? Any suggestions?"

♥

Jeff sighed, bored. Far from living the high life he craved, Janice wanted to stay home all the time, ever ready to get him into bed. She pounced on him at the most inopportune times and then got angry if he failed to perform to her expectations. Not that he would ever turn down sex so willingly given, but it became annoying that every session must be spent making sure she got her jollies even when he was tired of murmuring the words of adoration she needed to achieve her climax. Janice was older than he, not that it mattered, yet in the harsh light of day when she decided they would make love beside the pool, he saw the wrinkles, the sagging skin, the age spots on her hands.

He sighed again as he looked around the lavish room. To him this represented living with a capital L and he loved it. Yet was their relationship as solid as it seemed? Somehow he knew she would grow bored with him, as bored as he was with her, and then where would he be? Would she take him with her when she left Maine? Somehow he doubted that, so it was time to leave this life of luxury, of sexual slavery. Time to make his way back to Toronto. The only decision needed from him was whether to wait until she ended it, or leave of his own accord. Putting back his shoulders, he decided he must leave. Not today, not while a delicious aroma came from the kitchen where her daily cook had arrived to fix a sumptuous dinner.

"Coo-eee, Jeffrey!" Shit, she was back from the beauty parlour, nails sharpened.

♥

Evelyn was chatting to one of her phone friends when she first felt it. Like something inside her had switched off and she waited, breath held, until it switched back on again. She felt fine after that and dismissed it.

It happened again when Christine arrived home from her trip and was chattering excitedly. She took a deep breath and held it until the feeling subsided.

Christine held up the sweater she had bought for Harvey and said, "What do you think?"

Evelyn nodded. No use alarming the child.

"What's the matter, Gram? You look a bit off colour." Christine tossed the sweater on a chair and rushed to Evelyn's side. "Are you all right?"

"Do stop fussing, Tina. I am fine, it's a spot of indigestion."

"Oh, you sure?"

"Of course I am. Now show me the rest of your purchases."

Christine brought out the rest, but she watched Evelyn closely, the spontaneity gone from her chatter.

Later she sought out Mrs. Grant. "She looked funny, like she felt ill."

Mrs. Grant patted her shoulder. "Look love, she's well past ninety and things are bound to start failing. She's never been really ill in her life, but things start to wear out when you get to her age. Take her to the doctor's and get her checked out again. The doctor will know if she has a problem."

Christine's eyes filled with tears. "Oh Mrs. Grant, whatever will I do if she gets sick? I couldn't stand it. I always think of her as going on forever, but I know she can't. I don't want to think about her dying."

Mrs. Grant put her arm around her shoulders. "Now, come on, who said anything about dying? I'm sure she'll see a hundred if not more. She's a strong woman in both body and will. You wait and see."

Christine wiped her eyes on a serviette. "You're right, but I'll take her to see the doctor anyway. She won't like it, though."

"So here you are. What are you two planning? Something for Christmas?"

Evelyn stood in the doorway, smiling widely.

"No, in fact we were saying that a visit to the doctor was in order for you. We'll go tomorrow." Christine used a firm voice and Mrs. Grant nodded.

"Really? Nice of you to plan my day, Tina, but I have no intention of going anywhere near the doctor tomorrow. Listen to the weather forecast before you make plans like that."

Christine looked dismayed. The announcer had said two inches of snow was expected overnight and the storm would continue for two days. She had forgotten that.

"I forgot about the weather. Good job we travelled today, isn't it?"

"Now, come along. We'll have tea and biscuits, Mrs. Grant, thank you."

♥

Milly decided the time had come to again visit her mother. At a loose end because they had called off one of her meetings due to bad weather, she cast around for another way of killing time. Strange how time lay heavily on her hands unless she was organizing events or people. Hobbies did not interest her, and reading seemed far too boring for someone with her mental agility. Television was for morons, the computer did not beckon her, apart from inputting her monthly budget calculations. Housework was beneath her, and that included laundry and shopping for food.

She sighed and picked up her address book from the desk, tutting with annoyance as she saw dust on the window sill. Maybe it was again time to beg Mrs. White to return. Nobody had looked after the house like her. She flicked to the page and dialled the number.

"Mrs. White!" she made her voice lively, full of warmth, well as warm as she could make it. "How are you?"

"Who's this?" an old voice asked.

Milly laughed merrily, realizing it was Mrs. White's mother. "This is Mrs. Armstrong. Is Mrs. White at home?"

"What do you want?"

"I wanted to know if she were working."

"Of course she's working. She won't be home until six. What was your name again?"

"Never mind. I'll call another time."

Milly put down the phone and stared at it. So Mrs. White had another job, and no wonder since she was an excellent cleaner. This was all her own fault: she should have kept her mouth shut. Now what was she going to do?

She had a list of twenty or so women whom she intended to interview on Friday. Most had atrocious accents and were probably refugees but she could not afford to be choosy. The catering bill had staggered her when she opened the letter. To think a few dinners could cost so much, and what made it more annoying was that she must use her own money.

Going to the bedroom, she browsed through the closet. Might as well wear something less ostentatious if she were to make an impression on her mother. She chose an older suit, a Chanel she had purchased many years earlier. It showed its years but she still liked it. Mother would not know a Chanel, or any designer, would only notice its age. Oh well, this was not going to be a good meeting, not with Christine in residence. Her mind flashed back to the phone call.

"Mrs. Grant, I wish to speak to Christine. It's her mother."

"I don't know if she's home right now. Hang on, I'll check."

The phone went silent and then she heard them talking. Christine said, "I don't want to talk to her. Say I'm out somewhere."

Evelyn said, "Now, darling, talk to your mother. It's only common courtesy and a phone call can't possibly hurt."

Mrs. Grant said, "Come on, she's waiting. What do I say, or will you answer it, Miss Christine?"

Christine said churlishly, "Oh, all right. I'll talk to her. I bet she's going to ask me to come home again. I'm staying here."

"Hello, mother." The tone was sharp, no nonsense.

"Well, you surprise me, Christine. Not wanting to talk to me? I heard everything you said. You should teach the housekeeper to put the phone on hold before wandering away."

"We don't have a hold button. This isn't your house, you know. What do you want now?"

"Really, Christine, where are your manners? I taught you better than that. At least we could talk. You could tell me about your business. Are you still employing my mother as your secretary?" She laughed to denote it was a joke.

Christine took the receiver away from her ear and pulled a face. "She's not my secretary, as you put it. She's only answering the phone when I'm out, or did you expect Mrs. Grant to do that?"

"She answered when I rang, I notice."

"She was dusting right by the phone. If it were a business call I would have taken it or if I were out, Gram would have. Why the sudden concern about my business? Looking for a partnership?"

"Good gracious, no!"

"The business is doing well and we're very busy. That being so, I must say goodbye."

"No, no, wait a moment. I wondered if I could come over and see mother? I know she was annoyed at my visit last time and thought I would test the waters."

"She won't see you, I can tell you that. You annoyed her and anyway, as I said, we are very busy. Go and annoy someone else, mother."

Christine hung up abruptly and left Milly seething with anger.

♥

Jeff took the housekeeping money from the kitchen drawer and counted it. Almost three hundred and eighty dollars. It was more than enough to buy a ticket back to Canada and suddenly he wanted to go home.

For the last week Janice had been nattering about going to her Florida house and he did not want to head south. Maine was closer to Canada and he could get a direct flight to Toronto. He was not going to stay around until she dumped him. He would dump her and the sooner the better.

Tonight they were to attend a dance at the country club in honour of the retiring manager. While he did not want to go because he hated the snobs at the club, mainly because the men snubbed him, Janice had purchased him a new evening suit and he wanted to wear it in public. Years ago he bought his first evening suit off the rack, more of a tuxedo with matching trousers, and had it altered to fit. No doubt that the new suit, made to measure by a master tailor, made him appear taller and slimmer. It suited him, he thought, admiring himself in the full length mirror then stepping into the mirrored triangle to admire his back and sides. Yes, he would feel and look good tonight and bask in the admiration. The months of good living had erased the worry lines from around his eyes and mouth. He ate well but gained not a pound because Janice was a fitness freak. They not only golfed every day, they jogged, spent the late afternoon sailing on her small sloop, and had hours of sexual activity. It was, he thought, the lifestyle of the rich and it suited him. The women would truly admire him tonight and that made the outing more acceptable.

"Jeff?" Janice called, "Where are you?"

He jammed the money back into the drawer, opened a cupboard and took out a mug. "In the kitchen," he called, "Want some coffee?"

"No. You know I never drink the stuff." She walked into the kitchen dressed in a short tennis outfit. "We've got a date to play with Marge and Pete this afternoon. Don't eat lunch. It'll weigh you down."

He laughed and sipped his coffee. "Come on now, Pete weighs about two tons and the ground shakes when he runs."

"Ah, but Marge more than makes up for him. She's good enough to be professional."

Jeff sighed. Tennis was not his favourite sport and he disliked Marge and Pete, who were the 'creme de la creme' of snobs. Indecently rich, everyone lionized them, though he figured that was more for their money than their charm.

"Come on, finish that drink and we'll go. Don't want to be late, do we?"

He mimed her silently behind her back and grinned. Soon he would be out of this place, soon he would be home.

"I saw that, Jeff." She turned around and pointed to the stainless steel freezer.

"It was in fun. I knew you could see me," he said. "Come here and let me prove how much I love you."

She stood stock still as he put his arms around her and kissed her deeply. Soon she started to respond and he felt her relax.

Whew, almost messed up that one.

♥

Harvey received a bonus and could hardly wait to show Christine the cheque. For £25,000, it seemed to scintillate as he gazed at the numbers. Realizing he had earned such a large sum was incredible and he laughed. So much for his mother's comments about playing computer games being a dead end occupation. In his hand was the proof she was wrong. He wondered what his father would have to say.

His parents were still unaware of his job. More of a position really, he thought wryly. They did not know that he worked flexible hours and worked when the whim took him. Sometimes he started work in the afternoon and worked through the night. Sometimes he took a day off to work at home on his own computer and relayed his results back to the office. Christine was so proud of him, but he still felt reluctant to tell his parents, though he had no idea why.

They met at the Cyber Web and chatted with old friends for a while. People came and went over the weeks while the regulars remained stalwartly in place. Now old friends, they shared their failures and successes. More failures from the others, but Harvey and Christine had made the grade and the others admired them for their industry.

"I mean, why bother? I've got four degrees and the only job I could get was stacking things on high shelves in a supermarket," Johnny West whined. "What's the point of trying?"

Susan Houson said, "I managed to get promoted to manager at the Dairy Queen and then got laid off. I think it was because I was earning too much money and the part timers managed without me when I was on a vacation."

Everyone jumped in with their own hard luck stories. Bearded young Andy said, "I think you're all right. The people who do the hiring have a hidden agenda. They don't care about your education, all they see is your appearance. If we all wore business suits and shined shoes, they'd hire us. They don't seem to realize that the world has changed since they were our age. Even the government offices allow their employees to wear running shoes and that's something."

Eric jumped in. "What difference does what you wear make? Most stores insist you wear their overalls or jackets. I can't see why they don't realize my many qualifications entitle me to a good position."

He shook his head, sighed, and said, "Sure, I know why. I figure they're afraid we might get their positions. Most got where they were because of attrition, not education."

"That's true. One man who interviewed me, said "You'se."

They all laughed.

Susan looked around the table. "Andy may have a point, though. Look at us, dressed like we get our stuff at the Salvation Army. I did wear a blouse and skirt when I attended interviews, but I won't wear shoes with heels and men like high heels. That's the problem when men interview young women. Subconsciously they see them as sexual prey."

"I don't think that's right, Susan," Christine said. "All men aren't like that."

"I did say 'subconsciously."

"I know, but they must have some smarts or every woman in the city would be unemployed, apart from strippers and exotic dancers."

Susan sniggered, then said, "I bet even *they* have their problems. No, they stack the cards against people of our age. We have a better education than our parents, we're computer literate, we have many interests and yet we're out of work."

Christine sat quietly. It was not the time to say that they could make their own jobs, just as she had.

Harvey took her hand. "Tina and I are going to chat on line." He rose and pulled her to her feet. "Come on, the end station is free."

They sat at the end station and started to chat to Enid in Australia, who was bemoaning the heat and an approaching wild fire.

When Christine signed off and moved her chair so Harvey could use the keyboard, he sat still for a moment and then said, "They're all losers, you know."

"Who?"

He gestured with his head. "That lot over there. They won't make any effort."

Christine eyed the group who still sat bitching. "Yes, they think the world owes them a living. We were like that once."

"We were, but we saw a chance and took it. Let's face it, if it weren't for a chance meeting in the mall, I wouldn't have my job."

"No, and if I hadn't looked for a niche, I would never have found it. Eldertrans is already in the black and we've only been incorporated for eight months."

He put his arm around her shoulders and looked into her eyes. "We're the living proof that anything is possible, Tina."

"Are you two going to start snogging?" Susan asked testily. "If you don't want the computer, move away and let me have it."

Harvey sighed. "Okay, take it. Come on, Tina, let's get a coffee."

Susan glared after them as they moved back to the large table.

CHAPTER SEVENTEEN

"Oh my god!" Christine dropped the phone. She stood with her face in her hands, gasping.

"What's the matter?" Evelyn asked hurrying to her side.

"The bus crashed, Gram."

"Oh no! Was it bad?"

"Not that bad, I don't suppose, but they're all old people. It can have repercussions."

"Sit down and tell me all you know. Who called?"

"A police officer. The bus went off the road near Waterloo. The driver tried to steer clear of an accident and hit an icy patch. The shoulder was iced over and the bus slid into the ditch."

"That doesn't sound too bad, darling. I'll get us some tea and we'll talk. Don't answer the phone whatever you do." Evelyn rang her bell and Mrs. Grant appeared quickly.

"Tea please, Mrs. Grant, put the sugar on the tray. Tina has had a shock."

"What's the matter?"

"We need the tea now, we can talk later."

Christine sat huddled in a corner of the couch. "This is so awful, Gram."

"I know, darling, I know, but it's over and done with, so no need to worry like that."

"Maybe but suppose one of the passengers sues us?"

"You have insurance for that and so does the bus line."

She bit her thumb nail. "Still, they're all so old and a lot of them are very cranky."

"Stop worrying, child. Nothing bad will happen."

Then the door opened and Mrs. Grant entered with the tea tray.

"Now then, tell me all about it. What's happened?"

Christine groaned and Evelyn repeated the story. Mrs. Grant shook her head and clicked her tongue. "I always thought something would happen. You're too young to be running such a venture. I told you, didn't I, Mrs. Wallace, that . . .,"

"Stop it at once, Mrs. Grant. I'm not so old that I cannot remember what you did or did not say. You never mentioned a word of this anytime apart from glaring at me when a phone call was from a customer."

"Well. .," Mrs. Grant started sulking and Christine smiled. The pair of them were like five-year-olds when they started arguing. She poured the tea and handed out the cups.

For some minutes everything was silent as they sipped tea and munched on biscuits, then the phone rang. For hours after that the phone was busy: the couriers, the bus line, the police, the customers, the relatives of those on the bus, on and on until finally Christine unplugged it from the wall.

After supper they watched the television news and saw the accident scene. The shot of the sideways bus showed only the bus company name and it looked undamaged. The assembled passengers, now seated on another bus, were laughing and joking with the reporter. Alan, delighted with his moment of fame, gushed and postured.

Christine laughed at him. "Seems like you were right, Gram. Nothing happened and that police officer made it sound as if the accident had killed everyone."

"Now we can rest easy. We'll contact the insurance company tomorrow. Today we'll forget the incident. Come on, let's have supper early and watch that movie they've been pushing on ITV. What's it called?"

"Willie Wonka and the Chocolate Factory. You're going to enjoy it."

♥

Milly decided to visit Joyce Rawlings. About time she saw the results of the last interior decorator's work. Like herself, Joyce completely redecorated her home though she did hers once every five years. Once everything was Oriental, once French. This time she had decided that 'country modern' was the 'in' thing. What on earth was country modern?

The eight-year-old Rawlings house stood in a small grove of trees in a secluded area of Richmond Hill. The exterior resembled an English country manor and she stared at the frontage as she neared the end of the drive. How on earth had the gardener managed to get the ivy to grow so rapidly and cover such a large area?

Now nearing winter, the leaves were dropping and Virginia Creeper was bright red against the fence. Remnants of last night's snow still lingered between the trees and on the lawn. Massed gold chrysanthemums filled the borders and Michaelmas daisies stood tall and vivid, a cloud of royal purple. The flight of flagstone steps held baskets filled with cedar branches and apples and the dove cote was alive with sound. She shut the car door and stood for a moment inhaling the brisk air. How good the country atmosphere felt. Here only the purling of the doves, the sighing of the wind and the distant cawing of rooks disturbed the peace.

The front door opened and Joyce came to the head of the steps. "Milly. How very nice of you to call. I was about to go down to the supermarket. Never mind, it was simply to fill a few minutes and now we can have a long chat over lunch."

They entered the house, a house redolent with the fragrance of apples and cinnamon, a house warm and inviting. Country modern was comfortable, Milly decided, as she admired the overstuffed chairs and couch.

"Love this style, Joyce. It's so inviting."

"Yes, Gerrard is a wonder and I love it too. Come on, let's sit and I'll call for some tea." She picked up the house phone. "You will stay to lunch? Good."

A smartly dressed maid arrived with the tea trolley. Joyce nodded and said, "Thank you, I'll pour, Daisy."

Milly grimaced. Imagine being polite to a maid. "You seem to treat the servants as equals, Joyce."

"Of course I do. They have the same feelings as we do and I like them to feel appreciated."

"Tosh! They are menials and you should treat them as such."

Joyce smiled. "I think you have the impression that we live in the Victorian age, and that servants are dumb animals."

"I don't care to consort with the lower classes, that's all."

"The lower classes?" Joyce handed her a tea cup and laughed. "Honestly, Milly, you do talk a load of rubbish."

Milly's nose rose even higher. "One does not converse with servants or thank them for the work you pay them to do. Do they thank you for their pay cheque?"

"No, but that's different. I can't treat the help like strangers, particularly when they work so hard."

"Honestly, I expect you have them share meals with you. Why didn't the maid sit down and start in on the cookies?"

"Don't be sarcastic, Milly, it doesn't suit you."

Milly put down her cup and stared around. "Yes, I like this new furniture but then Marty is doing very well for himself these days. Lucky you. By the way, have they rescheduled the AIDS meeting?"

Joyce lowered her cup and was about to answer when the house phone rang. She picked up the receiver. "Thank you, that will be wonderful," she said after listening for a few minutes. She replaced the receiver and turned to Milly. "Sorry. You were saying?"

"I asked if they had rescheduled the meeting."

"Not yet. I don't suppose anyone will call until they've heard the weather forecast for the next week."

"I hate these winters and often wish I had bought a place in Florida. It must be nice to get away from the cold."

"I don't like our place too much these days. We rent it out in the off season but the temporary people make such a mess of the place. We've got a live in housekeeper who does her best, yet somehow the place seems tainted. I'm thinking of selling it. Interested?"

"Not very, if what you say is true. Maybe I'll do the usual and stay at a hotel for a couple of weeks."

"We've got a lot on this month and are having five or six dinner parties. You're invited, if you wish to come, that is. Find yourself a suitable escort."

"Thank you very much, Joyce," Milly said waspishly, "Always there to remind me of my solitary state."

"Now, Milly, what did you expect me to say? That I'd find a suitable escort *for* you?"

"No, of course not. You should assume that I would not come alone. That's so very demeaning, isn't it?"

"I wouldn't know."

They glared at each other for a moment, then the door opened.

Mrs. White, clad in a housekeeper's uniform of black and white, her hair freshly permed and wearing cosmetics, entered. Milly, whose back was to the door, did not see her until she stood in front of Joyce. She gasped, looking back and forth between them.

"Mrs. White? Joyce? What is this?"

Joyce smiled beatifically and took the list Mrs. White handed to her. "This is my housekeeper. I think you know each other." She glanced at the list and nodded. "Very suitable, Mrs. White. You're marvellous with the menus."

Mrs. White smiled and almost dropped a curtsey. Milly looked furious and her face was set in rigid lines. How dare Joyce? How dare Mrs. White? She rose, picked up her purse and sailed out of the room. Her heels clacked over the marble floor in the foyer. The front door opened and closed.

Joyce put back her head and laughed and Mrs. White joined her. "That," Joyce said, "was so very satisfying. I finally got one over on Millicent Armstrong."

♥

In a foul mood, Milly drove slowly and carefully back to the city. The roads were slick in the sunshine and the snow banks dazzled her. As she reached the section where her mother lived, she changed her plans and decided to drop in for a visit She was in the mood for a confrontation and hoped Christine was at home.

The radio announcer started reading the news. One item caught her attention.

"…another bus took the elderly passengers to the General Hospital for examination. All were released. A spokesperson for Eldertrans declined to make any comment, but said they did not plan to reduce the number of tours. We could not reach the bus driver for comment."

Milly felt suddenly energized. That was the crackpot company Christine was trying to run. Armed to the teeth with outrage, she put her foot down, eager to reach her mother's house.

♥

Harvey bought himself a new Porsche. It positively glistened even when standing in the garage.

They were eating dinner one evening when his father looked at him. "Do you rent out the space in my garage to your friends? What on earth are you thinking of? About time you got yourself a job and earned some proper money."

Harvey chewed on his roast beef and nodded. Let the old man talk.

"Harvey, is this true? Whose car is in our garage?" His mother placed her cutlery on her plate to speak to him. Very proper. She patted at the corners of her mouth with her linen napkin. God, he knew every move she made and every word she uttered. He continued chewing.

His father put his elbows on the table, a terrible no-no in this house, and stared at him. "Well, Harvey? Your mother is talking to you. Have you lost all your manners?"

"Sorry, I was chewing. Not nice to talk with food in your mouth, is it?"

"Harvey, I wish to know whose car is in the garage." Mrs. Wright stared impolitely and Harvey knew he must answer.

"The car is mine," was all he said.

His father's eyes bulged. "That car is brand new. Where did you get it? Surely you didn't steal it?"

Harvey laughed. Look at them, the old man all goggle eyed and his mother positively white around the gills. "Calm down, Dad. I paid for it."

"Where on earth did you get the money? Are you involved in drug trafficking, or did you . . . ?"

"Jeepers! Don't start thinking I stole it. God, the way you think of me. Did you raise a criminal? I have a job, a good job and I got another bonus. I paid cash for the car."

"Work? You work?" His mother looked utterly confused. "When do you work? You're always here under foot."

"No, I'm not. I work flex hours. Goes to show that you don't miss me when I work forty-eight hours straight and don't come home. I don't think you know I exist until I pop into view."

"What is this job?" his father asked, looking attentive for a change.

"I work for Symelinx and design programs for video games.

"Computers?" His mother said, shaking her head. "I told you time and again that playing games would get you nowhere."

"No? Well now I earn over a hundred thousand a year and get regular bonuses for playing video games. Matter of fact, I write them." Both gasped as he tossed down his napkin. "I don't need this, you know. I need you to treat me like an adult and that being so I intend to get my own place. You won't need to worry about me at all then." He pushed back his chair and walked out of the dining room.

That showed them. Harvey grinned as he ran up to his room. He'd pack, get a hotel room and then look for a condo or small house.

"Harvey?" His father stood at the bottom of the stairs, looking up at him. "Come down here, son, we'll talk. I appear to have misjudged you."

"Too little, too late, Dad! We have nothing to discuss." He moved away from the bannister and almost ran to his room.

That told him, the stupid old sod. Now he would live life properly, without the parents telling him what to do, without being castigated for not measuring up to their expectations. He had no idea what went on in their old minds. Poor Dad, he would never understand today's generation; his mind stuck in a time warp, somewhere around the 1930's. As for his mother, a stay at home mother, who had never had to work for a penny, he shuddered to think of her plans for his future.

Wait until he told Christine.

CHAPTER EIGHTEEN

"So I've moved out and I'm staying at a hotel. How'd you like to help me find a flat or townhouse?"

Christine squealed. "Wow, you've done it! Sure, where do you want to live? What part of the city?"

"As far away from my own home as I can get. No, that's not it. I want to live close to downtown, close to work, close to the action."

She laughed. "So does everyone else. The rents are astronomical downtown. You've got a new car, so why not move to a suburb?"

"I don't want to use the car for work. Too congested on the parkway and the parking prices are killers. I could use the bus or train."

"Then you must live either east or west. I'll come over and fetch the papers and we'll check the want ads."

For almost a week they checked the papers and twice went to see apartments.

"I think I'd like a condo better or a townhouse," Harvey decided. "Those cramped buildings are the slums of the future, even if the flats are expensive."

"Oh my, shades of my mother. She thinks only the poorest people live in such buildings surrounded by drug pushers and rapists."

They laughed.

"No, maybe a condo would be better. It would be an investment. Not like paying rent for something you can never own."

"True, paying rent is lining someone else's pockets. Okay, lots of condos for sale, look . . ."

♥

"Another thing, Mother, you cannot allow Christine to continue with this farce. Imagine her thinking she could run a company. Why, she's had no schooling, no training."

Evelyn sighed. Milly had arrived red in the face, spoiling for a fight yet Evelyn stubbornly refused to rise to the bait. "Christine has a lot of experience now, Millicent, she learns as she goes. Her company is very profitable."

"Still, this accident . . . I hope she's got lots of insurance."

"Of course she has."

"She must cease with it at once, and she has you answering the phone at all hours. It isn't right that she . .,"

"Look, before you continue, I should tell you that I am her partner. We own equal shares in the company."

Milly smiled widely. "Ha-ha! I knew it, I knew it. You have the Midas touch when it comes to things like this. How dare she tell me that she runs the company? You run things, she's your front."

"Baloney. I promised myself that I wouldn't lose my temper, but you're annoying me. Go home and take your offensive remarks with you."

Milly stood tall and crossed her arms. "Oh no, mother, I won't leave until I've seen her. She must return home where she belongs."

"Fine, sit and wait. She's gone on a bus trip to Brampton. I don't know when she'll be back. It depends on the weather."

"Brampton? What on earth is there in Brampton?"

"A concert given by a senior's home, if you must know."

"A child her age should not be mixing with old people. She should have friends of her own age."

"I find that remark very strange coming from you. When she was younger, you didn't allow her to mix with others her own age. You vetted every person she liked and drove them away. We all know that resulted in her running away from home and you."

Milly's face grew red with suppressed anger. "Mother, you are impossible to talk with. Send for your helper and order us some tea."

"Mrs. Grant is out today, gone to visit her sister."

"So you were left here all alone? Oh my God! I think it's a good job I chose today to visit."

"Do go home, Millicent. You annoy me and give me indigestion." Evelyn rubbed at her stomach and pulled a face.

"You're sick. I shall call your doctor at once." Milly almost ran to the phone, her face a mixture of relief and horror.

"Do put down that phone. I don't need a doctor and I don't want you bothering him for nothing."

"Mother, I am telling you now that you look pale and ill. Hello, this is Mrs. Armstrong, my mother Mrs. Evelyn Wallace is one of your patients. Mrs. Wallace is not very well and I want the doctor to pay a house call."

"Millicent!" Evelyn warned.

"Oh, I see. I must say that the health system is now a shambles. I cannot drive in this weather and my mother is ill. What do you suggest?"

Evelyn rose and using her cane, yanked the telephone plug out of the wall connection. "Put down the receiver." Milly stared at the cane and cowered as if Evelyn might use it on her next. "Sit down."

Milly sank into a chair and put her arms around herself. "I don't know what's come over you, Mother. Here you are, all alone, and yet you refuse help."

"I don't need any help from you. Go home and let me rest. The phone is not going to ring since we have nothing planned until after the holidays, and I can look after myself. You saw to that by your protracted absence from my life. Millicent, and only came back when you wanted money. Is that the reason you came today?"

"No, it is not. I'm insulted you would even think such a thing. I want to see Christine."

"She doesn't want to see you, though, and neither do I."

Milly put her face in her hands and sat completely still. Evelyn watched her, knowing this was done for effect and not out of any feelings she might have. Milly was always too wrapped up in herself to think about anyone else. When she didn't move, Evelyn quietly walked out of the room and went to the kitchen to make herself some tea.

Milly sat for the longest time and, when her mother said nothing, raised her head. The room was empty.

Might as well make some tea, she thought and rose.

Evelyn was sitting at the kitchen table eating pound cake with butter and jam. The kettle was on the verge of boiling and Milly noticed only one cup was set.

"Nice. Very nice, Mother, that you couldn't even make some tea for me."

"Considering my age, it is you who should be making the tea. Help yourself."

Milly opened the china cupboard and took down a cup and saucer. She ran her finger along the edge of the shelf and looked at it. "Dusty. Doesn't that woman of yours ever clean properly?"

"That woman is Mrs. Grant and you know that she does a wonderful job with this old place. Nothing here is sterilized or decontaminated as it is at your place. How is Mrs. White these days? Did you ever get her back?"

"No, I have a service that comes in once a week now. More expensive, of course."

Evelyn laughed. "Did you ever think of cleaning the house yourself and saving the money? I have no idea where you got all those airs and graces. I know you didn't learn them here or from me."

"I appreciate the finer things in life, Mother. I am accustomed now to having menial tasks done for me."

"Oh la-di-dah! Make the tea while you're on your feet. You pour boiling water into the tea pot, swish it around to heat the pot, then...."

"Mother! I do know how to make tea." She busied herself, showing her knowledge.

Evelyn grinned. "Good. I had wondered what you lived on between visits from your service."

"I eat out most days. I have many invitations."

"Good for you."

"If you eat any more of that cake, you'll be sick. That's far too much butter and you must watch your cholesterol."

"You watch it. I've eaten cake this way since I was a child and I'm still here, I notice."

Milly fell silent. She sat at the table and brushed away some breakfast crumbs. "Tt-tt-tt."

Evelyn smiled. "That's right, dear, you do some cleaning."

♥

The country club dance was a bore as he expected, but all the women admired him in his new evening suit, and that made up for it.

It was past midnight and most of the older members had left. Now the band played disco music and Janice was in her glory showing off her moves to anyone who would watch. Jeff half-heartedly gyrated with her and glanced at his watch when she turned her back. His legs were beginning to ache from the constant movement and he felt his energy running low.

The music stopped and the break riff played. He took her hand and they went back to their table. "I'd like to be at home with you right now," he whispered in her ear.

She turned and smiled at him. "Me too."

"Than let's leave. Come on, last one in the shower is a rotten egg."

"I want to stay here a while longer. They haven't drawn all the door prizes yet."

He sighed. "They all look like bottles of booze and you don't need them."

"Nevertheless, I might win. No, we'll stay."

When the band started again, she rose and walked onto the small floor, expecting him to follow.He did.

It was almost three by the time they arrived at the house. As usual, all the lights were blazing. Janice said it deterred crooks, and he supposed it did, but he bet it added a lot to her electricity bill.

When they got inside, he kissed her. The sooner he got her into bed and satisfied, the sooner he could leave. She kissed him back and started pulling at his shirt. Not wanting her to ruin the best shirt he had ever worn, he picked her up and carried her up the stairs. God, his legs were killing him, and she weighed a ton as she lay in his arms like a dead weight

He dropped her on the bed and started to make love to her. She writhed under him and he started to remove her gown. When she was almost naked, she pushed him aside and got off the bed. "In the shower, come on, I want it in the shower."

Jeff smothered a groan. Janice was very athletic and sometimes she was too much for him. Tonight was one such occasion.

She clung to him as the shower started running and slowly unbuttoned his trousers. He took off his shirt and stepped out of the pants, taking care to place them on the chaise longue.

Once under the warm water, she was all over him, he tried to hold her but she wriggled and laughed. While she was pretending to struggle, he slipped and finished up on the floor. She laughed hysterically. Annoyed, he grabbed at her ankle, yanked sharply and she fell over backwards, her head hitting the taps at the other end. He pulled her toward him and noticed that her face was white and expressionless, her eyes blank. She was dead.

Quickly he lifted her head and saw nothing but her wet hair. Somehow the controls had hit her somewhere without breaking the skin. Dead! God, what did he do now? He turned off the water, then turned it back on again. Who would ever know that he had caused her death? She could have slipped in the shower.

Clues, what clues would the police look for? Traces of his DNA? He snapped the shower head free and rinsed every part of the shower he had touched, watched the water run down the drain. All the time, Janice looked at him through dead eyes. When he thought he had removed every trace, he wiped his fingerprints off the doors, off the controls, off everything he might have touched.

He took his clothes into the bedroom and packed everything he owned. His possessions filled two large soft bags. Janice had been generous and he owned gold cufflinks, a gold zodiac medallion on a thick gold chain, a gold Rolex, and even a gold bracelet.

Quickly he went to the kitchen to get the housekeeping money, glanced around at the luxurious space and checked the living room. When he felt assured that nothing of his remained, he again went through the house with a duster and cleaned off anything he might have touched, even the items in the medicine cabinet. He was very thorough. Then he got his bags and his new vicuna overcoat and left the house, leaving the door unlocked. Keeping to the centre of the drive, he walked down to the main road.

The nearest civilization was about two miles and there he could possibly catch a bus, or rent a car. No, a car rental would want an address and his insurance. Better he travel the way he had before, thumbing lifts or taking the bus.

Nobody would know he had killed her, would they? Everyone knew he lived with her, all those people at the country club, all the neighbours. Still, if he took off the glasses he usually wore, had his hair brush cut again and maybe died black, he would change his appearance enough that people would hardly see him.

Eventually a truck stopped and he climbed into the cab. "Where you heading, chum?" the driver asked.

"Home. Up north."

"I'm going that way. I like company on these night trips, keeps me awake. Of course it's against company policy, but they won't know."

"Where are you going?"

"Buffalo."

"Terrific. I'm going there, too."

"I'll have to drop you off before we get inside the city centre."

"No problem."

They spent the hours chatting about baseball, hockey and basketball.

♥

Harvey found a condo in Ashton. Part of a small complex, it was home to many upwardly mobile youngsters.

Christine enthused, "It's super, Harvey. Look at the pool. Wonder what it'll be like in summer?"

The pool stood in the centre of the complex, covered now for winter. Tall trees stood around the perimeter and the landscaper had arranged bushes to shield near naked bodies from those whose kitchens overlooked the area.

Christine loved Harvey's place, which was an end unit and had a garage separating him from the neighbour. The windows were large and triple glazed, the hall floor was of marble tiles and the interior floors were varnished hardwood. A large kitchen overlooked a small fenced back garden. A toilet, pantry and laundry room was to one side. At the front a large L shaped room was for living and dining. Upstairs, he had two bedrooms, a small room suitable for storage or an office, and a large bathroom.

Now they were discussing furniture.

"Nothing like I had at home," he said. "Nothing that looks like my mother might like it."

Christine laughed. "True, you must get something modern. We'll take a day to visit the shops downtown and I know of two or three places in Newmarket."

♥

Christine was humming as she opened the front door. Mrs. Grant arrived simultaneously, her arms filled with grocery bags.

"Thanks, dear," she said as Christine opened the door and took one of the bags.

Milly stalked into the hall. "About time, too! How dare you both leave my mother on her own? Have you no common sense?"

"Seems to me she wasn't on her own if you were here," Mrs. Grant said with a sniff. Christine ignored her mother and walked into the living room. Gram was sitting by the fire reading a magazine.

"Hello, darling," she said as Christine kissed her forehead. "So pleased you came home early. I need rescuing from the wicked witch."

"I heard that, Mother," Milly said. "You are impossible."

"I am? I thought that honour went to Christine." She smiled up at her granddaughter and both giggled.

Milly glowered at them. "I'm leaving now, but I shall return."

"Shades of Patton," Christine said, saluting.

"I don't think you realize the gravity of leaving my mother on her own for hours at a time."

"Come off it, Mother. You could care less about her. Why the sudden interest? I sure wish Dad had stayed around. Listing his sins kept you occupied."

"Well, really!"

"Yes, really. Get a job mother, find something useful to do with your life. Forget those snobby clubs you belong to, come and live in the real world for a change."

"I don't need a child to tell me how to live. You have not heard the end of this, Christine. I want you to stop with this bussing nonsense. They have mentioned our name on the news and I will not have our family name sullied in such a manner."

Christine laughed. "Sullied? Where on earth did you dig that word up from? Mother, you're a relic. Even Gram here is more up to date than you. It's pitiful that a grown woman can't find something to do that will benefit mankind. All you do is make trouble between people. Grow up!"

"Well! I will not be spoken to in that manner."

"So, leave," Evelyn said. "Then you won't hear a word from either of us."

"All right, I'm leaving, but as I said, you have not heard the end of this." She turned on her heel and stalked out on her Ferragamo heels.

"Whew! How long was she here, Gram? I wish she'd have the manners to phone before she drops in on her missions of mercy."

"She came shortly after Mrs. Grant left. I was at my wit's end, but I had her nicely simmering the entire time and told her a few truths. She gets most annoyed when she can't make you angry, doesn't she?"

They laughed and shared the visit with Mrs. Grant when she brought the tea tray.

♥

"I'm afraid to say that you can do nothing," George Fielding said in response to her question. "Your daughter is an adult and your mother has invited her to live at her home. Your mother is now legally her guardian because she thought you might cause trouble. Surely this arrangement is best for your mother? She needs someone on call, someone at hand."

"She's got her daily woman."

"Not the same as family."

"No, but Christine belongs at home with me. She's become involved with a most unsatisfactory business."

"You mean Eldertrans? That's a terrific company. They're wonderful to the seniors. My mother goes on all their trips and spends weeks looking forward to something planned. She likes . . .,"

"What does your mother have to do with my situation? My mother has turned my child against me and that can't be right."

George sighed. "I have a feeling that you did the turning, Milly. You're not very tactful at times and Christine ran away from you once. Do you want that to happen again? At least this time she ran to your mother."

"You're useless as a solicitor. I don't know why I bother to speak to you."

He narrowed his eyes. "No, I wondered that myself when I heard about my colleague . . . the one you lured to your bed, I might add. Ha, I see you look startled. People in my profession talk to each other, you know. I wouldn't try that again."

She sniffed, pleased in a way that they had been talking about her sexual activity but surely solicitors were like doctors and priests, and they never disclosed a client's personal matters? "Honestly, is nothing sacred even between solicitors?"

"The matter was not one of juris prudence but of your imprudence, Milly. Have you heard from Jeffrey?"

"No, and I don't expect to either."

"So are you planning to divorce him?" He took in her polished look, every hair in place, every garment so well chosen. She was well preserved and beddable. "You need a man in your life."

"What if I do? I don't intend to divorce Jeff until he pays me back every cent of the money he now owes me."

"Yet the dealership is doing very well I hear and things are now solvent. I'm sure he'll be grateful for your concern."

"My concern? Hardly likely, George, since everything now belongs to me. He has no say in things, unless I wish to hire him as a salesperson. He's incapable of managing anything."

George tapped his pen against his teeth. "Not yours yet, Milly. We need his signature. So you do think he will return?"

"He'll come back sooner or later. He left Nassau leaving behind a string of debts. One of my friends heard about it when they were there on vacation. A nasty looking man asked them if they knew Jeffrey, said he owed him money. Of course they said they didn't know the name, but they told me quickly enough when they returned."

"Jeffrey sounds like a crook to me, Milly. I think you should divorce him and marry again. Get something out of life for a change."

"You too? Everyone seems to think my life needs changing. I am perfectly content as I am. I have lots to occupy my time and have many friends. Why would I need a man cluttering up the house?"

"Look, Milly, we've known each other since we were children and I'm telling you this with your best interests at heart. Unless you change your lifestyle soon, you are going to finish up alone. You constantly antagonize those who know you, me included. Try to change your outlook, think positively, forget the negative."

"Oh George, you sound like a Gershwin song. I am perfectly all right as I am. Now I must go. I will consult someone else, some organization like the welfare people to find out how I can get Christine out of my mother's home."

George sighed as he stood and extended his hand. "Leave it alone, Milly. Let the girl live her own life and let your mother be happy in her last years."

"Humph!" Milly shook, his hand, picked up her purse and sailed from the office.

He watched her go, shook his head and turned back to his work.

CHAPTER NINETEEN

J oyce Rawlings and Marty drove along the Don Valley Parkway
with the top down. Early May, the weather was exceptionally warm.

"What's this shindig in aid of?" Marty asked.

"Oh the usual, shelters for battered women. We need more homes."

"Has the crime rate gone up? Are more men taking it out on
their wives?"

"Seems like it. Milly organized this bash and most of the elite
are coming. At two hundred a plate, they'll need to be rich. Still, the
auction should be terrific. I've seen some of the donations. Lots of
paintings, lots of real jewellery, lots of antiques."

Marty chuckled. "So 'Milly the Magnificent' has done it again, eh?"

"More like poor Joyce did most of the work for her. Mind you,
they seem distant with each other these days and I heard a whisper
that Milly's Mrs. White left her and went to work for Joyce."

"Boy, that must have put the cat among the pigeons."

"Yes. Anyway, I hope you've brought your checkbook."

"Of course."

♥

George Wright watched the news on TV - all bad, of course. He picked up the remote and flicked through the channels.

"I wish you wouldn't do that, George," Grace said tetchily. "Turn to the info channel to see what's on or look in the guide." She tossed him the TV Guide. "Look through the listings, that channel flipping gives me a headache."

He continued to flip and suddenly spotted the name Harvey Wright on the credits of a show. Turning to the TV Guide, he discovered he had missed a documentary on new animation techniques . . . and to think they named his son in it!

"Harvey got mentioned on a show, Grace. Look," he pointed out the listing in the guide. "Animation, that's what he's doing now."

She sneered. "Cartoon characters?"

"I suppose, but he must be doing well. I'm proud of him. He did it on his own."

She pulled another face, unimpressed. "You helped since you bought him the computers and the programs."

He shook his head. "I didn't help at all, and we both ignored him most of the time. You spent your time nagging him about things that didn't matter and I was always on at him about his laziness. He isn't lazy, that much is evident and I think we owe the lad an apology."

"I guess." She didn't sound sure. "It surprised me when I heard how much money he earned. That's more than you earned in a year when you were thirty."

"Yes, and I went to school for most of my life up to that point." He grinned. "Let's face it, the kid is a genius."

Grace suddenly smiled, if George said her son was a genius, surely that was her doing? "We must get in contact with him again, George. I don't want to drive him away forever."

"Yes, that's what we'll do. I'll get someone on it first thing tomorrow."

♥

Jeff slept in a motel overnight. He bought a tasteless coffee from the machine outside his room and drank it as he made ready to leave. Today he wore the second hand clothes bought at a Goodwill store, nondescript, forgettable. He felt better when he blended into the background.

None of the morning papers he read at the library had an article on Janice. Last night he had watched each of the news stations, and breathed easier when none mentioned it. Now he made his plans. First thing to do was change the American money into Canadian, then he must get to Toronto airport.

♥

Harvey throughly enjoyed his new home. It was easy on the eye with its expensive leather and plush furniture with a few chrome and glass etageres. He and Christine had spent two months searching for the pieces. How they had laughed as they haggled. Two or three pieces were antiques bought on a whim, though the eclectic mix blended well and the rooms were comfortable.

He hired the woman who cleaned for two other bachelors in the complex and, through her, met new friends. Two of the other single men, Graham and Laurence, were in the high tech business and they quickly became buddies.

Christine would arrive every Friday evening at seven and they sent out for Chinese or pizza, later going over to number five where Graham held a Friday evening bash. Chatting until the wee hours, they formed a new group of friends and rarely went to the Cyber Web Cafe.

Things between them were slowly changing. Both felt it. Harvey had kissed her a few times, not passionate kisses, but warm enough to show he cared. It irked him that Christine seemed attracted to Graham, a tall rangy young man with a thick head of red hair.

It felt like she had slapped him when she remarked, "I never liked red heads before now but I find his white eye lashes very appealing."

"Not exactly a thing that other people would notice," Harvey said laughing while the jealousy consumed him.

Tonight they had spent time chatting and drinking wine with the gang. Harvey was in an earnest discussion about robotics with Stewart when he noticed Christine go into the kitchen. Looking around, he saw that Graham was not in the living room and figured he was also in the kitchen. His heart started to pound and his hands formed fists.

Taking a deep breath, he saw Stewart looking at him strangely. "Sorry, you were saying?"

In the kitchen, Christine found Graham arranging canapes on a microwave tray.

"Wow, the little woman at work?" Christine laughed as she turned on the faucet and let the cold water run.

Graham turned around, his face lighting up when he saw it was her. "I'll have you know I spent all day cooking, and that's all you can say?" His tone was falsetto.

"Mother talk?"

"Yeah, she hated it when we didn't go into raptures about anything she served."

She laughed. "My mother can't cook, you know. She always had someone to do it for her."

"Jeez, nice for some. My mother spent days creating masterpieces that we scarfed down before she even managed to sit at the table." He laughed. "Still, we always ate everything and that should have been compliment enough."

Christine laughed. "Silly. That's not how mothers operate."

"True, and they expect you to help with the washing up."

She leaned against the counter sipping her drink. "Thank the lord for the men who invented microwaves and dishwashers."

When the microwave pinged, he removed the canapes and set them on the table. Turning he stared at her, eyes filled with hope. "I'd like to meet you away from here," he said, pinning her against the kitchen counter, one arm on each side of her.

"Graham, does this mean you like me?" Christine decided to treat it as a joke.

"Of course I like you. Why do you think I drool every time I look at you?"

She laughed. "I thought that was part of your condition, and didn't like to mention it."

"Come on, Tina, I want to take you out. Any hope?"

"Sure. Why don't you ask Harvey? We could make a foursome."

He groaned and moved his arms from the counter. "Okay, I get the message. I didn't know you two were an item."

"We're not. Just good friends."

His eyes lit up and he smiled widely. "So there might be hope for me after all?"

"Could be."

Harvey joined them, his eyes flashing from one to the other, testing the atmosphere. "Any more of this Italian?" He brandished an empty bottle.

"Sure, on the floor in the pantry. I'll get a couple of bottles."

The other guests had decided to play charades with many ribald remarks and laughter.

"Come on, let's get in on the game, Harvey."

Graham came back into the kitchen to find it deserted. Shrugging, he opened the bottles and set them on the counter.

♥

Evelyn felt ill. She put a shaky hand to her forehead and found it hot. Mrs. Grant came into the living room and checked the fire.

"I don't feel well, Beth. Maybe I should lie down for a while."

Mrs. Grant became flustered. "Oh dear, come along, we'll get you upstairs."

"Please, don't fuss. I'm not that sick. I just want to lie down. Here, on the couch."

"Are you sure? I'll cover you with the Afghan. There, that's better. Now close your eyes and try to nap."

"Go away, Beth. I'm not sick and you make me nervous with your fussing."

"All right, dear. I'll be nearby. Just ring the bell."

"I will."

Mrs. Grant tiptoed to the door and Evelyn watched her. "Go on, go back to your work and stop that creeping around."

"Humph! Not much wrong with you that a nap won't cure."

When she left, Evelyn gave a sigh. She felt awful, like a heavy load was pressing down on her and confining her limbs. Within seconds, she was asleep.

"That's what she said, Miss Christine, better come home right away," Mrs. Grant said, "She looked very pale and she was shaky."

"Thanks. I'll be right back. The library can wait."

She was back at the house within ten minutes and ran up the steps. Opening the door and closing it quietly, she crept to the living room double doors. Slowly she pushed the right-hand one open and stood for a second and looked at her grandmother. Evelyn lay on the couch, the Afghan over her legs, fast asleep, snoring softly.

Christine decided to let her sleep and went to the kitchen.

"She's asleep, Mrs. Grant, so I thought I'd let her be for now. Let's have some tea. One thing about Gram, she always knows when tea's being made. Bet you her radar wakes her and she'll ring."

"Oh, I do hope so, dear. She didn't look at all well."

"Did you call the doctor?"

"I was going to, and then I thought I'd wait until you came home. We'll see what she's like after she's had a cup of tea."

"Good. It's not like her to profess sickness, even when she's coming down with a cold. You know how she is about frailty."

"I know, I've worked for her now for over thirty years and I know all her foibles."

Christine smiled. "Tell me about her. What was she like when you first met her?"

Beth smiled widely, thinking back. "Oh, she was a right goer, always on the run, always busy with some project or other. Tall, slim and energetic, she was a real beauty and the lads must have fought for her company before she married. Yes, Evelyn was like a pea on a drum. I mean, you couldn't hold her down back then, not that she's changed much. I recall when her grandmother once called her a 'whirling dervish.' I worked for the family too back the, until your great-grandmother died," She sighed. "Old age takes the vim out of a body, but Evelyn's mind is as active as it ever was. She's a grand old lady, almost a sister to me. Oh, you wouldn't think it to hear her talk to me, but she and I have shared our moments, and we're more than friends."

"Tell me about my grandfather. I've only seen old photos of him."

"A real gentleman. He was very well respected in business and was practically a millionaire by the time they married. This house cost thousands and that was in the days when a house cost only a few hundred to build. It must be worth a million now."

Christine pulled a face. "Sad to think my mother will inherit this lovely house. She'll sell it for as much as she can get."

"Maybe."

"No maybe about it. I know her, as I'm sure you do. She only loves money."

Beth touched her arm. "Now, Miss Christine, that isn't very charitable. Mrs. Armstrong is practically a widow by all accounts.

She hasn't heard from your dad and it cost her an awful lot to pay off his debts."

Christine thought about that for a second. "Oh, she's probably making another pile of money. She never does anything for anyone else, only for herself."

"Miss Christine, I never knew your mother to be very friendly, but she's sticking by your father even if he did leave her. She won't hear of divorcing him. That's real loyalty."

"You can call it what you like, Mrs. Grant, but my mother is a cold, heartless bitch and nothing you say or do will make me change my mind."

Mrs. Grant gasped and crossed herself as if Christine had uttered a curse. "I don't like such talk."

"So don't listen."

"Why are we arguing? Your grandmother is sick and we're squabbling about nothing."

Christine stood and put her arms around the older woman. "I'm sorry. We're both entitled to our opinions so forgive me. Now we'd better take the tea into Gram. Strange she didn't ring."

Evelyn was dead. Both knew it the minute they approached the couch. They stood, shocked and numbed. Neither said anything. Christine dropped to her knees and kissed Evelyn's cheek and Mrs. Grant said a prayer, then put down the tray.

Evelyn Wallace looked peaceful in death, a smile on her lips, the worry gone from her expression. Mrs. Grant went over and drew the drapes, turning on the small side lights over the fireplace.

"Better call the doctor. We can talk about the rest later. I won't stoke up the fire. Better not."

Christine rose and nodded. She felt so bereaved, so alone suddenly, so abandoned. "We'd better unplug the phone in here. Poor Gram, I already miss her." The tears started and she couldn't stop them, her throat felt constricted and she had difficulty swallowing.

Beth Grant turned her away from the couch and led her from the room. "Come on, dear, that's right. We'll stay in the kitchen until the doctor arrives."

Christine sat at the table and put her face in her hands. Oh, why was she thinking about herself at a time like this? Gram was over ninety and her last years had been happy. It was good that she had died in her sleep, good that she didn't suffer . . . yet how hard it was to accept.

Mrs. Grant bustled around making work for herself, and Christine saw that she too was grieving.

"Come and sit with me, Mrs. Grant. By the way what's your name? I've known you for so long and I never did hear Gram call you anything but Mrs. Grant."

"I'm not even a Mrs. because I never married. I only lived with Harry. That sounds awful, but nobody thinks anything of it these days. Not in my day, though. That's why I never had any close friends. It was shameful back then, 'living in sin' as they called it. When the government declared war, they called him up and Harry didn't want to go. However, he had no choice and then the Germans got him." She touched Christine's hand. "My name is Elizabeth Grant. You can call me Beth if you like. It doesn't seem to make much difference now. Evelyn sometimes called me by my name when we were alone. Strange how she liked the old established customs. Not that she ever treated me like a servant, you know. She and I shared so much and now she's gone." She mopped at her face with the dish cloth.

"Don't cry, Beth. Tell me about when you first started working here. I never did ask Gram too much about the old days. She did tell me some things, but now I wish we'd talked more about it."

"That's the way with youngsters in any age. They never think of asking why and how they got here, how their parents managed, or even how they met. It's at times like this that you realize how much you need to know about the past."

"I must be growing up at long last, Mrs. Gr . . . Beth. Gee, it's nice to talk to you now without your surname. It makes me feel closer to you."

"I'm an old lady too, Miss Tina, practically sixty-seven now. I've seen some things in my life and I'd like to share them with you."

The door bell rang. "Oops, that's the doctor."

They left the kitchen to let him in. He took very little time with the body.

"I'll write the death certificate. No autopsy. She died of old age and peacefully. Now I presume you've called the solicitor?" They shook their heads. "Right, call him. From what Mrs. Wallace told me some years ago she wanted him to arrange her funeral so he will know."

They sat in the kitchen commiserating with each other after they had called the solicitor, who said Evelyn had prearranged her funeral.

"Nothing for us to do right now, but I bet we'll be rushed off our feet once word gets out. Mrs. Wallace was well known and well liked here in this city. I suppose you'd better call your mother."

She shook her head. "No way. You can call her, but I won't. Wait until they make all the arrangements because she'll want to change everything, last wishes or not."

Mrs. Grant sighed deeply and nodded. "I expect you're right."

Christine looked at her but Beth was contemplating the clock over the stove.

Soon the undertaker would arrive to carry Evelyn from her home on earth.

♥

It was a week before he saw news of the death of Janice Merton. It was not much of an article, but reported the authorities were treating it as a murder case.

Jeff blew out a deep breath of aggravation. Back in Toronto, he had temporarily taken a room at the YMCA. Every day he visited the main library to read all the papers . . . and now he found himself a wanted man. The next day and the day after, he read the New York Times, the more lurid daily, and found two more mentions of the mystery man the police sought for questioning and thanked God he had assumed the name of Garry Whalen. The name had popped into his mind when he applied for the job of caddy and he stuck with it. Surely they could never find Garry Whalen? Not when he didn't exist. Though now he came to think about it, Janice had always called him Jeffrey.

Today he was going to scout out the dealership. He had seen the full page ads in the Toronto Star and knew it must be doing well. How had Milly managed it without using her own money to pay off the loans? Or had she? Good old Milly. Wait until he got home, he would show her how much he had missed her.

Not that he missed her, but she was solvent and he *was* her husband. Maybe she had sued him for divorce. He shook his head, no way would Milly stain the name of Armstrong, not when she was almost on the 'A' list of Ontario society.

He took the bus and made his way on foot to the dealership. Wow, the lot was packed with the new season's models and many customers were walking along the rows. Inside the showroom looked busy, the salesmen showing the better models on display.

Yes, it was good to be home. He felt tempted to walk back into the showroom then decided not to when he saw only one face he recognized. Not much of a welcome home to be found here, better he wait until he had spoken to Milly.

♥

When his superior asked Harvey to attend a trade show in Calgary, he was thrilled and excited that the company had chosen him as their representative. They gave him a cheque for expenses: two thousand pounds. Harvey felt like a millionaire as he signed his traveller's cheques at the bank.

He bet this trip would make Christine look at him in a new light. How far he had come from the dirty running shoes and orange Mohawk days. Now he dressed casually in good quality clothes, wore Gucci slip-ons, had his hair styled. The new Harvey was definitely an improvement, and he was getting up nerve to propose to her. He knew she liked him, but did she like him more than she showed?

They were still at the fond kissing stage and he had never pushed her to go further. Somehow Christine was an innocent to him and he figured she was a virgin. That she was not the clingy type appealed to him. Other young women he met at the condo parties were all over him, knowing of his well-paid job. He did not like gold diggers and wondered why they picked on him since he was not exactly handsome. Tall and slim, he had the Semitic look of an eastern race. On the other hand, he was better looking than a lot of the guys.

Christine appealed to him even more when he noticed the way other guys' gaze followed her and how they spent time talking to her. Graham, he noticed, was always standing near and watched her every move. Once he saw Graham put his arm around her shoulders and she did not move away.

Soon, he told himself, soon he must speak to her about the future. Show that he thought more of her than as a friend. Maybe it was something in his genetic nature that made him hold back while the others were screwing any female that did not object. Apparently sex meant nothing to them, other than a sport, and he could not be like that, although in the past he had experienced many one night stands.

Yes, he decided. He must talk to her and soon because he did not relish life without her support, her company, her loveliness.

A mass of indecision where she was concerned, he didn't want to wait until Graham made a real play for her and insinuated himself into her life.

♥

The Wallace house was in full mourning. Since Evelyn had prearranged everything, the world seemed to move in slow motion. The solicitor's office contacted the funeral home, the florist, the car company and the church. Christine sat in the empty living room, her business forgotten, as she thought about life without Gram. It already seemed empty.

Mrs. Grant was busy baking and cooking and making lists of people they should invite to the funeral tea. Christine stayed out of her way after she refused her offer of help. Then the solicitor's secretary called to say they had booked the restaurant and had hired extra staff for the afternoon.

"What?" Mrs. Grant shrieked when Christine told her, "I've spent a fortune on supplies, and filled the freezer and the pantry with baked goods. How could that man not say anything earlier? Oh dear, I've got to sit down. This has upset me. Mrs. Wallace knew that I would look after things, I know she did."

"Now, Beth, Gram probably wanted you to relax for change. Not be under all this stress. Never mind, we can eat everything later. Freeze the lot, Beth. Maybe we should have a memorial tea at the house."

Beth pounced on the statement and dried her eyes. "Yes, she would like that. Yes, Miss Christine, that's what we'll do. Only her very best friends and maybe some of the phone ladies she so liked chatting with. Oh dear, I'd better plug in the phone so I can talk to them."

Christine had often heard Gram say 'life goes on' and knew her life must become normal again. Yet she felt this was too soon, much too soon. She called Patrick to tell him the latest.

"I'm so sorry about her passing," Patrick said, "She was such a lovely lady."

"Yes, she was. Anyway, life is for the living and she told me that often enough so I should get back to work when the funeral is over. The ceremony is Thursday so I'll start work again Friday."

"We're invited to the funeral?"

"Of course. That goes without saying. We've had condolence cards from about four hundred people, so if only half of them attend the internment, we're going to have a packed church."

"Wonderful, a fitting tribute to a grand old lady. I'll tell Alan and the nurses."

"Do that. Maybe they might like to attend the service, and do all come to the memorial tea here at the house next week. I'll E-mail you all with the time and date."

♥

Milly never read the papers, considering them a waste of time. They also soiled her hands. Why she still got the paper, which was Jeff's, she could not imagine, but rain or shine it arrived on the front step. Sometimes she read the social columns, though stalwartly refused to read the bad news knowing that if anything happened that might affect her ordered world, someone from her social set would let her know.

A small notice caught her eye. "A memorial service and funeral for Mrs. Evelyn Wallace, 93, will be held Thursday at 2:00 p.m, at Christchurch Cathedral."

Her mother dead? A sense of triumph quickly replaced a surge of annoyance. Soon she would own the house and the estate. Yet how dare Christine not call her? She flipped the paper over and scanned the obituaries. There it was and yet surely as daughter and heir, someone - the solicitor maybe - should have called her. Already they had arranged everything and without her input. Well, they would not get away with this.

She ran upstairs to wash the ink off her hands. Then she changed into a new black suit and added the appropriate accessories. Her stupid daughter was going to regret not calling her.

♥

"Marvellous, isn't it? That solicitor's office seems to work like greased lightning when it comes to closing an estate," Beth Grant said, still miffed about her wasted baking and the compliments she was missing from invited guests.

"Sure is," Christine agreed. "Gram was always annoyed with them and their shillyshallying as she called it. She said they charged by the minute and worked as slowly as possible."

Beth picked at her finger nails. "Never mind, it'll soon be over and we can get back to normal. Not that anything will be normal now Evelyn has gone."

"I sure miss her. I miss having her always ready to help solve a problem." Christine's eyes filled with tears.

Beth put an arm around her. "Now, Miss Tina, don't start or we'll both be at it."

"I know." She swallowed the lump in her throat. "The tea next week will be different, Beth. Only her close friends and those who loved her."

The phone rang. "Oops, I plugged it in this morning to call the solicitor. Sorry."

Mrs. Grant pulled the lead out of the outlet. "That's better. We don't need that thing ringing right now and it can't be business related."

"No." Christine walked over to the window and pulled back the drape to see what the weather was like. "Oh damn it all! My mother has arrived!"

"Crikey. I'm back to the kitchen. You answer the door." Beth scurried away.

As the bell rang, she stood debating on whether to answer it or pretend no one was home. No, better let her in: better they got the arguments out of the way or her mother would start in public.

"Christine!" Milly said in a shrill voice. She walked past her daughter and into the living room. "Good grief, open those drapes. What is this? We don't live in an age where we must sit Shiva, or whatever they call it. I'm surprised you haven't put cloths over the mirrors."

"Hello, Mother." Christine made her voice as soft as possible.

"Why don't you answer the phone? I let it ring forty times and I knew you were home."

"We do go out occasionally. We're not quarantined."

"I fail to understand why you didn't have the decency to call me when my mother died. She was *my* mother. Well? What reason can you give?"

Christine made her voice firm. Mother must always be in the right but this time she wasn't. "I thought the solicitor would call you."

"Well, he didn't. I do think that as my only daughter you would have called me yourself. I can bet that you called your father."

She shrugged. "Father? I don't know where he is. Do you?"

"No, I do not. The less I see of that man the better. Now, about the arrangements . . .,"

"All made. The solicitor did everything according to Gram's wishes. She prearranged everything, so all he had to do was make phone calls."

"Give me his number. I must speak to him."

"What for?"

"I'm sure my mother did many things wrong and presenting a dignified and proper ceremony for our friends and associates is vital."

"You can't change a thing, Mother. It was her last wish."

Milly picked up the phone and put it to her ear. "This is not working!" She looked under the desk and saw someone had unplugged it. Stooping, she reconnected it and turned to Christine with a look that would melt glass. "Where is the solicitor's number?"

Christine shrugged again, knowing it always annoyed her mother. "In the phone book, I suppose."

As Milly opened the desk drawer and took out the household phone listing and began to thumb through the pages, Christine walked out of the room and went to the kitchen.

Beth was washing the counters and humming to the radio. She looked up as Christine sat at the table. "She started already?"

"She's calling the solicitor to make sure he does things her way."

"She's got a nerve. He won't listen to her . . . I hope."

"No, he won't. Jeepers, things are going to be uncomfortable around here now she's turned up." She poked at the fruit bowl, looking at each piece.

"Tell her to go home, then."

Her head shot up. "I can't do that. She won't go until she's made us both so angry we could kill her."

Just then Milly sauntered into the kitchen, sniffed and stood in the centre of the bare floor. "I see this place is still as antiquated as ever. I shall change all this."

"Oh no, you won't!" Christine stood, fists on hips. "I like it this way and it's only proper for a Victoria kitchen. We've got a microwave and a new stove. Why should we change anything?"

"That's right, Miss Christine," Mrs. Grant said fervently. "This kitchen is very efficient. I like it."

Milly looked her up and down. "I don't need an aged housekeeper, and I certainly won't require you."

Mrs. Grant stood, arms on hips and glowered like an avenging angel. "Who put you in charge? Mrs. Wallace may have changed her will, you know. She had me get the solicitor for her about two years ago."

"What? *I* am her legal heir and will inherit everything. Oh, why am I bothering to argue with staff? Christine, into the living room, we need to talk."

"No, we don't. Go home, Mother, we don't need you here." She walked into the pantry and started looking along the shelves.

"How dare you! Come along, we must talk about things."

Christine came out and stood, hands on hips. "Do go away. I won't talk to you."

Milly looked at her set face, glanced at the smirk Mrs. Grant wore, and flounced out, saying over her shoulder, "Very well, I shall make some phone calls and we'll see who is now in charge."

They looked at each other and grinned.

Mrs. Grant nodded. "Oh yes, she's going to be trouble. Wouldn't you think that she'd realize that her strong arm tactics never get her anywhere? Come on, let's have a snack. Leave her to fume on her own."

CHAPTER TWENTY

H arvey had a wonderful time in Calgary. It was true that everything was bigger and better, he thought as he gazed down at the packed floor of the trade show from the mezzanine. He had eaten the biggest plate of lamb chops ever and rubbed at his full stomach as he sipped on a soft drink.

Then he saw her: the woman of his dreams. A dark haired, beautiful woman with large expressive eyes. She was looking up at him from a stand on which were displayed large video monitors. Their eyes met and he could have sworn a spark hit him. Quickly he moved toward the stairs, keeping his gaze on her, and ran down toward her.

"I'm Harvey," he said, mesmerized by her loveliness.

"I'm Linda," she said, her voice soft and filled with promise.

"Do you live in Calgary?" God, it sounded so stupid but his mind was on hold and words failed him.

"Naw, I'm from New York City. And you, are you English?"

"No, Canadian, Toronto."

"Ooh, you talk like those people from Boston."

He felt insulted in a way but she was such a delight. "I guess it's the way we cross our T's and sound our G's. I mean, you've got an accent, too. My accent is Canadian, that's all."

"Wow, Toronto, eh? I've always wanted to go there. Tell me all about it."

They talked as people came and went and the monitors sold themselves via a pile of handouts.

That night they ate together at a Mexican restaurant and Harvey ate things he had never seen before or tasted.

"I love talking to you. You're special," he said to her as they drank their coffee.

She smiled. "I love to hear you talk, Harvey." Even the way she pronounced his name gave him shivers. "Can we go to your hotel?"

"Of course." Adrenalin surged through his being, made him a man among men. She wanted to come to his room. That meant only one thing and he cursed himself for ordering the second bottle of wine and the liqueurs. His mind flashed to Christine. This was wrong, he loved her and she would never sleep with someone else, he knew it. He wrestled with the problem as they strolled to the elevators, told himself that this didn't count . . . but it did!

As they walked across the road to his hotel, he debated how to tell her that he didn't want to sleep with her, since that was obviously her aim. She pawed at him, kept kissing his neck, squeezing his hand, winking at him. Inwardly he groaned, realizing one moment of unguarded lust had brought him to this.

As they rode in the lift, she wrapped herself around him and moaned, "I sure want you, baby."

Mercifully the door opened and a couple got on. Standing apart from her, he decided: he would not do this. He would stay faithful to Tina. Tina, Tina, Tina, he repeated it to himself like a mantra. Linda almost dragged him to the room, where despite his efforts to push her away, he succumbed. Never before had a woman lusted for him this way, never before had he felt so aroused.

Before he knew it, they were lying on his bed, kissing passionately. His mind started spinning, he felt nauseous, wanting to extricate himself from her grasp but his body had its own intentions. His previous sexual encounters had been with girl friends, women he knew. Not that he was a great lover, and was usually finished within two minutes, now he prayed that the liquor would help him hold back until he had satisfied her.

Dawn broke and he opened his eyes. The bed was a crumpled heap of sheets and he was alone. Alone? Groggily he pushed himself up, thinking she was in the bathroom. He waited, rubbing at his coated teeth with his finger, pushing back his hair so it was neater. No sound came from the bathroom and he staggered over to the door. It was empty. She had gone.

Groaning, he stumbled back to bed and slept for another four hours.

When he woke, he readied himself for the day. He put on his jacket, went to the bedside table and picked up his wallet. It felt thinner and he realized the money was gone. Shit! How stupid could he be? She had robbed him. Why had he cashed the last of the travellers' cheques? Why had he brought her to his room? Stupid! He had wanted her, had thought he had found paradise but she was nothing but a predator, waiting to steal anything lying around. His laptop was gone, as was his radio alarm. Cursing, he went to the trade show, planning to find her before he took stand duty. She didn't show. Served him right for being unfaithful to Christine. Now strangely he could not remember anything about their session in bed. Best he forgot it anyway.

♥

Christine went through the day of the funeral in a trance. People came and went and yet she saw nobody as they swam in and out of her vision without registering. Milly began orchestrating things at the restaurant, moving people around, the hostess with the mostest, dressed in a designer original by St. Laurent and collecting her share of glares and smiles.

Christine and Beth sat at a table with Milly and the solicitor.

"I'll read the will today at the house, if that is convenient," he said.

"Yes, today," Christine said.

As she said that, Milly jumped in brightly. "I thought tomorrow would be nicer. Give us time to change and have decent night's sleep. Surely it is customary to read the will at the family's discretion?" The solicitor, Arthur Appleton, glared at her.

"Read it later today, please," Christine said stonily.

"Of course," Arthur nodded. "It is usual."

Milly looked daggers at Christine and Arthur. "Oh well, if you must, you must. Oh dear, look at those people laughing. This is not a party, don't they know that?" She rose as if to speak to them, but Appleton took her arm and pushed her back into her chair.

"I don't think you understand, Mrs. Armstrong. Mrs. Wallace specifically wanted a party. Wait until the jazz band arrives, then you'll see."

"Jazz band?" Milly's jaw dropped and she looked enraged. "My mother ordered a *jazz band*?"

Christine smiled for the first time. "Oh, how wonderful. We'd been talking about the funeral processions in New Orleans after seeing one on TV, and she thought it a wonderful sendoff. Good old Gram."

"How like her, that is," Beth Grant said grinning. "Yes, that will be lovely."

"I think it is deplorable!" Milly simmered with anger. "A jazz band! What *will* people think? It's bad enough that we are sitting in a large restaurant when the usual venue is the house. Mother had no idea about etiquette."

Appleton stood as a group of musicians entered and stood in a cleared space near the end of the room. "Excuse me. I must make an announcement."

A waiter handed him a small microphone. "Ladies and Gentlemen," The guests fell silent. "Evelyn Wallace was a free thinker. She lived a long time and knew the value of laughter. Today she wants you to remember her with laughter, with joy for her long life, and without tears. These musicians are to play her home to the Lord and bring lightness to your hearts. Celebrate her life. Enjoy. Stay as long as you wish. The bar is now open and free of charge."

The mourners applauded and started chattering as the band played their version of, "When the Saints go Marching In."

Christine and Beth clapped along and smiled delightedly. Milly sat erect, hands on her lap, her face miserable. For half an hour they sat, listening and watching as some mourners got up to dance and laughter filled the air. The guests consumed bottles of wine, champagne, whisky and gin. It was a real party.

Christine drank a glass of champagne and toasted her grandmother with tears in her eyes. "Here's to you, Gram. You always did know the right thing to do. The party is wonderful."

"Amen to that," Beth said, her face red from two glasses of champagne. "To Evelyn, my friend and companion." She raised her glass and burped. "Oops, sorry." She and Christine giggled as Milly looked daggers.

"Hmph!" Milly snorted derisively. She turned to the solicitor. "Well? When are we going to the house? This is noisy and not very nice. How much did mother spend on all this liquor? To give away free drinks is the height of stupidity."

Christine, brave on one drink, said, "Shut up, mother. This is Gram's party. It's her money and her last wish. You have no say in anything."

"Well! Christine, stop drinking that swill immediately. A lady always remembers temperance. Do not drink in public like a common person."

Christine thought this extremely hilarious and started laughing. Beth joined her and they sat laughing at Milly until she stood and imperiously stalked off to the bathroom.

Drying their eyes on napkins, they had another drink as the solicitor tapped his hands and feet to the music and looked happy.

"I wonder if he ever heard traditional jazz before?" Christine said, her eyes bright with the affect of the champagne.

Beth said, "Probably not, it's a common music and he's so top drawer. Anyway, it sure is lively."

Milly came back, her back straight as a broomstick and her nose in the air, bestowing looks of animosity on everyone. People who noticed her nudged each other and laughed.

An hour later, Arthur suggested they leave. They rose and made to leave the room, but laughing people stopped them to offer condolences. Christine accepted them politely. Milly was her usual haughty self and would not acknowledge anyone she did not know, or who looked 'common.'

Beth and Christine ignored her and her miserable face. They giggled when a man said, "Guess you won't be throwing a great party like this, eh, Millicent? If I know you, you'll probably make us pay for the funeral tea."

His party collapsed with laughter. Milly pushed past them and marched into the lobby.

"She's upset by her mother's death, so we'll make allowances today," Christine said, wondering why she wanted to defend a woman she didn't even like.

By the time they reached the house, Christine felt subdued. She wondered what surprises were in the will. Gram had never mentioned a jazz band, and imagine Gram throwing a party to celebrate her life.

Manoeuvred by Milly, they sat in the dining room. The solicitor sat at the end of the table and they sat down one side. Milly drew her finger over the shining surface and inspected for dust. Beth glared at her and rolled her eyes.

"Well now," Arthur said, as he clicked open his briefcase, "this won't take long."

Evelyn had appointed Arthur as executor of her estate but Milly expected that. After the minor bequests, which included instructions for an order of four mini buses and a party for Eldertrans, he started on the part that interested Milly most. She sat straight up and prepared to look surprised.

"My companion Elizabeth Grant is to remain in the house that is now her home until she decides to leave. It is her home in perpetuity and to ease her life, I leave her fifty thousand pounds."

Milly glared, but said nothing as Beth cried into her hands, overwhelmed by Evelyn's generosity. Christine hugged her. "That's wonderful."

"To my granddaughter Christine Armstrong, I leave my house on Bedford Place and my entire estate after other bequests and taxes."

Christine gasped and looked stunned. Milly looked like she was having a heart attack. She sat grinding her teeth and clenching her fists.

"To my daughter Millicent, a daughter who never did know I existed, I leave ten thousand pounds and my good wishes."

"This is preposterous," Milly said. "Mother was not in her right mind. Look at that travesty of a party. The woman was mad. I intend to contest this will immediately."

Arthur cleared his throat. "I will read the codicil. 'In the event that my unfeeling, uncaring daughter, Millicent, decides to contest this will, which I am sure she will, I must add that I have a doctor's certificate on file that proves I was perfectly sane when I dictated this document. Save your time and money, Millicent. If you stupidly decide to contest my wishes, then you forfeit everything. If you had ever shown me one speck of affection, I might have thought better of you. You treated me with indifference, let me know that I annoyed you. You did, however, play the dutiful daughter when you came to beg for money. "As ye sow, so shall ye reap." Need I say more?'"

Christine and Beth exchanged smiles. This was Gram at her finest.

This incensed Milly. "This is completely outrageous. How do I know that you didn't add that nonsense yourself?"

"Mrs. Armstrong," He showed her the document. "A Notary Public and my secretary witnessed it. Mrs. Wallace thought of everything."

"So I see. Well, I'm leaving. This house can fall to bits as far as I am concerned. I can see that my daughter wormed her way into my mother's confidence and brainwashed her." She turned to glare at Christine. "I will never forgive your actions."

Christine stood. "Mother, I knew nothing about this. Not that you will believe it. All I can say is that whatever Gram said to you in that will, I concur with her. I think she's right about you."

"Do not call me again, Christine. Today we part company."

"Hurray!" Christine threw her arms into the air and did a dance. "At long last I can live my own life."

"Traitor!" Milly, rigid with anger, stalked from the room. Christine sat and took Beth's hand. "You are going to stay with me, aren't you?"

"Of course, Miss Christine. My word, imagine her leaving me all that money. I can buy that new winter coat now."

Christine hugged her. "And a whole lot more, too."

Beth sighed. "It was so nice of her and to think I had wondered over the years what might happen when she passed away. I thought I'd have to find some place to live and get another job. I was saving every penny for all those years, and now I don't even need them. It's so wonderful."

"Yes, well," Arthur said, "Time I was going. Come to the office when you're ready, Miss Armstrong, and I'll advise you on the details of the estate. It is considerable, so plan on staying for some hours. We can, however, work at it in stages, if that's what you would prefer."

"Wow! Am I rich?"

"You are a *very* rich, young lady."

♥

"Tina? How are you? I heard about the funeral. Are you all right?"

"Harvey!" Her heart leapt in her chest then beat rapidly. She had missed him so much. "How nice that you called. Yes, I'm fine. Guess what? Gram left me everything."

"She did? Congratulations. Are you pleased?"

"Sure am. I'm now a wealthy woman. Imagine that. She left me all her stocks and shares and money."

"Are you still talking to me, a poor downtrodden drone?"

Christine laughed. "I'll tell you all about it when I see you Friday. I'm assuming that the Friday night get together is still running?"

"Sure. Come early and we can talk before we see the others."

♥

"How was Calgary? Did you have a good time?"

"It was okay." He sighed, ashamed of himself. "I was glad to get home though. Those westeners live too large for my liking."

His small smile widened to a huge beam, a grin of delight as he suddenly realized how much he loved her.

Christine smiled back. In all this time she had felt frigid toward men, could not stand the thought of one touching her in that way and now it was as if something inside her had unlocked and she wanted him. It was like a rebirth, as if her eyes had been at long last opened. Their eyes sought each other and they sighed in unison. She could not recall anything that they had said, only knew they loved each other and felt content.

CHAPTER TWENTY-ONE

Jeff noticed the dealership doing fantastic business. He took a street car to check it out every day and counted the number of people coming and going. Each day he called in at the library to read the paper and situations vacant, and scanned the full page car ads that cost a bomb. Unemployed and practically penniless, he had to do something.

Time, he decided, to see lovable old Millicent. Time for knee bending, apologizing, grovelling, time to make a play for her. God, the thought turned his stomach but in his present situation he considered it unavoidable.

He got his one good suit dry cleaned and his shirt laundered. The one pair of leather shoes he owned would suffice. The old clothes had served him well, allowed him to blend in with the furniture, but he ached to get back to his life of comparative luxury.

At nine the following day, closely shaved and neat, he inserted his key in the lock of the house. It would not turn. It struck him then, drat her, that she had changed the locks. He rang the bell, expecting Mrs. White to open the door.

A strange woman in a white overall answered. She had a duster in one hand. "Yes, can I help you?"

"Is Mrs. Armstrong home?" Darn it all. This was not what he had expected.

"I'll see. Who is calling, please?"

What to say? His mind flipped through possible answers and said, "Jeffrey. Tell her Jeffrey is here."

Milly sat in the library writing a 'thank you' note to a volunteer on her 'Save Don Valley trail,' project.

"Mrs. Armstrong, someone is here to see you. Says his name is Jeffrey."

She didn't look up. "Get his other name, you stupid woman. I know about a hundred Jeffreys."

"Yes, Mrs. Armstrong."

She went to the lobby and saw him looking into the living room. "Mrs. Armstrong wants to know your other name, please."

A rush of anger flowed through him. "Tell her, she knows who I am," he said stiffly. "She's my wife."

The woman gasped, her hand went to her mouth and she went back to the library.

"Well?" Milly still did not look up from her work.

"It's your husband. Mr. Armstrong."

Milly rose, her face like thunder and the woman shrank against the door as she stormed out, then scuttled back to the kitchen.

"Jeffrey! What are you doing here?"

"Hello, Milly, my love. How are you?"

"Get out of here."

"Is that any way to treat me?" He extended both his arms. "I've missed you so much. You're the only woman I've ever loved."

Milly walked into the living room and he followed her. One glance showed she had changed the decor to something vaguely French provincial.

She sat at the desk and turned back to her correspondence, dismissing him. "Stop lying. I don't want you here, nor do I need you. Unless you can repay the money I spent on clearing your loans, I don't want to see you again."

"You cleared the loans?" Relief washed over him and he felt liberated. "Oh, thank you, Milly. I'll pay you back when I can." He felt like hugging her but did not move.

She turned to him. "I don't think you quite understand. I now own everything and I no longer require you in this house nor in the business. Please leave. I will need to contact you for your signature on some papers, but other than that I never wish to see you again. Please go."

"Leave? I came all this way to . . ."

"To what? To worm your way back into my good offices?"

"Still talking like a Victorian novel, I see. Why can't we start again? We understand each other, we . . .,"

"I understand you well enough. You're a womanizing spendthrift who only thinks of his own pleasure. Did your latest amour, Brandi with an 'i', kick you out?"

He gaped and broke into a cold sweat. "How do you know about her?"

She smiled patronizingly. "I have contacts all over the world who inform me of your every indiscretion. I also know about your gambling debts and the man who is searching for you. That being so, I do not want you here in my house."

"Come on now, Milly, it's my house too. You only co-signed the papers."

She stood and faced him, smoothing back her already smooth hair. "I also paid off the mortgage with my money and can prove it. I made sure everything was done legally. Since *you* deserted *me*, I don't want you back and you cannot make any claim against me. Everything, and I mean everything, is documented. Now get out. Call me with your new address and my solicitor will contact you." She turned her back on him and glared at his reflection in the mirror.

"You can't do this to me. How am I going to live? I want back in the dealership, I want back in my home. Come on, Milly, let's make up and forget all this sniping."

"Go away, Jeffrey. If necessary I will call the police and take out a restraining order against you. You are not welcome here."

Jeff begged and pleaded, but now she would not even answer him. She walked over to the phone and raised the receiver to her ear.

"Shall I call the police, or will you leave of your own volition?"

He dare not have the police involved, not now. "Oh, all right, but I warn you, you haven't seen the last of me, Millicent Armstrong. I'm still your legal husband and I have rights. What about our child? What about Christine? This is going to affect her."

"Leave that brat out of it. She's all right where she is and I won't be speaking to her again. This situation is all your own fault and I'm sick of the sight of you. Now get out and stay out!"

Jeff turned on his heel, his hands clenched. He wanted to wallop her, wanted to scream his hatred of her. He walked away, knowing she could employ the best solicitors in the city and that he was penniless . . . but she would pay for this.

As he got onto the bus, he wondered about his daughter. Maybe the old lady would know where she lived. He headed for the Wallace house.

♥

Christine sat in the living room answering the phone. She had been answering it for two hours and as she hung up on the latest call for a reservation, she sighed.

"About time for your elevenses, I thought," Beth said as she entered with the tea tray. "Come on, love, leave that thing off the hook and have a drink in peace."

"You're right." She took the phone off the hook as it gave a tinkle. "Oh dear, I cut someone off."

"If it's important, they'll call back. Now you've got to get some help or an answering machine, one or the other. You're looking positively peaky these days, and don't put all that down to grief, it's more than that."

Christine nodded. "I never imagined how much work Gram did. She didn't say that she was stuck on the phone for hours."

"Well, she was. She loved it too, made lots of nice phone friends that she liked to chat with."

"Yes, so many people ask about her. She was very popular with the ladies of the seniors' centres. Imagine, she must have pored over maps and directories for hours because she knew where all the malls were and the nicest tea rooms. Gram was a real wonder. I do miss her, and not only for the work she did."

"You needn't run the business now, you know. You could sell it or cancel it. You've got more than enough money to last your lifetime."

She grinned. "I have, haven't I? Still, I like doing this and I can't even imagine sitting around doing nothing."

Beth smiled and nodded. "That's what made Evelyn so happy when you came, she had something to do and someone to worry about."

"That's the front door bell," she moved to the door. "I wonder who it could be," she was still muttering as she walked into the hall and Christine smiled.

She drank her tea and ate a cookie and waited for Beth to return. Beth seemed more content since Christine had stopped making messes in her kitchen and worked full time on her business. They had become friendly and confided in each other. She could not visualize the house without her.

"Christine."

She looked up and saw her father.

"Dad!"

"Where's the old lady? Having a nap?"

Her jaw dropped. He didn't know? Her faced whitened. "She's dead. She died about two weeks ago. The notices were in the papers and I thought you might have read them. I looked for you at the funeral."

Jeff held out his arms. "I just got back into town," he lied. "You poor little thing. Come here and let me give you a hug. We used to hug a lot when you were small." She stepped into his arms and he cuddled her close. Tears rose to her eyes and she sniffed.

"Now, now, Daddy will make it all better." He rocked her and kissed the top of her head. She smiled through her tears. The familiar aroma of cigarette smoke and aftershave took her back to her childhood.

Mrs. Grant cleared her throat. "Will you be wanting more tea, Miss Christine?"

"Yes, fetch another pot, please. Dad and I need to talk." She stepped out of his arms and resumed her seat in the wing chair.

"So, tell me about it," she said. "Where the heck were you and why have you come here?"

He sat in the other arm chair and looked around appreciatively. Then he looked at Christine and hoped she would let him stay.

"I went to see your mother and she threw me out. Imagine that, she took my business and my home and left me with the clothes on my back, and that's it."

"I have no idea about your finances, Dad, but mother said you had embezzled from the company and the taxes were outstanding. It must have been bad because she was hopping mad. What did you do?"

"Well, thank you for that much. At least you think she exaggerated, which she did, as usual thinking only of herself. Granted I owed some money on the taxes but I arranged a loan with the bank and made sure we paid them." She did not need to know that he had co-signed a loan with Milly.

"Where did you go?"

"I went to Nassau. I stayed there for about six months and then got tired of the constant sunshine and the slowness of life on the island. Then I ran out of money so I came back."

"Where are you living now?"

He laughed. "At the YMCA, if you can believe that. It's awful, noisy and filled with druggies. I've got to find somewhere to live and a job. I never thought I'd have to start from scratch at my age."

"Poor Dad." Beth came in with the teapot and a fresh cup and saucer and set them on the coffee table, then stood inside the door listening.

"Have you applied for any jobs?" Christine asked as she poured his tea.

"To do what? I can get a job anywhere as a car salesman, with or without experience. It isn't rocket science."

"No, that's true. Can't you find another type of work? I don't think you'll like having a boss after being the man in charge for so long."

He sighed. "You're right about that. I'll have to pound the pavements and seek something. Maybe in a shop, maybe in an office. What I could do in an office that doesn't sell cars, I can't imagine, but I need to work."

Beth sent telepathic messages to Christine knowing of her penchant for helping those in need.

"I don't suppose I could stay here for a while?" he asked softly. Beth shook her head violently and waved her arms as if to erase his words.

Christine looked at her over his shoulder and smiled. "You can stay for two days and after that you must leave. We can't manage with a boarder, even if you are family, and mother will be over here like a flash if she finds out about it."

"Come on now, this house is huge and you have so many rooms that I doubt if we'd see much of each other. I need a proper address for my resume and I doubt the YMCA address would make a good impression. They'd think I was shifty."

Christine laughed mirthlessly. "You probably are. You walked out on us, left debts that I can only imagine, then you come wandering back and expect us to slaughter the fatted calf. No way, Dad. I'm not as gullible these days and have many business meetings here. I'm going to be hiring a secretary soon."

His heart sank. "Do you have a job for me?"

Beth started her shaking and waving again.

"No. I run my own business with properly trained help. It keeps me busy."

He glanced around. "I wondered how you could afford to stay here. This place must be a money pit. Look at the upkeep and maintenance alone."

"Yes, it's expensive, but I manage and Mrs. Grant helps with the house."

"I could do some odd jobs for you," he offered.

"No thanks. I've seen your handiwork and it isn't good. Look for a proper job. You can stay for two days, but then you must leave."

He sighed and picked up his tea cup. It had not gone the way he wanted but he had two days to work on her.

♥

Harvey decided the time was right. He even picked out the ring, a large solitaire diamond set in platinum. Now he opened the black velvet box as he strode along the street. The ring sparkled in the afternoon sunshine and he imagined her face when he gave it to her.

Christine, independent in a lot of ways, made him feel as if he were a knight in shining armour. Since her grandmother's death she had changed, but for the better. She had become more confident in her abilities and had hired a manager to run Eldertrans while she concentrated on her new venture: a mail order company that catered to shut-ins.

When would he would ask her? He clutched the ring box in his pocket and tried to decide. Maybe he would automatically know when the moment was right. Longing to see her right now to propose, his mind told him that her answer may disappoint him, and maybe he would return home either ecstatic or in agony. It was the most important decision of his life and his nerves quivered with the major impact this might have. Who would have thought he could feel this way about another person?

♥

Milly marched through the lobby of the downtown office building heading for the elevators, determined to put her investment banker in his place. Twice she had requested a statement of her financial estate and received nothing. Unused to having her wishes ignored, she became furious that he had not even sent an apology.

The fourteenth floor seemed quiet as she stepped out of the elevator. Not a busy building anytime, housing as it did, accountants and investment firms, the hushed plushly carpeted corridor welcomed her.

In broad gold lettering, the door proclaimed. "Anthony Andrews Senior & Associates", and underneath in smaller letters, "Investment Services. Pension Fund Management, Estate Planning, Portfolio Management."

The door, unlike the other wooden doors on the floor, was a double door of engraved plate glass set in a marble surround, substantial and reassuring. She pushed open the air-assisted door and entered the lobby of the two-storey office.

The pretty receptionist looked up and smiled. "Good morning, Mrs. Armstrong."

"Good morning. I'm here to see Tony Andrews junior. Is he available?"

"I'm afraid Mr. Anthony is away right now. Could anyone else help you?"

Milly snorted with annoyance. What a waste of her precious time. "Is Mr. Anthony senior available?"

"Mr. Anthony has retired, Mrs. Armstrong, but I'm sure one of the associates could help."

She sighed openly and rolled her eyes. "Get me the senior man. I know I don't have an appointment, but this is the only time I could take out of my busy schedule."

"Please have a seat while I get someone for you." The receptionist checked a board that listed who was in or out and made a call.

"Mr. Greenberg will see you, Mrs. Armstrong, if you would like to follow me." Milly marched behind the receptionist, noting that she wore run down shoes with her discount store outfit and felt vastly superior.

Mr. Greenberg had an outer office with floor to ceiling windows. From behind an expansive and expensive marble topped desk, he rose as the receptionist ushered her in.

Grasping her hand in both of his, he said, "Good morning, Mrs. Armstrong. What can I do for you today?"

"Good morning." She wrested her hand from his and sat in a visitor's chair. "All I want is a statement of my account, an accounting of my investments. Twice I asked for a statement and didn't even get the courtesy of a reply."

He looked dismayed. "Dear me. That is most unlike this office. Let me check it right away and I'll get someone to print out your statement. If you would allow me to leave you here, I'll get my secretary to fetch you a hot drink. Tea or coffee?"

"Tea, please. With lemon."

Mr. Greenberg was a gentleman, that much she could see. He wore a subtle shade of grey tie with his grey pin striped suit and his aftershave was expensive. As he placed the call, she looked him over, noting his neatly styled hair and air of confidence. Yes, a man of the old school. She relaxed a little.

The tea arrived in short order along with digestive biscuits. The cups were of egg shell china and the tea pot a mastery of Chinese art. She sipped and nibbled and mentally added the cost of the walnut panelling and custom made cabinets as she wondered why it took so long to get a printout.

The door opened and Mr. Greenberg entered with another man she knew as Douglas McDonald.

"Mrs. Armstrong," Greenberg said, smiling genially, "We hate to keep you hanging around like this, but we are having a computer glitch. We've put two of our best accountants on it and they will make you a summary by hand. Trouble with computers is that they often fail to provide that which you require in a timely manner. I do hope you will make allowances for this delay."

She nodded. So computers again, dratted things, everyone always blamed the computers. "How long will it take to process this manually?"

McDonald smiled. "Maybe a couple of hours, so I have stepped into the breach and will take you to the Royal York Hotel for lunch. Is that convenient?"

She felt annoyed but well mannered enough not to let it show. "I had planned to attend a lunch meeting at the West End Hotel, but I could cancel that. I want that statement and I want it today." She eyed McDonald, very presentable, very suitable for an escort.

The men exchanged glances. "Very well, we will lunch," Douglas McDonald said. "I must leave word with my secretary about my next meeting and will come back to get you."

Mr. Greenberg sat behind his desk and began to play the drums with his nails on its polished surface. She glared at him, and he ceased but started to rummage through his desk drawers, unable to face her. Something felt very wrong, Greenberg looked nervous and McDonald looked tense.

♥

Christine finished her meeting with Hans Schultz, the accountant hired to look after the company books. Tax time had come around quickly and she could not handle the now complex financial figures. How simple it had been at first when all she recorded were incomings and outgoings. Presently they had fifteen paid employees for whom she provided benefits. The company purchased four more Voyager mini buses: now booked solidly by two of the largest retirement homes. Yes, it had surely changed and she wondered if it were for the better.

"So I'll e-mail the balance sheet to you when I've finished it, Miss Armstrong. I'm sure you'll have to pay tax this year, but I'll make sure we use all legal methods of reducing the payment."

"Thanks, I'd appreciate that. I never thought we'd ever make so much money, and we don't even charge that much."

"Your service is very valuable to our seniors. Not many people can be bothered with the aged and infirm. The fact that you always have a registered nurse on each bus makes a great deal of difference."

"I know, and yet we have had not one major incident." She tapped her head, "Touch wood."

He continued putting the papers in his briefcase. "A day out gives these people a new lease on life, and I think you deserve a commendation for taking the plunge and starting this business. I'm going to nominate you for Woman of the Year."

She protested. "Oh, come on now. That's going too far. All I do is manage things."

"Very well too, if I may say so. Well, I'd better get back to the office. Talk to you later."

"Thanks, Hans. See you soon."

Christine showed him out and stood for a moment on the top step. Two tourists were taking snaps of the newly decorated house. After reading a book titled "Painted Ladies" by Elizabeth Pomanda and Douglas Keister, she decided that her grand old house would also benefit from a treatment. Now a decorator had painted the scrollwork and embellishments in various shades of blue, while the windows and doors were royal blue. The fancy fretwork on the gables was off-white and looked like lace. It was out of place in Trawton but very attractive against the other houses that had brown or dark green paint. She smiled as the tourist asked if she would stay on the verandah for a shot and nodded.

Another project she had started was the restoration of the interior original features: the cut glass French doors, the ornate ceramic floor tiles, the original brass light switches. Even the bathroom looked as if it belonged to Queen Victoria because cupboards or trim concealed all modern conveniences. Beth, delighted with the upgrade, remembered all sorts of things Mrs. Wallace had removed and stored in the attics over the years.

Oak plank floors gleamed after they removed the wall to wall carpet. She replaced the top part of the windows with the original stained glass to allow a patchwork of coloured lights to dance over the floors. Gram saved anything she thought might be back in fashion and the packed and roomy attic was a veritable treasure trove.

Now she smiled as she entered the living room with its ten-foot ceiling to floor pink marble fireplace. This was home, the place she wanted to live the rest of her life and Gram had made it so easy. With money behind her, she lived well and soon found herself dismissing thoughts of 'how much is it?'

Harvey had telephoned last night and arranged a date for lunch today. She wondered what he wanted because they usually only saw each other Friday or Saturday.

The phone rang. She didn't even move toward it, knowing her new secretary, Jill, who worked in the library, would answer it. What a joy it was to have money, how very satisfying. Then she wondered why her mother always looked so sour. Money had not made her happy, in fact it made her positively miserable.

CHAPTER TWENTY-TWO

Milly enjoyed her lunch for its company and not the food. She noticed many women glance at Douglas with interest and felt delighted to have such a handsome man escorting her. Over the next two hours she posed and postured and flirted, as she picked at small green salad and ate two mouthfuls of grilled sole. Douglas McDonald ate well, steak and potatoes, salad, green beans, four dinner rolls with butter, a bottle of wine, a huge hunk of chocolate cake. He talked a lot and complimented her. This warmed her to him and she smiled genuinely. An expense account meal, she guessed, as he signed the hefty bill. She patted her flat stomach as she rose, proud of her self control when she refused even to look at the delicious desert trolley.

They arrived back at the office where he showed her into Mr. Greenberg's office.

"Good lunch?" Greenberg asked.

"Adequate," Milly said, unsmiling.

Then Douglas entered with two accountants, one of whom carried a file folder.

Greenberg gestured to the other chairs. "Sit, gentlemen. Now what have you brought us?"

The older man, grey haired and bespectacled, cleared his throat. "Could we have a word in private, Mr. Greenberg?"

Milly sat straight up, her eyebrows in her hairline. "What is wrong?"

"Er, er, well it's like this. . . ." he paused and swallowed.

"Come on, man, spit it out." Mr. Greenberg put out his hand for the folder.

"I think we should talk privately, sir."The man reluctantly handed over the file.

Greenberg opened it and scanned the contents. "What? What is this?" he roared.

"What is it?" Milly asked.

Douglas McDonald took the file and stood looking through it. "Bad news, Mrs. Armstrong, very bad news."

"What's happened? What has gone wrong?"

Greenberg and McDonald exchanged glances and Milly felt her heart grow cold.

♥

Beth finished making the scones with raisins and sultanas for Miss Christine. She cut the dough into squares and placed them on a baking tray.

The door opened and Jeff walked into the room. "Morning, Mrs. Grant. Any tea or coffee going?"

"On the counter. Help yourself." She opened the oven door and popped the tray inside. "There, that's done." She went into the pantry and brought out the evening's roast of beef and began to lard it, then inserted cloves of garlic under the surface.

"You're a good cook, Mrs. Grant," Jeff said as he sat at the table with his mug of coffee.

"Thank you, but at my time of life I've had lots of practice." She did not look at him, nor say that Christine had taught her how to cook properly.

"Any chance of something to eat? I'm starving."

"Don't look at me, Mr. Armstrong. I'm too busy to start cooking. I've got the bedrooms to do yet and the bathroom. There's a pile of washing and the hall floor needs polishing again."

He sighed. "Okay, don't start the martyr act. So you do housework, but surely that's what you get paid for, isn't it? If it's so hard to look after the house, Christine should hire someone younger to help you. All I wanted was a snack."

Beth decided Tina's decision not to tell him about the change of ownership made sense, though she felt like screaming at him that it was also her permanent home.

"He'll think I won't throw him out if he knew it was my house," Christine had said. "Let him think my mother inherited everything. I don't want him here so keep quiet about it."

Now Beth pointed around. "There's the pantry, that's the fridge, there's the bread bin, that's the cutlery drawer. Make yourself something, but don't make any mess."

"Not very hospitable, are you?" He walked into the pantry and started scanning the shelves.

"No, maybe not, but Miss Christine told me I wasn't to work for you. Said you were only staying two days and would be leaving today."

He popped his head around the door, surprised. "She said that?"

"Yes, she did. Now I've got to get to work. Maybe you should start looking for a job. Miss Christine said you needed one."

"Huh! Miss Christine this and Miss Christine that! She's my daughter and I don't believe she would ever throw me out of the house. We're family."

Beth took her cleaning kit out of the cupboard under the sink "Family or not, she's not the type to be blackmailed, Mr. Armstrong. I hope to find you gone when I get back."

Jeffrey slumped into the chair. Surely Christine would not be that cruel? Look at this place, a veritable mansion with all the bedrooms and only two occupied. It puzzled him why Milly let her continue to live here. Maybe he should ask Milly if he could stay as well . . . but then Milly did not want to talk with him. He sighed. Where *could* he go? He decided that if he kept out of sight, except for meals, soon Christine would accept his presence as normal.

After making himself bacon and eggs and toast, he washed the frying pan, plate and cutlery and left the kitchen. The old woman could not complain about that.

♥

Milly went home in a blue funk. The blasted man had swindled her, he had moved around her investments so that it looked as if money still accumulated from interest, meanwhile embezzling the lot. No wonder he went away: probably to some country that did not have extradition. It was not only her portfolio that he ruined, she learned, other people suffered the same fate. From all accounts, Tony Andrews junior had embezzled more than twenty million pounds and those old fools had not even noticed. Andrews, a smart man, had written a computer program that showed things were continuing as usual, even while he continued to syphon off money. Computers.. . . huh! It went to prove that those blasted machines were unreliable.

She wandered around the house, her mind racing. Where did this leave her? She had asked them, but neither Mr. Greenberg nor Douglas McDonald answered, because they did not know. They had sent for a forensic auditor who would eventually give them a clearer picture of the situation, and she insisted they call the police in her presence. Blasted man, how dare he rob innocent people! His father was such an honourable man too. Good job the company carried insurance.

With a severely depleted income, she wondered how she would manage. She cancelled her cleaning lady; her first economy. With only herself in the house, how dirty could it get? She prided herself on her neatness. Then she looked out at the gardens and wondered if she should fire the gardener. Better not. That would be too obvious. She must save face at all costs until she heard the final results of the audit. Anyway she could live on her income from the dealership in the meantime, and her savings.

At a time like this, her mother would have helped but she was dead and little Miss Brown Nose had taken the lot. A thought occurred to her: maybe she should visit Christine and tell her the bad news. Surely her daughter could hardly refuse to help her own mother, not after Christine had stolen her inheritance.

♥

Harvey told Christine about his latest idea when they met at a coffee shop. He wanted to start his own company, wanted her opinion, and his enthusiasm grew as he spoke.

"Symelinx has been good to me," he said, "what with the bonuses and a large pay cheque. Still, I think I can do better on my own, plus I would retain the rights to the games I write. As it is, Symelinx takes all rights and I get a mere pittance for my ideas when you consider the global implications."

"Then take the chance," Christine said, "If you've got enough savings to start a small outfit, I don't think you'd regret it. You could always go back if it fails. If you don't leave under a cloud, they would welcome you back."

He grimaced. "It's a long shot, though, don't you think?"

She nodded. "But everything in life is a gamble. Yet you know what they say, 'the longest journey starts with a single step.' I think you ought to start walking. You can do it, Harvey, we both you know you can."

He nodded. "That's true. Right! I'll do it. First I'll write up a business plan and see the bank manager about a start up loan. If that goes okay, then I'm out on my own. Gosh, I'll have to hire a couple of guys. Oh lord, it's going to be so messy at first."

"Come on now, Harvey, it can't be that bad. Look at me. I worked out of our living room and kitchen and now I've got a staff of twenty-seven. Not counting part timers and volunteers. Take the plunge. Go for it!"

"Thanks, Tina. You've made me feel better. I knew I could count on you for support." He took her hand and kissed it. "I think a lot of your opinions, you know. In fact, I think a lot of you."

She grinned. "Me too. I have great confidence in you, Harvey and know you'll set the town on its ear."

He kissed her hand. "A mutual admiration society, I'd say. You've been through a lot and you've come through smiling."

"In my case I didn't know what I was getting into, so let's not make me into a paragon of business acumen. Without Gram prodding me, I wouldn't have had the nerve. I'm on your side, like you were on mine."

How she wished she could tell him that she loved him. That would never do: being the first who said it was scary, in case the other person didn't say it back. She looked at him with love and hoped he got the message. "I think you'll make a terrific boss."

"Spoken by someone with a bias. Oh well, I've got to learn sometime and this is the time. I wonder if Bill Gates felt like this."

"Ah, but Bill Gates started when he was too young to know better. Stop worrying, and get on with it."

"Tina?"

"What?"

She looked into his eyes and saw he looked deadly serious. Was this the moment she had prayed for?

"I love you, Tina. I love you so much." His eyes filled with tears and she gulped as the tears came to her own eyes.

"I love you too, Harvey." As one, they stood and embraced. He did not kiss her.

"Come on, let's get out of here and do some serious talking. This is our future at stake. We need to be sure we're ready for it."

"I want to be with you day and night," he said, unable to free her hand, wanting her close. "It would be wonderful if we were never separated."

She smiled, knowing he meant it and yet knowing it would never work. What was it they said, 'familiarity breeds contempt?' Well, that could happen, they could fall out of love just as easily. So they would stay separate until the feelings became too strong to overcome and they would marry.

As he left, he glanced back and saw her standing on the steps, her hair loose and blowing in the wind. She raised her hand and waved, blew him a kiss, and he felt ten feet tall. That beautiful woman loved him, him Harvey Wright, the one chosen most likely to fail by his classmates in that joke graduation ceremony. Christine was perfect and belonged to him.

CHAPTER TWENTY-THREE

As Milly dressed in her best outfit, she wondered if she had enough money to renew her wardrobe for the winter. She changed her outfits with the seasons and after having worn a garment two or three times, would donate it to the Salvation Army or some other charity. For her to be seen wearing something too often would embarrass her, though she kept some of the better labels to wear on her 'at home' days.

She felt nervous about speaking to Christine, but needs must and she was desperate. Looking in the hall mirror, she checked her hair and settled the small feathered hat carefully so as not to disturb the waves of her new hair style. What a terrible time for this to happen to her, how demeaning to have to beg her own daughter for help.

The house looked cheerful as she drove into the driveway and she realized that Christine had repainted it. Something else was different but she could not figure it out. As the door chimes sounded, she stood looking out at the garden. That was it. The garden was beautiful with massed flowers that complimented the colours of the house. Christine was not as stupid as she had thought.

Beth Grant came to the door. "Oh, it's you," she said brusquely, drying her hands on a dish cloth.

"Is Christine home?"

"No, she's out." She kept her face expressionless as she checked out the latest designer outfit, thinking the shops must really roll out the red carpet when they saw her coming.

Milly looked at her watch. "Will she be long?"

"How would I know?"

"Is she attending a meeting or on one of the trips?"

"I don't know. Want to leave a message?"

Milly glared at the stupid housekeeper. To think the woman had received more money than she had from her mother's estate was enough to curdle her stomach. She caught a movement behind Mrs. Grant and thought it might be Christine. Was the woman lying?

Then, peering around, she saw a man. Was Christine living with someone now? That nerdy computer geek that she talked about?

Suddenly he turned to go upstairs and she saw it was Jeff.

"What's *he* doing here?" she snapped.

Beth smiled. Time to get another one over on Mrs. Armstrong. "He lives here since you threw him out." It gave her a great deal of satisfaction to say the words and Mrs. Armstrong's face turned puce.

"What?"

"What I said. Now I've got work to do. It's all right for some." She made to close the door, but Milly stepped forward, pushed her aside and entered the hall.

"I wish to speak to my husband, if you don't mind."

Beth glowered. "I do mind, and suggest you leave."

Milly pushed her aside and went to the bottom of the stairs. Then did something she hadn't done since her teens, she shouted.

"Jeffrey Armstrong, come down here at once!"

Beth stifled her snigger, thinking the poor man would be sorry if he did.

♥

Jeffrey thought he had avoided Milly. He ran up the stairs to hide in his room and stood watching for her departure through the bay window.

Her voice shrilled up the staircase and echoed in his brain, "Jeffrey Armstrong, come down here at once!" Shit, now he was in for it. If he didn't go down, he felt sure she would co me up.

Slowly, he walked along the upper hall and looked over the bannister. She stood in the vestibule, looking murderous. Sighing, he slowly made his way down the circular staircase, one slow foot after the other, sliding his left hand down the bannister rail. All the time his brain was working feverishly, seeking words that would placate her, looking for some reason why she should take him back.

"What is this?" she asked, her foot tapping impatiently.

"I'm staying here with Christine." He tried to sound nonchalant but failed.

"I can see that, but how did you manage to worm your way into this house?"

He grinned. "She's my daughter. She didn't want to see me on the streets."

Milly grimaced. "Such colourful language from a man who has no imagination. Have you found work yet?"

"Not yet. It takes time."

"Let's face it, Jeff, you have no intentions of working. Your plan is to live like a parasite off our child."

"Come on now, that's a bit thick."

Beth Grant stood listening as she absentmindedly rubbed the same circle of hall table with her duster.

Milly saw her. "Don't you have something else to do?" sh e snapped. "How very rude to stand listening to a private conversation."

Mrs. Grant drew herself up. "I'm working. It's my time to clean the hall and you shouldn't be here anyway. Miss Christine won't . .,"

"Miss Christine is my daughter and she will do as I say. Go to the kitchen and make coffee or something. I wouldn't mind a drink."

Mrs. Grant glared. "I'll not be cooking or doing anything else for you. I'm not the housekeeper, no more than I was when Mrs. Wallace was alive. I was her companion and she made it clear in her will that this was now my home."

"*Your* home?" Milly's voice rose shrilly as she laughed derisively.

Beth moved forward. "That being so, I must ask you to leave. I didn't invite you in and Miss Christine won't want you here."

Milly exploded. "Miss Christine, Miss Christine! She's not royalty, nor is she any better than any of us. Call her Christine without the Miss. The very nerve of that brat brainwashing my mother, and now owning my birthright!"

Jeff leaned against the wall and crossed his arms. If the old lady was giving Milly heck, he was safe. It sounded like Christine had gazumped her mother and now owned the house. Good for her.

The front door opened and Christine entered.

"What's going on here?" She dropped her shoulder bag on the hall table. "Mother, what are you doing here?"

"I saw your father and could hardly believe my eyes. Why is he here? Why have you given him sanctuary?"

Christine laughed bitterly. "Sanctuary? This isn't a church. I'm more concerned about your presence."

Milly smiled, which removed her shrewish look and took a step forward. Her voice changed and was soft, caring. "I came to see you, Christine. I wanted to talk to you. We can't remain estranged, not when life is so short. Don't you think we should make up and be friends again?"

Jeffrey and Mrs. Grant exchanged glances. It was as good as a soap opera.

"Huh! Friends? We've never been friends. Not even when I was a small child did you as much as show any sense of caring about me. You treated me as an imposition for most of my life. I ran away from you, but you didn't even welcome me back and now you come here asking to be friends?" Christine took off her coat and dropped it on the table. "I've heard enough from you. Please leave. We have nothing to discuss."

"What? You're asking *me* to leave and allowing *him,*" she pointed at Jeffrey, ". . . to stay? What is going on? That man deserted me, and deserted you. He left a trail of debts that I had to pay. He was living with a prostitute until he managed to get involved with a loan shark or a mafia type who is now chasing him for his unpaid gambling debts. How *could* you?"

Christine smiled wryly. "Easy, Mother. If you think he is living here, it will drive you crazy." She shook her hands around willy-nilly as she shook her head like an idiot. "That gives me a great deal of satisfaction."

"You've become hard and unfeeling."

She smiled. "Then I take after you, wouldn't you say?"

"Oh, this is too much."

Christine walked over to the door and opened it. "Out, now."

Jeffrey raised his hands as if he would applaud, but then shoved them in his pant's pockets. Beth Grant smiled widely and gestured to the door as Milly glared at her.

Milly raised her nose. "I'm leaving. Evil fills this house."

"It won't be evil once you leave," Mrs. Grant got the last word.

They all burst into laughter as Milly walked down the steps. "My poor mother, she'll never learn," Christine said as she wiped her eyes. "Tomorrow she will have sanitized this visit in her mind and I'll be in the wrong. She's a real character, but I admire her in a way. She never deviates from what she considers right. Not that I condone her attitude to others."

"Tea time, Tina?" Mrs. Grant said as she hung Christine's coat in the hall closet.

"Please, Beth."

Jeffrey turned and quietly went back to his room. Time to let them forget his presence and maybe he could stay. His stomach rumbled and he thought he might like tea and scones, but he knew he mustn't draw attention to himself.

"How long is he staying?" Beth asked, looking up at the ceiling.

"I don't know. Not long. I don't want him here, and if what mother had to say is true, then I think we'd be a lot safer without him."

"Hmm. I don't think you should have taken him in in the first place."

"I might not like him very much, but he *is* my father. He was homeless, " She gestured around, "And I have all this."

"This must be very upsetting for you, love."

"Not at all. I'm inured to my family after all this time. I don't let them bother me, and now treat them with the same contempt with which they once treated me."

"Shame that. Now what's the news about Harvey? Is he going to start up on his own?"

Christine shared everything with Beth these days, but did not say anything about the engagement. It was still too new, too thrilling. One day, after Harvey gave her a ring, she would announce it to the world. They were closer than ever and now saw each other at least once a day, usually for lunch although their Friday night date was the same as always.

"Yes, he's been to the bank and they granted him a start up loan. His father will have a bird when he finds out Harvey went to his competitor for the loan." She laughed at the thought. "I think Harvey is going to make it as an entrepreneur. I'm so pleased for him."

"It's nice that you two have hit it off so well. You look positively radiant these days. Is love on the books, do you think?"

Christine laughed and blushed. "No getting anything past you, Beth, is there?"

♥

Jeff stayed in his room as long as he could. Apart from a trip to the bathroom, he sat staring out the window, waiting for Christine to go out. He felt bored and hungry, but realized his appearance could start another argument This morning they had argued when he asked her secretary to type up a resume for him and the young woman had taken it to Christine.

"Go to an agency and get them to do it, Dad. Jill has a lot to do this week with the new catalogue, and I will not have you using her time on trivialities."

"How can I get a job without a resume? Tell me that."

"You probably can't, but Jill isn't going to type it for you. Take it back, take it to a secretarial agency."

How cold she sounded, how unlike the Christine he knew.

"But darling . . .,"

"One more day and you're out of here. I can't have you here any longer."

"Why not? You've got all those empty rooms."

"No use arguing, Dad. I want you to leave tomorrow."

Now as he sat watching pedestrians and cars, he saw a tall young businessman open the gate and wondered who it could be. Someone answered the door and the young man entered. Within ten minutes Christine appeared with him and they sauntered down the street, clinging to each other. So Christine had a boy friend, had she? About time too.

She had told him nothing about her time in Edmonton, other than she had managed to escape from a cult. Cults were a terrible thing and he felt glad that she had managed to get away from those who held her. Milly had told him little, other than complain about the extra work made when Christine returned. Since she had a housekeeper, gardener and cook, he said, how could one small girl make any difference to her life? Then he became aware that Christine spent her time away from the house, and suddenly didn't see her at all.

His mother-in-law, not his favourite person at the best of times, had taken her in and left the whole shebang to her. Good old Evelyn, she always did know how to wind up Milly. Huh! Milly! She must now be living a good life funded by his company, the company she had stolen from him. Her and her high-priced solicitors!

He put on his jacket and quickly went down the stairs. Time to get some fresh air and pay a visit to his loving wife. If he found her in a better mood, maybe he could appeal to her as her husband, the man who still loved her. He shook his head. No way. That was ludicrous.

♥

Milly walked around the back garden, deploring the lack of colour. Without the necessary funds, she had cut back on annuals and the back garden looked drab. The front, with its large round flower beds, had taken all her money, but one must keep up appearances at all costs.

Her stupid daughter. How could she take that swine into the house? Him, standing there grinning like a Cheshire cat. He had a nerve. Yet what was she going to do now?

Tony Andrews & Associates, through insurance and other means, had returned about half her investments. They charged Tony Andrews, a man stupid enough to come home, with embezzlement and insider trading and he now resided in a jail cell. It irked her that she had lost so much money, though her new financial advisor was doing a superlative job and had invested wisely. Yet how could she get her hands on more money, the money she needed for her new car? Every year she had a new car and things must not change in front of her friends.

Her income from the dealership was adequate, she supposed, for someone who did not have the social connections she had worked so hard to form, but she had always lived above her means, especially when she relied on Jeff to supply most of her wants. She longed for a new BMW, a car that shouted expensive. No one in her clique had one and she wanted to be the first. How awful to have to drive a common import or English model from the dealership, but needs must. Maybe a top of the line car with all the extras would make a decent impression and, with the trade in on her Mercedes, she might manage.

On the other hand maybe she could get the dealership body shop to respray her Mercedes the newest colour. Maybe that might be best as she had personalized her plates and no one would know it was the same car.

She stewed over her misfortunes. First her stupid husband, then her mother, and then to add salt to the wounds, Tony Andrews. Her mother had a lot to answer for. Imagine leaving everything to Christine. What had she ever done that her mother would cut her out of the will? Surely she had been loving and caring, as much as any other married daughter would be? Maybe Christine had found time to turn her mother against her, but the child had always had such a high idea of herself and had probably told a pack of lies.

Marriage was an option, she supposed, and she knew many widowers who might like to have a well cared for female on their arm. Milly had reached a watershed and realized her life must take a new direction. Jeff was history and Christine was lost to her forever. Time for her to develop a strategy for the future.

♥

Harvey presented the ring to her after they attended a performance at the theatre. Sitting in a private booth at the Rathskeller, she felt her eyes fill with tears as he took out the small box.

"Will you marry me, please, Tina?"

"I already said yes, but yes without a doubt." She looked at the ring as he slipped it on her finger. "Oh, it's magnificent! Thank you, love. I just fell in love with you all over again."

Harvey pulled her close and kissed her eyelids. "I love you, Tina, love you with all my heart and soul. How soon can we get married?"

She laughed then. "Spoken by a man peering down my cleavage! I love you so much, Harvey. Wow, I can't wait to show everyone my ring! Come on, we'll go home and celebrate the happiest day in my life."

They stood and, arms around each other, began to leave. They reached the wide lobby.

"Well, if it isn't my old friend Christine. Tina, baby, come to daddy!"

Christine and Harvey stopped and gaped at the tall man who stood arms open wide in front of them.

Christine's heart plummeted. Good grief, it was the Ed the pimp from Edmonton! He smiled, and gestured, moving forward until he could pull her into his arms.

He hugged her and than pushed her back, still holding her arms, his face serious. "You owe me, baby, owe me big time. I've been looking for you and here you are. Lose the yobbo and we'll talk."

She struggled out of his clutch and clung to Harvey who looked flabbergasted. He put a protective arm around her. "Who the heck is this?"

"Harvey, this is . . .,"

"Harvey? Harvey? God, what a name." Ed put back his head and laughed. Dressed in a tailor-made suit and handmade shoes, he looked surprisingly good. A stranger could take him for a successful businessman . . . but he wasn't!

Christine felt cold inside. Now it would all come out, her sordid past. God, how could she have been so foolish as to think her past would not come back to haunt her? How would Harvey take it? Three minutes ago she had been so very happy, and now . . .

CHAPTER TWENTY-FOUR

She lay huddled into a small ball and tried to stop shaking. Who would have guessed that Ed would show up here? Harvey had not accepted her explanation that she had worked for Ed in Edmonton. She mentally relived the nightmare of her ruined evening.

"Ed owns a department store," she had gabbled, praying that he would not contradict her. To her relief, Ed simply stood smiling. "I worked on the cosmetic counter."

Please God, she prayed, please make it all right. Ed now looked too smooth, too gangster-ish, his hair too long, his jewellery cheap and flashy.

Harvey looked down at her. "Oh yes, what was the name of the store?"

She could not speak, couldn't think of a name. What could she say? She had hoped Ed would come up with a name but he stood, smiling grimly and she felt frightened.

"Well? What's the name of your outfit?" Harvey asked Ed, his eyes narrowed.

"I didn't have a store, mate. She's making it up. Ask her what she did." He grinned evilly, "Go on, ask her."

Her heart dropped inside her. Ed was going to ruin her life, even knowing him was bad enough, but for him to turn Harvey against her, when she was so happy. She burst into tears.

"Oh, there she goes again, always turning on the waterworks." He took her arms and shook her. "Stop it, you stupid cow, I've told you it don't work and never will."

"How dare you talk to her like that!" Harvey pulled Christine away and moved forward, fists raised.

Ed waved his hands. "Now, now, sonny boy, let's not make a scene. She knows what she did for me, and I'm sure she's going to tell you. She owes me money and I intend to get it. A contract is a contract and she ran away with the takings."

"I did not!" She shouted now, angry and mortified. "We had no contract. You're nothing but a parasite."Realizing what she had said, she covered her face with her hands. Now she had done it, made it worse.

"Take her out of here, sonny boy. I'm sure we'll meet again." Ed stood back and gestured to the door. "I'll soon find her and get my money back."

Harvey looked at Christine, he did not take her hand or touch her and her tears started afresh. He moved to the door and held it open for her.

As she passed Ed, she hissed, "Damn you, and damn all your race. How could you?"

He grinned. "Easy, darling, I don't like double-crossers. I always manage to find them that runs off, so don't try skipping out this time. Go with your fella and think about what I said."

Harvey did not touch her. He slouched along to the car and opened the door, silent and angry. She didn't know what to do or say.

They travelled home in silence and her mind raced to find the answers to his coming questions. What could she say? Ed was not an ethical man, she could not say he was and Harvey looked so angry. She glanced at him and his face was set in lines of discontent.

Harvey pulled into her driveway and sat. "Get out!" was all he said and she stared at him.

"Harvey?" her voice was hoarse and tiny.

"Get out I said."

"But . . .,"

"Look, Tina, I'm very angry. Something happened between you and that horrible person. I don't want to know right now, but tomorrow maybe, when I've cooled off, I want to know everything. Now get out."

She stared at him, his knuckles were white on the steering wheel and he shut his eyes. "All right," she said, "We'll talk tomorrow. Goodnight, Harvey."

He did not answer but looked out the side window away from her. Sighing, she got out and stood as he rammed the car into reverse and shot out onto the road. As she put up her hand to wave, the street light caught the diamond on her left hand and the tears came again. "Oh Harvey, what did I do?"

"Where's Harvey?" Beth asked as she bustled into the hall. "I've got a hot drink and a . . . Oh dear, what's the matter, lovey?"

Warm arms held her as she sobbed and this made her feel better. "Come on now, don't take on so, Christine. Come along, we'll sit by the fire and you can tell me all about it."

Later they drank cocoa, Beth's panacea for all ills. "Seems to me that you've got to tell him the truth, lovey."

She groaned. "How could I do that without making him walk out of my life? No man wants spoiled goods, now do they?"

"Harvey's not judgmental from what I've seen of him, and he's very impartial. You did what you did to support yourself, so if anyone is to blame for the circumstances, it's your parents."

"Oh, he'll not accept that as an explanation. I was wrong to do what I did but at the time Ed seemed so caring and I was alone and penniless."

"There you are, then."

She put down her mug and dried her eyes. "Nevertheless, I needn't have done any of it, Beth, when you think about it. I could have picked up the phone and called home. I could have gone to the authorities and sorted it out. No, I can't possibly find an excuse. I did what I did and I'm at fault."

"Look here, you're a nice girl, and Harvey fell in love with you. While accepting this might be hard for him, it's history. Like your Gram always said, it made you into the person you are today. Don't forget that even Harvey has done things in his life that he might not be proud of and he's no different than any other young man. *Nobody*, not even Harvey, is a saint. He fell in love with you as you are, not as you were."

That sounded reasonable and she felt a bit better. "I suppose, but I dread talking to him. I was so happy last night until that man showed up. Look," she extended her hand and showed the ring. "Isn't it fantastic? I bet he wants it back now."

Beth admired the expensive ring and sighed. "He's not much of a man if he can't accept your explanation. Don't put yourself down so much and make sure he knows that it will never happen again."

"Oh my God, I never thought of that. How can he possibly trust me now?" the tears started again and Beth reached for the Kleenex.

"When you get to my age, lovey, you'll realize that this minor glitch was not the earth shattering event it now seems. When I was your age, I had my moments of self doubt, but looking back on it now, it was all such a waste of time. Now, you get a good night's sleep and things won't look as black."

Christine sighed and wiped her eyes. "Thanks, Beth. You make a lot of sense."

CHAPTER TWENTY-FIVE

Christine smiled coldly as the sales rep ogled her. "I see you're not married," he said staring at her ringless left hand. "Or are you divorced?"

"Single, and I intend to remain that way." She hadn't meant to snap but that's the way it sounded.

He opened his briefcase and picked up the books and papers from her desk. "Sorry, forget I spoke. Is that all for today?"

"I didn't mean to sound nasty. I'm sorry." She smiled, one of her full volume smiles that usually charmed the men. "Call in again next month. I'm planning a fall sale."

"Fine." He smiled too then, his umbrage forgotten.

Christine watched as he chatted to her secretary, Jill, at the other end of the library. A real ladies man, she thought, always on the search for a willing female.

She sighed as she sorted through her 'in' basket. So much to do and so little time, but she loved every pressure packed minute. It had been her saviour, this mail order catalogue. Still catering to the elderly, she sold all sorts of things: gadgets that made things easier for arthritic hands, canes, walkers, large dial phones with enormous numbers for those with sight problems, stools for the bathtub, rails and handles to help them stay independent. Items suitable for Christmas presents filled the fall issue.

At the small rented warehouse for her catalogue items she had a staff of four working four days a week. Internet sales were spectacular and her flyer had gone to every seniors' residence in the country. Inquiries were now coming from Europe, and various companies who specialized in those items she carried were now bombarding her with literature. Who would have known that such a limited business would catch on so quickly?

Where had the years gone, she wondered then as she glanced at the calendar? Two years now she had been alone. Where, she wondered, was Harvey? Did he ever think about her? Somehow after their confrontation where she angrily handed back the ring, they had lost touch. His attitude had hurt her back then, his righteous indignation when she confessed to her lurid past. His callous words still rang in her ears. Maybe she was well shut of him if his mind was so closed. In her mind she had made peace with herself and did not feel so touchy about the past. It was her own fault and she had accepted the blame. She even gave Ed a wad of money to get him off her back and thankfully he had not come back for more. When later, the headlines blared that the police had captured and charged Edward Rawsthorne with drug trafficking, she cheered. Had Harvey read those same headlines?

She still missed Harvey, still loved him, yet at other times she felt nothing but contempt for his attitude. How could he have blamed her for something she did when she was only fourteen? Why hadn't he understood? Her thoughts constantly turned to him, although the days of crying herself to sleep had passed and her new business took her mind off things. Harvey was the one who had shut her out of his life, and he might never come back into hers. When he first left, every minute of every day she looked for reasons why he had not forgiven her. It had all happened so long before she met him and, as her Gram used to say, our past makes us what we are today. He had fallen in love with the person he knew, not the old juvenile Christine.

At first she had spent her nights tossing and turning, feeling lost and alone. During the day she retreated into her business, and let no one speak of personal matters other than their own. When alone, she talked to the silver framed photograph of a younger and more vibrant Evelyn, and felt better for saying the words aloud. It was as if Harvey were dead and she had to struggle to find her motivation for continuing to work, to make her days productive. Yet the work was her salvation, her *raison d'etre*. At the back of her mind, she knew he was somewhere out there and maybe one day would return to her. Nevertheless, those who knew her well, knew she had lost her sparkle.

The months flew by, Beth Grant passed away in her sleep and now she had a young woman housekeeper, Martha, who was, as she liked to say, "more with it." The old house, repainted and refurbished with its gingerbread trim, stood on the street like a grand old dowager and she had completely modernized the kitchen and bathrooms. Of late she had received many lucrative offers, first from a woman who wanted to open a small select hotel, then from a restaurant chain. No way, this was her home and she would never part with it.

Her mother still flitted around like a wilting butterfly and the last she heard of her, she had taken Jeff back into the dealership, but only as a salesman. She smiled at the thought. Poor Dad must feel mortified. Then she reasoned that if he had accepted the job, then he did not care. She recalled the year when he had disappeared for some weeks and came back tanned as if coming from the tropics. Nassau, he had told her. Probably hiding from the mob, she had thought then. Strange how she had no feelings for her parents now, did not want to see them and did not worry about them. Love for them, always tenuous, had gone. Yes, that part of her life was over. Still, nobody ever said that she had to love those who gave her life, particularly when they had treated her so shabbily in her younger days.

♥

Walking toward his old home in the dusk, Jeff cursed as he saw a long black car pull into the driveway. A car that belonged to someone either very rich, or very criminal. He dodged behind the protection of a tall cedar hedge and thanked his stars that he had arrived now rather than earlier.

From his hidey hole, he stared at the house. Then he looked at the car. Oh lord, suppose it was the gangster that was chasing him? He snorted. If he knew Milly, she would deny even knowing him and probably call the police.

For two hours he stood behind the hedge, and for two hours he wondered what to do. Was Milly all right? Should he walk away and forget what he had seen? Somehow he felt less of a man for thinking of his own hide, but she cared nothing for him so why should he worry?

He jangled the change in his pant's pocket and shifted from foot to foot. It was getting cold and he was hungry. What to do?

Maybe this was not the time to speak to Milly. He should go home, back to the boarding house, and have something to eat.

♥

"You and I could be very happy, Milly," Gardner said as he poured more brandy into the crystal snifters.

A tall, well built man, Gardner was grey haired, and almost handsome. He had a commanding presence and people liked him for his candour and generosity.

"I'm a married woman, Gardner, and you know that." She simpered as he touched her cheek with one finger.

He smiled down at her. "I've loved you since I first met you at high school. I never could understand what you saw in Jeff Armstrong. Not a very intelligent man, nor an ambitious one either."

She sighed. "That's true. I was blinded to his faults and saw only his physique, I guess."

"Not like you, that, Milly. You were such an intelligent girl and our honour student. Where is he now? Gone?"

She shook her head. "We're separated, as you know, but he works for me at the dealership as a salesman." She laughed as if it were funny - and to her it was. "I discovered he was living with our daughter, but when she also threw him out, I gave him a job. He now he lives elsewhere and he isn't coming back here, I'll make sure of that. I don't want him in my house."

He laughed. "Boy, that must get up his nose. Being your employee. Now come here and give me a kiss. A proper kiss mind, not those little pecks you dole out at social events."

Milly relaxed into his arms and inhaled his Polo aftershave. She liked Gardner, had always liked him. He was right about so much, and she had made a big mistake with Jeff. Of course since Jeff's family were the richest people she had ever met, she figured he was heir presumptive to the family business. What she had not known until her wedding day, was that he had two older brothers. These siblings were away at university in England and Jeff never mentioned them. The eldest Gordon, was heir presumptive, his brother Grant next in line. Jeff, being the runt of the litter, was entitled to little other than a small inheritance. A good job her parents had provided for her because Jeff surely could not.

"Jeff has someone chasing him for money, a gangster," she said, apropos of nothing.

He pulled back to look at her. "Oh no. Are you safe here, Milly? Do you have a security system? I can get one installed."

"No, Gardner, I have a security system. I'm safe and it's not me they are looking for. If they come here, I shall be glad to point them in the right direction."

"Good for you." He glanced at the mantel clock. "Now, shall we watch that show you like so much?"

"All right." She clicked the remote and the painting above the fireplace slid up and the big screen television slid forward.

"That's some arrangement," Gardner said. "Did you design that?"

She preened. "No, can't say I did. I saw it in a copy of Architectural Digest and the builder installed it."

"Very classy. I don't like the blank eye of a dead TV staring at me in a room. I must get someone to install one in my place."

The opening credits of Upstairs, Downstairs started and she switched on the sound. Milly loved all things British: she admired the Royal Family, loved their country estates, their pomp and pageantry and tried to cultivate an upper class accent. As for the show, she was obviously one of those upstairs, and grinned at the antics of the servants who lived below stairs.

They sat entranced for an hour. Milly switched off the set when the closing credits started to roll. "A drink or coffee, Gardner?"

"Both. How about coffee and cognac?"

"Good idea. Come and keep me company while I make it."

Gardner whistled as he entered the huge kitchen with its stainless steel appliances and ceramic tiled floor. Milly moved so gracefully, he thought, watching her slim hips revolve the right amount. Her at home gown was long and flowing, very sexy. Like Milly: he hoped.

"Nice, isn't it?" Milly felt proud of her modern kitchen and its state of the art appliances. "My cleaning lady loves it, says it's so easy to keep clean." Going to the sink with the coffee pot, she smiled at her reflection in the shining sink. She did not mention that a fingerprint stood out like a neon sign on anything touched. Since she rarely used the kitchen for anything other than passing through or making the odd pot of coffee, she didn't touch anything and if her cleaner left even one mark on the pristine surfaces, she screamed blue murder.

Gardner sat at the glass topped kitchen table. "We'll sit here for our drink, shall we?"

"Why not? It's the nicest room in the house." Milly brought the cognac and glasses to the table and set down two place mats. "There, now we'll be cosy." She thought that sitting in a kitchen was for those below stairs, like the show they had watched. Still, early days and she must keep Gardner sweet and so concealed her distaste

Gardner represented stability, security and it did not hurt that he liked her. At school she had written him off as too gauche, too much of a jock. Back then her mind was set on a handsome man, not a clever one, and jocks were too full of themselves. Although looking back now she could well see why the girls pursued them. That alone gave them an inflated sense of importance. Not her though, she dismissed all jocks as morons and concentrated on those she knew came from established and old money. Yet little good that had done her. She was married to a cretin on the run from gangsters and Gardner was beginning to look better every minute. Milly smiled and touched his hand as she passed his cup.

As they drank coffee and cognac, Gardner started to talk about himself. Milly was content to listen. She learned a lot about a lot of people that way and Gardner thought her a very sympathetic companion.

♥

The man paced in front of the picture window on the eighteenth floor of the hotel, not even admiring the view of the docks or the bustling harbour.

"He's here. I know it and you know it." Grogsy Mulligan was one of the best enforcers in the USA and other countries. He had travelled the world to search out many welshers.

His companion, a thin man with a pale complexion, shrugged. "We know where he lives, don't we?"

"Nah, that was a phony address. People never heard of him there but with some searching I'm sure you'll ferret him out, Jimmy."

Jimmy pulled his face. "Sure. That's right, leave it all to me. Bet I get to off him, too."

"Come on now, when did you ever do anything alone? I do my fair share."

"Well, start tracking him. You got contacts here. I don't."

"Look, we'll split the difference, Jimbo. I'll give you some numbers to call and I'll call my close contacts on my cell phone."

They talked to people for about two hours and came up dry.

Grogsy put his phone into his pocket. "Sheesh! This guy is invisible."

"Maybe that's not his real name."

Grogsy slapped his forehead. "Sheesh! Right again, Jimbo. He used a phoney name."

He took out his cell phone and called Nassau where he spoke to his superior. The boss rang back an hour later to say that the name of the man who had rented the house on the cape was Jeffrey Armstrong.

"Jeffrey Armstrong! That's his name. Right. Enough for today, we'll start first thing in the morning.

♥

Milly garnered looks of admiration and hummed as she left the hairdressing salon. Today she had splurged on Mr. Vitelli, the best and most expensive stylist in Toronto, knowing she must look extra good for her next meeting with Gardner.

After weighing her options, she decided marrying Gardner was her best bet. He had wealth and social clout and it helped that recently bereaved widows and divorced women constantly pursued him. Yet he had told her how much he admired *her*. Her, plain old Millicent Wallace. Yes, the others were too predatory, he told her, and confessed that while he liked the thought of women chasing after him (and what man wouldn't?), he resented their conclusion that he was stupid. No, women who prowled were not attractive and he refused many invitations to dinners and events because he knew the hostess had her eye on his money.

She agreed with him that money was a curse, lying through her teeth. Money was the be all and end all of her existence, and without money she could not aspire to the upper echelon, which to her represented her arrival in society. Without money, she could not change her wardrobe twice a year, could not redecorate the house every other year, could not drive an expensive car. Money, and the accumulation of it, directed her every move. Married to Gardner she would move to the top level of society. He was filthy rich, though not one for outward show. His taste was superb, his tailoring magnificent. Yes, time to, what was it they said? 'gird her loins' for battle. To hell with Jeffrey: she wanted to get Gardner for her very own.

Jeff had gone to earth. He simply vanished and when she discovered he had not been at the dealership, she made a few enquiries. She spoke to the woman who worked as Christine's secretary in her search for him, but she told her Christine had said he had left the city. Darn it all: no Jeff meant no divorce, and a divorce was high on her list of priorities. She hired a private detective.

♥

Christine took possession of her new car. A Jaguar, it sparkled under the street lights as it sat in the driveway. Never had she driven such an expensive car and delighted in its easy handling. To spend such a large sum seemed silly, when she never drove any distance, but Hans the accountant told her they would write it off as a business expense and she needed to show more outgoings.

Always thrifty, though where she got that from she would never know, she spent as little as possible on nonessential things. Her profits were enormous and she expected a hefty tax bill this year. Not that it worried her, as her private worth was fantastic so she tended not to think about it. Her financial advisor was a genius, and her money made more money, much of which was put into various trust accounts for the many charities she supported anonymously.

The catalogue and Eldertrans kept her busy and she rarely took time off work. In a way, she thought it sad, that she, a young woman in her twenties, was living the life of a nun. Surely she should get out more, have a social life. Her housekeeper, Martha, said as much to her, bluntly.

"What are you saving yourself for, Christine? All the money in the world won't make you happy. Look at you, in your twenties, working night and day, and for what?"

"I know, I was thinking that myself. I should join a club or something. The only people I see are sales reps and the oldsters at various events."

"You trying to replace Mother Theresa?"

Christine laughed. "No, and I'm not doing good works, but making money for myself. I appreciate your speaking out because I know you're right. I have to change my life, live a normal life with outside interests."

Martha wiped down the counter and filled the coffee percolator. "You make more than enough contributions to charity, though. I know that much."

"I like to donate, but then who doesn't?" She smiled, thinking her mother had never heard of charity, other than sit on committees. She sighed.

Martha smiled sadly. "Thinking about him again, are you?" They had talked at length about Harvey but the talk had not changed her feeling of loss. "Look, Christine, don't set yourself up by thinking love is everything. You're young. Other people survive without romantic love."

Christine's lip curled. "Sure, nuns and monks. Some life *they* live."

She set out the coffee mugs and took down the biscuit tin. "What I mean is that life has a lot to offer; security, peace of mind and achievement."

Then she said it aloud. "I still love him." While that was always in her mind she never said it to anyone. Saying it made her feel lighter.

"That'll start to wear off eventually, and he'll become a memory."

She picked at her napkin. "We're talking as if he's dead, but he's not."

"Cheer up, Christine, put it behind you and live for the day. Try to live life like we do, a normal life with trials and tribulations, joys and sorrows. Wow, listen to me, a regular Agony Aunt." Both laughed. "But you know what I mean, ducky. Cheer up."

Yes, she must change her life, yet what chance did she have of ever being normal? Her childhood was fraught with fear, her teen years were spent as a prostitute and her parents had abandoned her. Not that she cared much about that, but surely it left a scar? In her heart she wanted Harvey, but knew she must put him out of her mind. Suppose she met another man, a man who loved her, could accept her as she was, warts and all, would she learn to love him? However, what man wanted someone who had slept with strangers?

Yes, Harvey was much more vulnerable than she. He loved her deeply and she knew it. However, he loved her as his first love and his first genuine passion, whereas she had slept with dozens, maybe hundreds of men and had felt nothing for them. The scar that these encounters had left on her soul provided some protection. Because no one had really loved her as a child, that also helped show her she could survive without love. Hadn't she survived before they met? Yet was that survival? Was it enough? Now she had tasted his love and had given her heart to him, she felt shattered when that trust had left their relationship.

No, better she join a club, make some friends. Yet where to start? She picked up the phone book

CHAPTER TWENTY-SIX

Milly dieted rigorously. She wanted to look her best when she and Gardner finally hit the sheets. How ludicrous, she thought, that someone of her age was behaving like a teenager. However, when she was a teenager everything was flawless without effort, her weight and her shape were perfect. Now it took a masseuse, a sauna and daily exercise combined with a rigid diet to make her look acceptable. She didn't mind it at all, look what she stood to gain.

The detective had found Jeffrey and the divorce action was in the hands of her solicitor.

♥

Jeff was shocked awake when someone crashed through the flimsy door on his room at the boarding house

"What the . . .?"

A dangerous looking man stood over him as he rubbed at his eyes. "Clothes on, we're going out for a walk," he rasped.

Jeff grabbed his jeans and a t-shirt and shrugged into them, his hands shaking. Darn it all, the money men had found him and he wondered how. Maybe through Milly. No. He scrubbed that thought, she had no idea where he was, and *they* thought he was Gary Whalen. He clumsily stubbed his feet into his sneakers without socks and cringed as he felt the damp insoles. Hardly able to tie a knot, he left the laces to dangle.

"That's better, lover boy. Come on, let's get out of here."

The man pushed at him with a fist as they walked along the dusty hall. Damn it all, the blasted door to his room stood open and someone would steal his stuff by the time he got back . . . if he ever got back.

It was cold on the street and he shivered as the wind forced its way under his T-shirt. He stuck his hands in his pockets and pulled his neck down into his shoulders.

His companion took his arm and led him along. They walked into a car park and he steered him to a long black car. Oh no, a long black car.

"Cold, are we? You're gonna be much colder soon, sonny boy."

A man got out of the driver's seat, opened the back door, then got back behind the wheel.

"There we go. All comfy now? Warmer here out of the wind, isn't it?" The man's tone was gentle, as if they were all pals together.

Bleakly Jeff nodded. How soon would it happen, he wondered as the car left the lot and headed for the expressway?

"What is this?" Jeff asked, suddenly finding his voice.

"You already know. You owe Jose some money and you ran away so you didn't need to pay it back."

"Who's Jose?" Jeff tried to sound surprised but it came out squeaky.

"The man you played cards with on the yacht. You know."

He decided to play it dumb. "What yacht?"

"Shut up with the lies. *We* know it was you and *you* know it was you. Time to pay for your supper, sonny boy. About two hundred thousand with interest we need and now."

"I live at a rooming house, for God's sake. Where would I get that amount of money?"

"Same place as you got the money to rent that house in Nassau, same place as you got your stake."

He groaned. "I don't have a cent to my name. Talk sense."

"We don't like that, sonny, don't like it at all. We have ways of making you see sense."

Jeff shrugged. It was over for him now and he knew it. "Go ahead, I can't get any money and can't pay you anything. All I own are the clothes on my back and I expect some jerk will rip off everything in my room so I won't even have a spare pair of socks." Tears threatened and he felt resigned to his fate.

The car pulled into a lakeside park and moved forward so it stood behind a tall hedge of cedars.

"We'll wait for a while, Jimbo. Why don't you see if you can get us some coffee from that van we saw back there."

It was like time had stopped. They sat side by side in the comfortable limousine, not speaking. Jimbo came back with two Styrofoam coffee cups and Jeff realized they had excluded him from their party. He sighed.

♥

Milly gasped when she opened her front door to find a stern looking police officer. "What is it, officer?" This meant bad news because he looked very grim.

"When did you last see your husband, Mrs. Armstrong?"

Her shoulders relaxed. It was only about Jeffrey.

"Would you like to step inside, please? So much nicer than letting the neighbours speculate, don't you think?"

She did not invite him into any of the rooms but stood in the spacious foyer. "Now what is this about?"

"Your husband is in the General with multiple injuries. A man walking his dog found him beaten up in a lakeside park. He was unconscious and still is."

She gasped. Might as well look concerned, but he probably had it coming to him. "Will he recover soon?" She almost smiled as she realized that if he did not recover she need not pay for a divorce.

"I have no idea, Mrs. Armstrong. I'm here to inform you of the event."

"Thank you, officer."

"I have instructions to take you to Queensway hospital if you wish to go."

"No, thank you. I have my own car and must get changed. I'll drive down shortly and thank you for coming to tell me."

He looked at her strangely, but said nothing as she let him out. She shut the door and leaned against it. Did Jeffrey still have insurance? Maybe he did and that might be the one thing that redeemed him in her eyes. No . . . George had told her that he had changed the beneficiary to Christine. Darn that child. Anyway, if he were broke, he would be unable to pay the premiums. She sighed and pushed herself away from the door. Might as well have a snack before she got ready to meet Gardner.

♥

When the Chamber of Commerce nominated Christine Armstrong for Ontario Woman of the Year everyone was delighted. Jill and Martha hugged her and said she deserved the recognition. She considered the nomination a great compliment and shivered with excitement. They were holding the provincial awards ceremony in Ottawa.

"I'll make a flight reservation," Jill said.

"No, I think I'll drive. Time to put some miles on the clock. The mechanic told me that an engine that size needs a good long run now and then."

"Drive? Are you sure that's such a good idea, Christine?"

"I'll drive, so don't argue. Boy, imagine me, getting an award. I'm so thrilled. Now, what about clothes?" She ran up the stairs, singing.

"Nice to see her so cheerful, isn't it?" Martha said as she came into the library with the tea tray.

"Sure is." Jill said, "She works too hard and though she is now doing volunteer work at the library, she should get out more. She'll meet a lot of people at this dinner, maybe even meet a man."

"She'll meet lots, but she won't see them again, not while she's still pining for the one that got away."

They shared a smile.

CHAPTER TWENTY-SEVEN

J eff groaned as the nurse changed a dressing.

"Feeling any better, dear?" she asked.

His voice was full of pain as he said, "Bugger it all. I feel like death. I'm wondering why they let me go."

"Who's they, dear?" she asked, knowing that the police would like to know.

"The thugs that beat me up, that's who. I thought I was a goner."

"Lie still now, while I change this dressing on your head."

Jeff suffered through her ministrations, and wondered if he were ever going to feel better. Plaster encased both his legs and lower left arm. The doctor had taped his ribs and immobilized his neck with a neck brace.

Strange how they had let him live, though. Surely that was not the usual way of doing things?

♥

"This man, Jeffrey Armstrong, I have a feeling that he isn't what he seems." Detective Cox said as he read the file. "That was a gangland style attack, yet he lived through it."

Harry Wells, his partner, shrugged. "So, he's tough, so what?"

"I think there's more to this man than meets the eye." He tapped the file. "He once owned a very lucrative car dealership and lived in a mansion. Why would he be staying at that dump?"

"I think he was in hiding, but they found him anyway."

"Yeah, but there's something more that I can't put my finger on. We got DNA from him?"

"Sure do. Took it when we didn't know who he was."

"I'm going over to the lab offices, want to do some snooping on this guy."

"Rather you than me, that lot are as easy to talk to as anvils. Think they know everything."

♥

With her softsider packed and her laptop in its case, Christine got into the car. Martha ran out of the house as she started it.

"Call us the minute you arrive."

"Sure will. It should take me about two hours to get there. At least we've got good weather for a change."

"Drive carefully."

Martha stood watching as Christine drove down the street and turned the corner. "She should have flown, got some rest, but would she? No, not her," she muttered.

♥

Harvey whistled as he looked at the passing scenery. He had always liked trains, liked the restful quality of watching the world go by without stress. Today's trains were more comfortable than when his mother used to take him to Vancouver to visit her sister. Now they had TV screens and movies to watch, good food in the dining car. When he was little, Grace packed a picnic lunch to eat on the journey and he drank warm soft drinks. Yet those days were when his mother loved him, when she doted on him. How had he changed, and why had she turned against him? He shrugged as he admired the distant hills and wondered what they were.

The purpose of his trip was to attend the Montreal Trade Show. Strictly aimed at high-tech professionals, he knew it was bound to show some surprises. High technology was moving so fast that some things were obsolete before they even reached the selling floor. Look at his cell phone, it took movies and photos, sent faxes, had a memory that held all his phone numbers and was also a tape recorder. What on earth had the world done before such things existed?

His company grew with each year, and they expanded into robotics. With several contracts from car manufacturing concerns, they had gone public this year and his worth on paper was several million dollars. He smiled, poor old Dad. He had almost had a heart attack when several TV news channels interviewed Harvey and his picture appeared on the cover of Time magazine and Maclean's. His mother wrote to him, almost begging that he come home to visit, but he tossed the letter away. They wanted him close by now that he had millions more than them, but he could not forget their nasty remarks so easily. If ever they had praised his efforts or tried to understand him, it might have been different and it was too late now to pretend they were friends. He still remembered their birthdays and their anniversary and never failed to mark the occasion with a card and a gift, but he did not want to see them. Not yet, but one day for sure because they were not going to live forever.

Christine, oh Tina, his heart longed for her still. Each time he thought of her, his stomach spasmed. He loved her as much now as when he walked away from her, never to return. Why, he asked himself for the trillionth time, had he not called her again, talked with her? What good had it done him, his high-handed attitude? Nothing at all, and he still loved her, she was in his mind night and day, and some good it was doing. His feelings of guilt overwhelmed him at times. Look at him, he professed to love her and yet had slept with a complete stranger in Calgary, and that was wrong. What she had done was long before she met him so how could he have made such a big deal about it?

Even now, he balked at being the first to make contact. He kept track of her through friends, knew she was doing well in business and the mail order catalogue was extremely profitable and doing great things on the Internet. Christine was intelligent, but she was also stubborn, stubborn enough to expect him to call her. He could, and he should, but somehow it went against the grain.

What had she done that was so bad? She had deceived him and that made him feel gullible. She could have told him the truth at the start and surely he would have understood? Still, no, he told himself, he would never have understood. That man Ed was a pimp. At first he had tried to rationalize the man's attitude. No matter how he looked at it, it seemed that Christine did not think enough of him to trust him. To think he thought her so innocent and yet she had been a prostitute. How innocent was that? Yet what did it matter? That was history, far in the past and long before he met her. Why had he not called her?

He closed his eyes as the train went through a tunnel and saw her face as clearly as ever.

♥

Jeff lay in the hospital bed waiting for the police. They had allowed him to lay healing for almost two weeks, now they were looking for an explanation.

The two men looked ordinary. One took a tape recorder out of his pocket and switched it on.

"Time ten forty-one, Queensway Hospital, room 577, attending officers James Shepperd and Kenneth Watts."

Jeff listened as he spoke. This was true to the television cop shows he had watched.

"Mr. Armstrong, did you know the men who attacked you?"

"No, never saw them before."

"Where did you meet them? Were you in the park?"

His mind skimmed possible answers, he chose to tell the truth. "They came into the rooming house on College street and took me out of my room."

"Why did they do that?"

"One man said I owed someone money and wanted me to pay up."

The other man took notes as he talked. "Did you owe the money?"

"I guess."

"Did you owe the money, yes or no?"

"Yes." Better to confess.

"Who did you owe it to?"

"A man I only met once in Nassau. We played cards on his boat and I was the big loser."

"Did he ask you for payment?"

"He knew I had nothing left when he took me to the bank in Nassau."

"Did he forgive the other part of your debt?"

He grimaced as he tried to shake his head. "No, but I thought he might when I left the country."

"When did you think this debt was void?"

"When I got back to Toronto. I used a false name when I was in Nassau and that's all they knew."

"I think they knew a lot more than that, Mr. Armstrong."

He shrugged and winced as the pain shot through his shoulder.

"I don't have any money. They know that now."

"However, you do have a wife and a large home on the outskirts. They can go after your wife, you know."

"They can?" He could not help the smile and turned it into a grimace of pain.

"We would like a full description of these men."

He talked about them, recalling their accents and what they wore, remembered their car, the silver vases with plastic deodorizer rosebuds in the interior, the plush seats and footrest.

After an hour he felt exhausted and the nurse rescued him by saying it was time for his medication.

"Interview closed at eleven thirty seven." He clicked off the recorder. "Until tomorrow, Mr. Armstrong," the detective said, "Get some rest."

They left, he swallowed the pills and sighed, groaning as his ribs jabbed at him. Tomorrow again? What were they after? The thugs surely would have left town by now, gone back home. Was it true that they could go after Milly? The thought cheered him no end and he grinned. Talk about a loving wife, she had not even called or sent him a card, and the police told him that she knew he was here.

♥

Gardner had just left after their lunch when the front door bell rang. Milly sighed with annoyance and put down the tea cup. Who would be calling at this hour, she wondered? Maybe Gardner had returned.

She looked through the peephole and saw two men. She did not know them and decided not to open the door. Checking the panel to make sure she had armed the security system, she walked back into the lounge.

The bell continued to ring and she became angry. Whoever those men were, they were uncouth and illiterate. If no one answered a door, surely that meant no one was home?

She took the back stairs from the kitchen and peered through the lace curtains at the car in her driveway. An extra long stretch BMW. Ostentatious, she thought, not a suitable car for anyone who was anyone. Sitting in the window, she watched and waited. Why did they not leave? The bell was going to be broken if they did not take their finger off the button. Should she call Gardner on his cell phone? Should she call the police? Who could they be and what did they want? She felt safe inside her securely locked home.

Then it dawned on her. Jeffrey . . .they were the goons who had beaten up Jeffrey. Yet what would they want with her?

She started pacing, weighing her options. The police were the better bet, although she did not relish seeing police cars near her home. How very embarrassing. How could she face the neighbours?

Darn it all, why was she worried about neighbours she had never met? These men were dangerous!

♥

Grogsy Mulligan swore again as, his finger firmly pressed on the bell, he peered through a small gap of the cut glass and gold leaded front door side light. "Shit, I can't see a fucking thing."

"There's nobody home. We're wasting our time here."

"I saw a figure I tell you. She's in there all right and we're gonna talk to her. Sheesh! Women!"

Jimbo looked around the door frame. "This place is wired up, got a security system."

"Go around back and check it out," Grogsy ordered, again putting his eye to the small opening. "Wish the windows didn't have all them lace curtains. We can't look inside."

Jimbo went around the garage and made his way to the rear entrance. The house had two other regular doors. One obviously led into the garage, the other was a kitchen door. Then he spotted a double sliding glass window opening onto the deck, silently moved toward it and peered inside. He saw a family room filled with plushy furniture and a small Siamese cat sleeping on the door mat. The woman had blocked the door. He saw the safety bar laying across the width of the door.

"Jeez! Fort Knox has nothing on you, lady," he said as he moved back toward the garage.

As he passed the solid garage door, he tried it. It was open! "Bingo!" he said as he ran to the front to tell Grogsy.

♥

Milly watched from the front bedroom window, but saw no movement. The door bell was no longer ringing and that was a relief. Then she saw the men get into their car. It turned around and went down the driveway. Thank God! She wiped her sweaty palms on her skirt and went downstairs. Now she was glad she had not called 999.

"You sure this is the way to do it, Grogs?" Jimbo asked as he pulled the car over onto the soft shoulder behind a thicket of tall rhododendrons.

"Sure, she won't suspect nothing Nobody will see the car and we can do what we need to do without anyone being any the wiser. Trust me."

They walked along the grass skirting the driveway and reaching the house, they made their way to the back garage door. Opening it and slipping inside, they paused to let their eyes adjust.

"Silly woman," Grogsy said, "I bet the door to the kitchen is open. Never think of garage doors other than the roll up."

They moved around, examining the contents. A new car, top of the line. An older well maintained Mercedes, a snow blower, a riding mower, a wall of storage cupboards - all locked.

"Come on, let's get on with it."

They moved to the solid door leading into the house and Grogsy turned the handle. It opened. Delighted, they grinned. Grogsy put on his gloves, as did Jimbo and they moved silently into the mud room off the kitchen.

"Whew, some setup!" Jimbo breathed.

"Shh!"

They split up, Grogsy signalling for Jimmy to take the left opening as he moved toward the right. The kitchen stretched the full width of the house, about thirty feet and had a walk-in pantry, a laundry room, a dining alcove in a bay window, leading to a small family room with large windows overlooking the garden. State of the art electrical appliances stood on stainless steel counters. A double stainless steel refrigerator freezer stood against the wall and reflected the two men as they crept around. Jimbo went through an archway and found himself in the dining room where Chippendale furniture stood gleaming and a silver cabinet displayed its contents. Another china cabinet held crystal. He whistled softly. This was some house.

Grogsy checked out the family area at the end. The cat awoke and stared at him. Its eyes got on his nerves and when he moved to touch it, it ran away and hid under the chesterfield. Good, he didn't fancy hurting a cat.

So where was she? The rich bitch who lived here, the one who could repay the money her husband owed? Why, he wondered, was the man living at the dumpy boarding house? Well, even if she *had* thrown him out, she must pay up or else.

CHAPTER TWENTY-EIGHT

Christine checked into the ritzy hotel in downtown Ottawa where the awards would be presented. In her tenth floor room, she stood at the picture window and looked down at the bustling area that housed the war memorial. The old street of where the sesate building stood ancient and revered to her right and the canal area where the tour boats moored were to the left. She admired an outdoor restaurant on the canal bank and decided she would have lunch there. Over all, she felt a sense of belonging, of pride that she was Canadian.

Her room had an interesting booklet about Ottawa and its history. This she read and planned for sightseeing. One of the award committee members was here alone and, after they had met at the reception desk, they decided to pair up for the two days of their stay.

Angela was a twenty-five-ish thick set lady who wore owl-like glasses. She did, however, have a wonderful way about her, was humorous and gregarious and Christine took to her at once. Picking up the phone, she rang Angela's room.

"All set?" Angela asked. "I was just about to call you. Let's meet in the coffee shop and talk over our plans."

They spent their day sightseeing: first a tour on a double decker bus, then a canal ride on a tourist boat, after which they visited two museums. By six pm both felt exhausted.

"That was far too much for one day, Angela. My feet are killing me."

"Mine too That's the trouble with having a job that consists of sitting in front of a computer screen most of the time."

"I know what you mean. I'm sure that my old ladies get more physical exercise than I do."

Angela rubbed at her calf. "Hell's bells, I know I've got to change my ways before my legs atrophy."

"Tomorrow we'll take the tourist steam train in the Gatineaus and see the countryside. Give our muscles chance to recover before we tackle the art gallery."

"I sure don't want to miss that pleasure. Now, what about supper tonight? Eat here, go out?"

♥

In Montreal Harvey ate at Quasimodo, a trendy restaurant where the food was fantastic, and ordered a bottle of Nuit St. George. His day proved interesting and now a bag filled with brochures, leaflets and CD's sat in his room. Things were moving fast in his world and he made some valuable contacts.

A tall, slim Asian woman with long black hair walked over to his table. "Would you like some company?"

He shook his head. "No, thank you. I'm waiting for someone."

Jeepers, they sure moved fast here, he thought. On the other hand, maybe she wanted company for herself. Looking around he noticed all the tables held couples and he was the lone diner. Oh well, what the heck, he felt happy with his own company. He sighed. Christine would love this place, he thought, then shook his head. Why did he still think about her? What was it about Christine that had him mesmerized? Time had gone so fast and it over two three years now and still he had not found the courage to make the first move.

He dated, of course, but none of them had anything that captivated him. They were attractive and sometimes beautiful, but as he got to know them, they all seemed so vapid, so unintelligent. Trying to hold a decent conversation with them was hard work and he soon lost interest. His phone still rang, other women made a play for him, but he was not interested. Since a magazine article about the wealthy young high tech entrepreneur hit the streets, every woman, and some married ones, made it their mission to snare him. He sighed and checked his watch. Time to get back to the hotel, time to catch up on his E-mail, time to check his messages.

CHAPTER TWENTY-NINE

Slowly, Grogsy crept up the stairs, pausing on every step, his ear pricked for the slightest sound. He could hear Jimmy behind him, his breath rasping and held up a hand and pointed to the right.

A wide corridor ran the width of the house with doors on each side. The right-hand branch had four doors, one of which was double.

"The master bedroom?" Jimmy hissed. They stood statue still as Grogsy listened. Then both heard a closet door closing. They moved to the door and stood each with a hand on the inset handles.

"Now!" Grogsy hissed and they flung open both doors.

Milly gasped as she saw the men, her eyes sought help, something she could use as a weapon, looked for the phone. Unfortunately she had left the cordless phone in the en suite bathroom. Her bedroom was sterile, no nicknacks, nothing, not even a vase and she saw nothing to use for defence. For what seemed like an eternity, they stared at each other.

"Mrs. Armstrong, I presume?" Grogsy asked in his best deep voice.

Blindly, she nodded. Her throat felt constricted and she could hardly breathe.

Jimmy pulled out the dressing table stool. "Won't you have a seat?" He grinned.

It was like a farce, she thought. Imagine inviting her to sit in her own home. She stood, unmoving. The tall man took her arm and propelled her to the seat. Both stood over her, their faces so grim that she covered her face with her hands.

"Nice rings, eh?" Grogsy said. "Take them off." He held out his hand.

"My rings?" she gasped, looking at them. The solitaire diamond was worth over a quarter of a million, the eternity ring worth half of that, the large sapphire was a family heirloom. She had worn her best to impress Gardner. No, they would never dare take them.

"Come on, come on," Grogsy said, putting his hand into his pocket as if reaching for a gun.

Milly shook her head. Her eyes were almost popping out of her head and her brain was reeling. How was she going to get out of this situation? Who would help her? Today she had no staff coming in to work since today she was usually out at meetings. No one would know of her peril.

Jimmy squatted and looked into her face. "Know why we're here?"

Shivering with fright, she shook her head.

"Your husband Jeffrey, otherwise known as Gary Whalen, owes a great deal of money to our employer. We have orders to get the money, either from you or from him. You know where he is right now?"

She nodded.

Grogsy sneered. "We managed to rough him up real good. Too bad he was tougher than old boots or he'd be a goner. We thought we'd done for him. Then we'd have come to you, anyway. His death doesn't let you off the hook, now does it?"

She stared at him, uncomprehending. How could she be responsible for gambling debts? "How do *I* come into this? You should get the money from the person who welshed on his debt."

"Oh, so you *can* speak then? You, Mrs. Armstrong, are as responsible as your husband. You have the means to clear his debt. Look at this place."

"I'm separated from my husband," Her voice was shaky and she felt nauseous. "He means nothing to me and I refuse to pay his debts." Surely such a level headed approach would make them see sense.

"Look, lady, you owe if he won't pay. He says he has no money. Well, we can all see where it is now . . . it's all right here."

She stood. "I will not listen to this nonsense. I'll call the police."

Grogsy grabbed at her wrist and wrestled her down onto the stool again. "You won't call anybody, lady. We'll take what we need from where we find it. Tie her up, Jimbo."

The men forced her to stand, then dragged her to the bed where they tied her wrists with a tie they found in the closet. "I'll get something for her legs," the little man, Jimbo, said and left the room.

Grogsy pointed at her, then shoved his fist under her nose. "Don't move, or else I'll knock you out."

Milly watched as he prowled the room, opening drawers and rifling through the contents. He found her jewellery box in the dressing table and started to put things in his pocket. Jimbo came back with a length of yellow plastic twine with which he tied her legs so tightly that she ouched with pain.

"That's too tight," she gasped.

He laughed. "So be glad I didn't wind it round your neck."

Then he took a roll of duct tape out of his pocket and wound it round her head and over her lips. She lay frantically breathing through her nose, wondering how she could get free.

Grogsy lifted a sparkling handful and showed it to Jimbo. "Worth a lot but not enough. Wonder where the safe is? All houses this size have a safe. Come on, we'll check the other rooms and look at the art works."

Casting a glance at Milly, they left.

She tried to free herself but could not. The tie around her wrists felt loose enough, but because she could not use her teeth to pull at it, she had no method of freeing her hands. The tough twine around her ankles constricted her blood and her feet were already white and numb. He had wrapped the duct tape three times around her head and hair so she was well and truly stuck. Closing her eyes, she pictured different scenarios in her mind, someway to free herself.

Grogsy and Jimbo looked behind the paintings as they appraised them. "Copies worth peanuts," Grogsy said. "No safe either. It must be in a closet."

They ransacked the house, found a few things of value and piled them on the hall table. The silver pieces, the silver cutlery in its velvet lined mahogany box, two small miniatures on ivory from the library, four first editions, a couple of Chinese bowls and a few items of crystal.

"The woman must have money somewhere. Let's check the kitchen. Try the freezer first."

"Bingo!" Jimbo said as he removed a plastic wrapped box from the deep freeze. "More jewellery. Stupid, these women, that's the first place we look."

Grogsy opened the package and looked at the contents. "Sheesh, a tiara! Still, the stones are large and look good. Look at this pendant. Good quality, very old, too." He examined the rings, bracelets, brooches and necklaces. "With this lot and the other things, I reckon we've cracked it. Come on, go get the car. We can get out of here."

♥

Jeffrey, allowed to move around the ward on crutches, spent his time gazing out of the window. He felt so lonely, so abandoned. Why hadn't either Christine or Milly even bothered to send him a get well card? Did nobody care about him?

No, they did not. Not one of his work mates at the dealership had bothered to send a card or flowers. Shit! He could be dead and no one would care. This had to stop. He was his own worst enemy if nobody gave a damn about him. Where had he gone wrong?

"Would you like some company?" A visiting nun stood smiling at him. "I can spend some time with you if you like."

"Yes, please, please join me." His eyes welled up in self pity. Someone wanted to talk with him and he felt grateful.

♥

The police caught Grogsy and Jimbo at the airport.

"Told you we shoulda rented a different car. The BMW is too obvious," Jimbo snarled.

"So were your faces and your ID," the officer said. "Toronto police are very competent and don't you forget it. This isn't the frontier anymore, no matter what you yanks think .Coming over here with hopes of having tea with the Prime Minister. Huh! As if!"

Grogsy scowled. "Do we have to listen to this moron?"

The other officer stuck his head in the car window where they sat handcuffed. "Not at all. I can tell you some dirty jokes if you like. Seems to me, you're going to need to laugh because you won't get much hilarity in the future."

"Look at this lot," the other officer said as he opened one bags in the Lincoln's trunk. "Thieves and enforcers."

♥

Christine and Angela enjoyed their second day of sightseeing. By this time they were the greatest of friends and found much in common.

"The art gallery was fabulous, don't you think? I thought it hilarious when I saw that toilet hanging from a door frame! They call that art?" Christine said.

They laughed.

"He probably got a grant to do it, too!" Angela said and they laughed harder.

"Honestly some things that they paid a fortune for I wouldn't put out in my dustbin."

"Our tax dollars at work, eh?"

"Still, I wish we had some say in what they buy!"

"The government is a law unto itself," Angela said firmly. "The man I voted for has as much say in what they do in Parliament as I do, and that's nothing."

"Listen to us! Anyone would think we knew the inside workings of government and we know squat."

Angela nodded. "Yes, but we agree on the same points."

"True. Too bad we can't make much difference but can only talk about it."

They parted in the lobby. "See you at seven?"

Angela agreed. "I must send some e-mail and then I can get ready."

"So we'll eat at Roger's Roast Beef House tonight?"

"Yes, it sounds terrific and we can walk to it from the hotel."

"Might as well have a good meal before the dinner tomorrow. Plastic chicken is my guess with wallpaper paste potatoes. You know hotel banquet food."

"Ugh! Sounds about right."

CHAPTER THIRTY

"Why don't you stop off in Kanata on your way back home? I'm sure you'll find our research facilities of great interest. We're making great strides."

"I'd love to do that. Let me make a couple of calls to rearrange my schedule, and thanks." Harvey shook Dave Lee's hand as they stood at the display stand.

Dave Lee, a third generation English of Chinese origin, lauded as the number one man in Robotics had built his empire from a space in his garage. Now his Kanata facility had attained world recognition. Knowing that, without asking, Harvey had received a personal invitation to a facility where no amount of money could buy entrance, was very pleasant. He finished his sparkling water and headed for the elevators.

The trade show brought him into contact with many new international companies and he felt satisfied with the trip. The stand cost was atrociously high but well worth it. Two of his top salesmen and a technician were manning the stand, which left him free to wander the other booths and do some networking.

After spending some time on his laptop, he rearranged his days. Thinking he might enjoy a few days of R&R, he arranged to take off the entire week. Who knew how long he would stay with Dave Lee?

"You're kidding!" Bob Ward, the technician almost fainted. "He *invited* you?"

"Hey, now, Bob, I *am* the president, you know. I do have some clout."

Bob shrugged. "I didn't mean it like that, boss. I know some guys would give their right arm to visit his place."

"I'm lucky, I guess. How did the rest of the day go?"

The trio sat talking shop for an hour then went their separate ways. Harvey wandered through the lobby, went down to the shopping concourse and window shopped. A sense of loneliness came over him as a young couple, arms around each other, stopped to kiss. He passed a high class boutique and paused to look at the display. Christine would look terrific in that gown, he thought. How he longed to talk to her again, to tell her how he felt. Still, he had blown that chance long ago. Was he to spend the rest of his life regretting his lack of action in gettng her back? He sighed and walked on.

A street walker approached him as he headed back into the hotel but he did not even glance at her and walked to the elevator, his mind picturing Christine in that beautiful blue gown. Maybe if he bought it, he could look at it now and then. No, that was silly.

♥

Milly lay on the bed, trussed like a chicken. Almost comatose, she realized she had wet the bed. Her silk coverlet would be ruined. How very embarrassing, she thought, even as her shut eyes saw nothing but spots and stars. What would they think of her when they came to her rescue? Still, accident victims must also foul themselves and surely medics had often seen this, but the utter shame of it all!

How long had she been lying here? Her mind refused to work and she had no way of knowing the time of day. It must be at least two days now, though.

Pushing down, trying to move she sensed that her feet were dead as the pain struck through her entire body. Below her waist everything felt numb and she could no longer move her legs. When would someone find her? Who was coming to clean or cook? Her memory failed her, but surely someone must call soon. They would see her car and know she was home, would rescue her.

Tears started to trickle down her face and she cursed herself, thinking she was stronger than this. It occurred to her that if her nose ran, she could not wipe it. How awful if people saw her with a snotty nose. Her memory came and went, images of Jeffrey, images of the two thugs, images of her daughter, her mother. Yes, her mother, Evelyn, the mother who had given her birthright to her ungrateful daughter. She hated her mother. Then in a moment of lucidity, realized she had loved her mother, in her own way of course, but she had loved her.

Jeffrey, she had once loved him too. Did she now? She had given him a job as a mere salesman and he had taken it willingly enough. Did he love her? Somehow she doubted it, knowing she had been a terrible wife to him.

Christine. The girl probably hated her. She had pushed her away at every opportunity and privately rejoiced when she ran away from home. Surely that was not a maternal instinct? Her own ambition had destroyed her entire family, had turned everyone against her - and she deserved it. Now she wondered if she could heal some of the wounds, make amends to those she had wounded so badly. In another part of her mind, she knew she would automatically revert to herself when she was well enough to take control of her life.

She listened. Was that a sound? She strained her ears, and heard nothing. Lying listening, she lost consciousness.

♥

Jeffrey clumped along in the day room, around and around, glancing out the picture windows as he circled. His legs were getting stronger but the crutches were playing merry hell with his arm pits. Soon, they told him, he would get different casts, soft walking casts that would stay on for another month. His less damaged arm had healed already, and he wore a short cast over his wrist.

Day after day, he had therapy, received counselling, had visits from doctors, nuns, the library lady, visiting social workers, when all he wanted to do was go home.

Home? It suddenly dawned on him that he had no home and his heart plummeted. Milly had locked him out of the house he called home. Though eventually Christine had come to see him, she had not said, but he sensed, he was not welcome to move back in with her. The Y? Another rooming house? No way, those were only pit stops. So where then would he go? His bank account held about four hundred dollars, but he probably would not work for some months yet. Where did that leave him?

He decided to talk to a visiting nun. She might have an answer for him. He sighed, thanking God for socialized medicine.

♥

Milly came to with a start. Was someone in the house? She prayed they were. The masking tape gag was still firmly in place and she could not make more than a growl. She lay listening. Her mind whirled from the effort and she felt dizzy.

Her mind told her she must try: she could not lie here and die. If she rolled off the bed, could she roll to the door? The door was open so maybe she could roll out onto the landing, and if she could get to the stairs maybe she could go down them, even if she had to roll down.

Each movement she made caused unbearable pain. It was as if she had frozen into position and could not break the hold the duvet had on her body. Determination, that's all it took, she told herself. If she could get her legs over the side of the bed, surely she would not hurt herself too badly when the rest of her tumbled over. Darn it, now she wished she had not bought such a high bed, but high beds piled with pillows were the latest style. They had tied her hands loosely but they were useless. Milly tried to wriggle her body to the left, the side where a lambskin side rug lay. It was agony as even a tiny movement brought cold sweat to her brow and made her feel nauseous.

It took hours, but she now lay on the edge of the bed, scared to move. She moved her head to look at the floor: it seemed miles away. This must be like the moment before you made a bungee jump, or what you felt before sky diving. She passed out again.

♥

Christine resumed her seat, her face flushed and her heart pounding. She clutched her award and smiled as the people on the table, led by Angela, gave her an extra round of applause.

"Terrific speech, Christine," Angela said. "You done good, girl."

"Well, if it weren't for my grandmother, I wouldn't be here today, you know."

"She sounds like a lovely woman."

"Oh, she was and I still miss her."

"Now, now. Don't get maudlin. This is a celebration. More champers?"

"Why not?"

"One glass only. That woman is going to interview you for the TV news at eleven."

"Yes, Mummy."

They laughed.

"I am so glad to have met you, Angela,"Christine said, "I missed having a female friend and I have a feeling we're going to be friends for a long time."

"Me too. We're sympatico, as they say. I think the only thing that will spoil our friendship is a man."

Christine giggled. "No chance of that. As I told you, I carry a torch and I still love him."

"Ah, but men have a way of popping back into your life when you least expect it."

"Not this one, he's too important now and I'm sure he's probably married or engaged."

"What's his name?" Angela asked. "You never did say."

"And I won't."

CHAPTER THIRTY-ONE

"Help me," her mind screamed, "Help me!"

She had fallen off the bed when she eventually managed to move very close to the edge. The impact had caused her to black out and now her every nerve shriekd with pain. Opening her eyes, she looked across the room. When her eyes adjusted, the door seemed so far away. Why had she chosen such a large room when she only slept in it? Acres of polished wood loomed, and she saw a dust bunny under the dressing table. The cleaner was slipshod. Oh hell, why was she thinking about staff at a time like this?

Suffering from severe dehydration and lack of food, she felt as weak as a new born. Every tiny movement, even of her eyelids, seemed to hurt. When would someone come to save her?

Milly realized that nobody cared about her. She had alienated every person with whom she came into contact. Her selfish outlook had caused this and maybe she would die alone and unloved.

Jeff, what she wouldn't give to see him now. Christine, too. Maybe one of them would come over to see her. Maybe one of them would find her. Oh God, help me, help me.

♥

"We have halfway houses waiting to help you, Mr. Armstrong. We are an outreach society that looks after the less fortunate."

Jeff knew what he meant: a doss house filled with winos and druggies. Somehow that did not appeal to him. The man talked to him for about an hour and as well meaning as the volunteer was, Jeff would not commit himself to anything.

It occurred to him that Milly might still come to his aid. She was still his wife and surely that stood for something? He clumped down the hall and asked the nurse if she would call his wife and ask her to come to see him.

"I'm not supposed to do this, Mr. Armstrong, but matron is downstairs. Here, I'll dial the number and you can speak to her."

"Thanks, nurse." Jeff gave her his best smile.

♥

Christine and Angela decided to go out on the town after they opted to stay for another day. Both purchased new gowns and shoes. They went to Rinaldo's high class salon for new hairstyles, had facials and their makeup done. Now looking ultra glamorous and sophisticated, they stood waiting for a taxi, fielding admiring glances and trying not to laugh and spoil the effect.

They had made a reservation at a genuine French restaurant a short trip from the city on the other side of the river.

"Lovely, having another culture so close, don't you think?"

"According to the concierge, this place is so expensive that you'd think it was in France."

They laughed as the doorkeeper ushered them into the taxi and saluted after he told the driver their destination.

"Boy, this is the life, Angela."

"Yup, too bad it's back to the real world tomorrow."

"Then don't spoil it."

"As if I would."

The restaurant on the outskirts of a village looked like an old farm house at the front but had a huge addition at the back. As they entered the foyer, they heard the sound of an orchestra playing.

"Wow! Fantastic, live music." Christine grinned as the maitre d' approached, his arms outstretched in welcome. He kissed each of them on each cheek in the Gallic manner and they smiled.

Ushered to a choice table, they looked around. The ceiling seemed miles high and four crystal chandeliers glistened expensively. Underfoot was plush maroon carpeting and their table had a pale pink table cloth and a vase of pink roses. Crystal stemware and silver cutlery added to the ambience. A waiter lit the candles and offered the menu.

It was wonderful and both relaxed in the heady atmosphere.

CHAPTER THIRTY-TWO

The phone rang and rang. That was strange because Milly always had the answering machine switched on. Heaven forbid she miss an important call from an important person! Although, he thought, if she had unplugged the phone it would sound as if it were ringing when it was not.

"No answer," he said ruefully to the nurse when she returned. "Do you think I can try later?"

"Not with me. I'm off shift in about ten minutes. Ask Nancy when she takes over. I'm sure she'll help you. Just don't let Matron catch you."

"Thanks." Jeff smiled his best smile. Thank God the goons had not broken his teeth, his one good feature. Although his eyes were nice, or so women told him. Neither blue nor grey, they were wide set and expressive and he had long eyelashes.

Strange that he was destitute and injured and yet his mind still strayed.

♥

Milly knew she was dying. She felt it in every fibre of her being. The fall had jarred her, but it had also doubly enforced her predicament. They would find her here, bound and gagged. How awful to be found in such a state. How terrible if any of her friends saw her.

Then, she thought ruefully, she'd be dead and it could not possibly hurt her. She could watch over them, see their reactions. She wondered if she could haunt them if they said unkind things.

Was that a phone ringing? Even as she listened, she lapsed into unconsciousness.

♥

"It's him, this Jeffrey Armstrong." The detective grinned as he passed the file to his partner. "I told you I sensed something about that man."

"Whew! You were right. Well, well, well, let's get the show on the road. Time we paid Mr. Armstrong another visit."

♥

Harvey eyed the restaurant where Dave Lee had invited him to supper. They drove from Montreal into the countryside near Ottawa. Dave had told him it was black tie and the place seemed very prosperous. The maitre d' escorted them through the room and he eyed the large ballroom where couples dined and danced. The ladies wore long gowns and most men wore a tailored suit. On a low band stand, a very classy orchestra with violins played show tunes.

The menu seemed fantastic and they chatted about shop as they enjoyed an aperitif.

"You're company is very cutting edge, I hear," Dave said as he buttered a slice of still warm baguette.

"I hope," Harvey grinned. "We both know robotics is the wave of the future and I think I've found some bright young men to work on our new project."

"University grads?"

"Not all. I find some of them through ads in the paper and resumes sent in on spec. Strange when you think I was an unemployed slob when I got my chance. I intend to repay the kindness shown to me when I needed it most."

"An admirable trait, I would say. Some of my best workers are those who have little or no formal education but possess an innate feeling for the work."

The orchestra played the Anniversary Waltz and an older couple stepped onto the small dance floor while their circle of friends applauded.

"Nice place, nice atmosphere too." Harvey glanced around at the affluent diners.

"A Korean gentleman introduced me to this restaurant, believe it or not. They sure know how to find the best places."

"Amen to that." Harvey tasted the soup. "This is terrific. I can taste the mushrooms."

"Not out of a can then?"

They laughed.

♥

Milly groaned as her eyes flickered open. Somewhere a phone was ringing. Downstairs? She moved her arms and tried to roll onto her side. If she could get on her side, she would roll off the rug onto the wooden floor and could pull herself to the door. If she could . . . .

CHAPTER THIRTY-THREE

Delighted when the doctor told him he would release him from the hospital, Jeff gasped when the detectives arrested him and charged him with the murder of Janice Merton. Incredulous, he could not believe that he had left any trace of himself in that house.

The detective would say very little but advised him to call his solicitor. He called Arthur Appleton, his mother-in-law's solicitor, thinking that Christine would pay the tab. Appleton came down to the station where he sat in a cell.

Two hours later, Jeff knew he was well and truly caught. They had found DNA evidence in the shower and also on the towels. The towels, shit! Why had he not thought about them? Appleton did not give much for his chances, though he made muttering noises about 'circumstantial evidence at best.' Well, that was true enough. He could not deny that he was living with Janice, everyone knew, every person who knew her, but that did not prove he had killed her, did it? Appleton mused and said he would have to do some research on the case and would get back to him.

"Will they extradite me?" he asked.

"They might well do so, and in that case, you will have to avail yourself of a court appointed solicitor in Maine. I'm not licensed to practice in the States."

He sat in the grungy cell and felt sorry for himself. He had not killed her, not really. Surely they would release him soon because he needed his therapy. Maybe they would let him go back to the hospital.

♥

The phone rang again and brought her back to life. She was now so weak that she could hardly open her eyes. Please help me, she thought. Even her thought process was slow and difficult.

It rang and rang. How much longer could she cling to life, she wondered. Would she die soon? Better make her peace with God.

She started trying to mutter. "God you know how selfish I've been, how very antagonistic to everybody, but you know why. You know how I longed for acceptance, wanted to be liked, wanted to be admired. You will forgive me, because You know I am sorry. How long ago it seemed when I used to attend church to worship you. These days a church visit is for show, to display my compassion, to show the world how much I am like them, benevolent and god fearing, but also to show off my designer clothes and shoes.

"Please God, forgive me my sins. If you let me live, I'm going to change." Even as she thought it, she knew she would not . . . and so did God.

♥

"Isn't this roast beef fantastic?" Christine said as she savoured the last mouthful. "The food here is marvellous."

"Hmm, I could eat that all again and still want more," Angela said, "Good job I chose this loose gown and not that slinky number I wanted."

Christine looked around, seeing the packed dance floor, the chatting diners and smiled. What a treat. She wondered if Toronto had anything like it.

"Any place like this in "T.O.", she asked.

"One or two. Why?"

"I think we ought to make it a routine to go out more often. I'm always sitting at home working when I ought to be out having fun."

"Me too. Gosh, we're a pair of old fogies and us not even thirty yet."

"Yes, and we'd better start having a social life or we'll die old maids."

A Chinese man walked by their table looking over his shoulder. "Want a drink at the bar?" he asked.

Christine looked to see who he was addressing and her heart stopped. Harvey! First she blanched, then she blushed.

"What is it? Are you all right?" Angela took her hand and patted it. "What's the matter? You look like you've seen a ghost."

Christine sat speechless, her wide eyes fixed on Harvey as Harvey stood statue like, staring back at her. He moved toward her and she rose in her chair.

He opened his eyes wider, trying to absorb her beauty. Surely she was more lovely than before? Her gown and her hair, her slim figure and trim waist, those dark passionate eyes, that soft mouth and white teeth, all had changed and seemed even brighter. He was aware of nothing else in the world but her beauty and the hypnotic gaze that warmed his heart. It brought back the love and made him whole, made him feel immortal. They said not a word and on some unheard command moved toward each other and whirled onto the dance floor as the orchestra played "How much do I Love You," as if on divine cue.

Dave Lee watched, astonished, and looked at Angela, also stunned, as she sat at the table.

"Do they know each other?" he asked.

Angela laughed. "Either that, or it was a *coup de foudre*. Who is he?"

"Harvey Wright. The top man in Trawton on Robotics."

"I'm Angela Ashton, by the way. I work with the Chamber of Commerce. We held our annual awards here and they named Christine 'Ontario Woman of the Year.'"

"I'm Dave Lee. I'm also in IT and other things."

She grinned. "I've read all about you, but I never thought I would ever meet you." They shook hands formally and smiled.

"Looks like they're in a trance." Dave said gesturing to the floor where Harvey and Christine swayed to the music but did not move. "Ah me, young love. About time I found the woman of my dreams too. I meet so many young women but they all have dollar signs in their eyes."

"Oh, do I?" she had to ask.

"No, I can't see any. Would you like to dance?"

"Love to."

♥

Gardner tried to call again. The phone rang and rang. Something was very wrong. Milly usually had the answering machine switched on, and for two days he had called with no luck.

He decided to drive over and see what was what.

♥

The police tried to reach Millicent Armstrong, as did Arthur Appleton. It came as a shock when they discovered Milly lay near death in the hospital. Gardner, who had found her, sat at her side for days until she came out of the coma. His was the first face she saw and she smiled as she sank into a peaceful normal sleep.

♥

They took Jeffrey to Maine to face the charges though Arthur tried to get the government involved. At the preliminary hearing, they decided that while they could not find anything other than circumstantial evidence, they would hold him until the trial, which was set for six months from that date.

At least he had a bed and good meals, he thought as he limped around the open grassy area called the exercise yard. High chain link fencing topped with razor wire surrounded it. His cell mate, pending trial for insider trading, was a jolly man who knew ten million jokes, all sexual, so Jeff prized this time to himself. His cell mate never stopped yakking and it drove him bonkers.

He liked the food. His work periods consisted of helping in the laundry or polishing floors. Overall, it could be worse. If he were free and still in Toronto, he would still be homeless. Meanwhile, he looked on this time as a holiday.

Yesterday he had written to Milly and today he would write to Christine. He wondered if they would answer.

CHAPTER THIRTY-FOUR

"I felt sure you were going to snub me and I was frozen in panic," she said as they sat in an alcove.

Harvey took her hand and kissed it. "I thought you were going to snub me!"

They laughed. "I love you, Harvey and don't want to ever lose you again."

"Me too. I thought about you every day, dreamed about you even and yet somehow after I had left it longer than two weeks, I couldn't do it. I thought you would tell me to get lost."

She laughed. "Never. I wanted to call you too, but I remembered Gram telling me a lady never made the first move. Oh, why, oh why did I listen to her?"

"Never mind. The thing is that we're back together. When do you want to get married?"

"I want my ring back first," she laughed, "and then we'll set the date."

"My parents will be delighted. How about yours?"

"Mother has been planning the wedding of the century since I was born and I shudder to think of her extravagant plans."

"Hmm. My mother will want in on the act as well. How about an elopement?"

"In our case I think that might be best. We can plan a wedding out of town, maybe out of the country, then send them a card."

"Sounds good to me, my love." He leaned over and kissed her softly.

"Ahem!" Dave Lee and Angela stood in front of their table. Christine noticed they were holding hands.

Angela grinned. "What did I tell you about a man breaking us up? I think you picked a good one there."

"You too." Christine laughed as Harvey and Dave looked at each other puzzled.

Dave said, "We're going back to Ottawa now. Are you coming with us or will you come back later?"

"Later, much later," Harvey said, winking.

♥

Milly accepted when Gardner proposed. She looked forward to a life of affluence and felt entitled to this new chance of happiness. The new Milly would be warm and outgoing, she vowed, she would try to be pleasant to everyone. Gardner especially.

"We'll go to Tampa when you get out of here," he said, "You need complete rest for a couple of months. My staff is terrific and you will love them."

She sat higher in the chair and smiled. "I'm sure I will. Thank you, Gardner, I appreciate everything you're doing for me."

"I may be an old dog, Milly, but I do know how to treat a lady. As my wife, you'll lack for nothing."

She smiled. "I know and I'm overwhelmed. It overwhelms me that you still want to marry me under the circumstances."

Garner smiled. "I always loved you Milly, and you know it. Have you heard from the solicitor?"

"Yes, the letter is in the side table. Read it and have a laugh."

Gardner took the letter and started to read. He grinned as he folded it and placed it back in the envelope. "Sounds like Jeffrey is in big trouble. Do you think he did it? The murder, I mean."

"No way. He's a coward of the first order. It must have been an accident and anyway the evidence is only circumstantial. He'll probably get a slap on the wrist and his time in holding pending the trial will count as time served. They'll let him go, I'm sure. Poor old Jeff. I wonder what he'll do once he's free again?"

He took her hand and squeezed it, looking serious. "Give him the dealership. Milly. It was his once and you sure don't need it now."

She closed her eyes and thought about that for a minute. Gardner was right and maybe this action would negate the guilt she felt about the way she had treated Jeff.

"Maybe you could write to him and tell him that, Gardner, and tell him he can move into the house. We won't need it right now and it should have a tenant."

"Good for you, Milly! I like your generosity."

She nodded and squeezed his hand. "I think I learned a lot while tied up all that time. It's not too late to make amends for my earlier actions. I must contact my daughter and speak with her before we leave."

♥

Harvey and Christine drove back to Toronto in her car. They drove slowly and carefully, taking the time to catch up on everything that had happened since their breakup.

They constantly rehashed the breakup. "I was so wrong to react that way when I saw that horrible man. My mind was working overtime and yet I never did let you explain anything."

"I was fourteen at the time, as I told you. I didn't think about anything but having someone protect me, someone who listened to what I said. At least it was like that at first, but I grew up fast and made some terrible mistakes."

"I understand everything now and will spend my life making sure that I never walk away from you again."

"I must talk to my mother. I want her to know that we're going to be married. Let her plot and plan then we'll elope, like you said. It will serve her right for being so awful to me for all those years."

"Oh my, your first flaw! Is that necessary?"

"No. It isn't, but I'll get such pleasure out of making her run around in circles."

Harvey looked at her and grinned, one eyebrow raised.

"All right, I won't tell her until after we are married. It seems so nasty, but I'm too happy to let it bother me. It sure will bother my mother, though!"

♥

Milly sat in the limousine and Gardner's chauffeur brought around her wheelchair. Gardner lifted her out of the car and tucked the rug around her legs.

Between him and the chauffeur, they lifted the chair up the six steps and onto the verandah.

Gardner rang the bell. "Chin up, now," he said.

Jill answered the door. "Yes, may I help you?"

"I want to see Christine, please. I'm her mother."

"Won't you come in. I'll get her."

Milly told Gardner to push her into the living room and set her near the fireplace. She was dreading this meeting.

Christine entered and saw her mother and a strange man. What on earth was she doing in a wheel chair?

Five minutes later she was speechless. Her mother was to marry Gardner and she was leaving Trawton for Tampa in Florida. She seemed quite composed when she said she had lost both legs below the knee but felt sure they could supply her with prosthetics, but that was for the future. Christine felt the tears well in her eyes. Images of her mother sauntering regally out of a room, her perfect legs in their sheer hosiery and high heels brought home to her how awful this incapacity must seem to Milly.

"So you see, your father will take over the dealership and the house. I'm here to apologize for the way I treated you, Christine. I know that making amends at this late date doesn't seem possible, but I would ask you to forgive me. I wish my mother were still with us because I owe her an apology too. Oh well, let's hope I never treat you that way again."

Christine knew how it had cost her mother to utter those words. "I forgive you, mother and hope you and Gardner are very happy. I know Dad will be pleased to get back to his dealership."

"Yes, poor Jeffrey. He always did like cars better than people." She laughed.

"I'm getting married, mother. To that nerd you didn't like. He owns Magnus Technologies, you know. Not a real nerd, more of a genius."

"Oh, how wonderful for you." Milly looked genuinely pleased. "I thought you would stay single for ever and blamed that on myself. I'd like to meet him before we leave to go south."

"Sure."

"Say I have an idea," Gardner said "Why don't you come down to Tampa and get married there? I doubt Milly will be wanting to travel back here for some time."

"I'll have to ask Harvey."

"Harvey Wright? *The* Harvey Wright? Gee, you travel in high circles, Christine!"Garner said, impressed.

"Please think about it, Christine. I'm your mother and as such should pay for the wedding."

Gardner beamed. "You can invite as many people as you like. I'll charter a plane to fetch you. I own two hotels so accommodation is no problem."

Christine felt stunned. Her mother had finally found the pot of gold!

-end-